THE SELKIE ENCHANTRESS

SEAL ISLAND TRILOGY, BOOK TWO

SOPHIE MOSS

Sea Rose
Publishing

Published by Sea Rose Publishing

ISBN-13: 978-0615801049

For my mom

CHAPTER ONE

*C*aitlin Conner tapped her scarlet high heel. She imagined ripping it off and tossing it in Liam O'Sullivan's ridiculously handsome face the moment he walked through her door. Maybe it would knock some sense into that thick head of his—the one he always had stuck in the clouds.

Sure, there were times she admired his penchant for daydreaming. But *this* was not one of them. If he didn't walk through that door in about three seconds, she was personally going to see that he suffered. She let the shiny heel dangle, catching the strap between her toes. She had good aim, too.

Candles flickered, wax dripping down their golden stems. Steam rose from an herb-crusted roast cooling in the center of the table. She poked at a glazed carrot threatening to spill over the edge. Liam wouldn't be the first to become a target for her temper. And that fire simmering under the surface was starting to boil.

She tugged at the neckline of her sweater dress. She'd worn a dress—a *dress* for Christ's sake. She hadn't worn a dress since Tara and Dominic's wedding three months ago. And, oh, how

Liam had liked that dress! Her lips curved. She could still picture the look on his face when she'd walked up the hill wearing the black dress Glenna had brought her from Paris. She was looking forward to having that same effect on him tonight.

And letting him feed her chocolate covered strawberries in bed.

But if he didn't get his fine Irish backside over here, he wasn't getting anywhere near her hand-dipped strawberries. Or her bed. Her smile faded as she glanced up at the clock. Oh, he was going to suffer all right. There was no way she was letting him off the hook for this.

FOOTSTEPS ECHOED on the deck of the passenger ferry. Alone at the bow, Liam O'Sullivan turned as a woman stepped out of the cabin and ducked her head against the frigid November winds. Wrapped in one of the captain's heavy wool blankets, she picked her way across the thick coiled ropes and storage crates. She rested her arms on the peeling paint of the railing to take in the view beside him.

The woman and her son were the only other passengers on the ferry tonight. Liam hadn't given them much more than a passing glance when they ducked into the warmth of the cabin an hour earlier. He preferred to ride up on the deck, no matter how cold, and watch the ocean stretch out until the first twinkling lights of the island came into view.

Home. He'd spent the last nine years in Galway working at the University, but he'd never considered the vibrant coastal city his home. He favored the solitude of the island. His family and closest friends still lived there, and part of him—a large part—wanted to move back someday. Glancing down at the bouquet of roses tucked into the crook of his arm, he wondered what

Caitlin's reaction would be when he told her that tonight. That he'd spent the last few months lobbying for a full-time research position at the University so he could move back to the island at the end of this term.

He smiled, lifting his gaze from the flowers to the ocean. The mists were thick tonight; the air cold and wet. Seawater lapped against the hull of the ferry, splashing up over the deck smelling of salt and kelp. "Not much to see this time of night," he commented to the stranger beside him.

"I just needed some air."

The woman's rich, lilting voice had him gazing at her profile. The hair that peeked out of her hood was moonlight blond and waterfall straight. High cheekbones framed fair, delicate features and thick lashes curled out from eyes that stayed fixed on the churning surface of the water.

"I heard talk of snow on the mainland tonight." Liam nodded to the thick clouds blotting out the moon and stars. "Won't get any of that on the island. But it's not the best time for a visit, I'm afraid."

"I don't mind the cold."

Liam glanced back at the woman curiously. They didn't get many tourists this time of year. Even the most adventurous travelers preferred the cozy villages along the coast rather than suffer the hour-long ride to the island. "What brings you to the island?"

The ancient motor hummed as they cut a slow path toward the faint outline of rocks in the distance. "I needed a few days away from the city. For myself, and my son."

"Galway?"

"Limerick."

Liam nodded. "I try to get away from the city as much as I can."

The wind whipped over the bow and the woman huddled deeper under her cloak. "It wears at you, doesn't it?"

Liam took in the slight downward curve of the woman's mouth, the sad eyes staring down into the water. "It does. I'm lucky I have the island to escape to."

Pulling her gaze from the water for the first time, she looked up at him. "Do you have a home on the island?"

Liam nodded, noting how pale her eyes were, almost like glass. He'd never seen eyes quite like that before. "I grew up there. My brother and grandmother still live there."

She motioned to the flowers Liam held. "Are the roses for your grandmother?"

"No." Liam shook his head, smiling. "The roses are for the woman I'm having dinner with tonight."

"They're beautiful." She gazed back at the water, her tone turning wistful. "She'll love them."

Studying the traveler more closely, Liam saw that she wasn't wearing a wedding band. Surely, she didn't have any trouble finding men to buy her flowers. Then again, he couldn't remember the last time he'd bought a woman flowers. This wasn't exactly normal for him. Glancing back down at the roses, he frowned. "That's strange."

The woman's gaze flickered back up to Liam's. "What?"

Liam pulled the bouquet from the crook of his arm and stared down at the velvety flowers. "Where did this white rose come from?"

She turned, her violet skirt rustling with the rhythm of the waves. "It wasn't there before?"

Liam shook his head slowly.

The woman's gaze locked on the single white rose sparkling in the center of the fragrant bouquet. "Maybe you overlooked it."

"Maybe," Liam murmured. "But I could have sworn they were all yellow."

～

Twenty minutes was one thing, but thirty? Pushing to her feet, Caitlin blew out the candles. Ignoring the little bits of wax that splattered onto the tablecloth, she crossed the room to the telephone. Something must have happened. There was no way Liam had purposely ditched out on their date. They'd been planning it for weeks!

She started to punch in the numbers for the pub and then stopped. What if Dominic answered the phone? What was she supposed to say? *'Hey, Dom, I thought your brother was coming over to my place for dinner, but he never showed. You haven't seen him have you?'* She shoved the phone back into the cradle. She hadn't even talked to Dom about this whole, *dating-Liam* thing.

Now *that* was going to be a fun conversation. Marching across the room, she grabbed her wool sweater off the hook and slipped her arms into the sleeves. Bracing herself against the cold, she pulled open the door. A thick fog swirled through the dark street and the scent of the sea rushed into the room. With one last fleeting glance at the romantic table for two, Caitlin lifted her eyes to the ceiling. *God help me, Liam O'Sullivan. If I find out you flaked on our first date, I will never forgive you!*

Icy winds stung Nuala Morrigan's face as she peered up at the man standing beside her at the bow of the ferry. He was taller than she'd expected—tall and lanky with a thick shock of black hair and sharp, lighting-blue eyes. He wore rectangular, wire-rim glasses and one shoulder hung slightly lower than the other, adding a studious vulnerability and boyish charm to his otherwise strikingly handsome features.

"Would you mind if I...?" She gestured to the bouquet.

"Oh," Liam stammered, his troubled gaze following the white rose as he handed her the flowers. "Of course." The tissue paper rustled in the wind. "I guess I missed it when the florist snuck the white one in with the rest."

"Long week?"

"Busy." Liam dipped his hands in his pockets. "But that's nothing new."

No. It wasn't. Nuala held the flowers up to her face, closing her eyes as she inhaled the sweet, intoxicating scent. She knew he stayed up until all hours of the night writing. She'd seen the lights burning in the windows of his apartment along the River Corrib long after the rest of the city fell asleep. She lowered the flowers, gazing back up at his attractive profile. "What do you do on the mainland?"

"I'm a professor at the University of Ireland in Galway." He turned, leaning against the railing. The wind blew his wavy hair into his eyes. "Irish mythology."

She smiled, like she didn't already know. It was his career that first drew her to him. It was one of the main reasons she'd chosen him. A scholar of Irish myths who not only studied them, but who *believed* in them? It was almost too good to be true. "I'm intrigued."

"Don't worry." He smiled. "I won't bore you with the details. I have a tendency to get caught up in my work."

"So do I," she said. The ocean lapped at the hull of the ferry. Seawater sprayed onto the deck. "I'm a writer. It goes with the territory."

Liam raised an eyebrow, regarding her with new interest. "What do you write?"

"Songs."

Her lips curved when she said the word 'songs' and she caught the slight shift deep in his eyes. As if something was registering, fragmented pieces of knowledge clicking together in that sharp, perceptive mind. "I'm sorry," he said slowly. "I didn't catch your name."

She held out a delicate hand. "It's Nuala Morrigan."

"Nuala the songwriter from Limerick," Liam repeated, taking her palm in his. His grip was firm, his strong palm callused from working on the island's docks to burn off steam on the weekends. She liked that about him. That he visited his family and friends so often. That those relationships meant something to him. "I'm Liam."

"Liam the professor from Galway," Nuala echoed. "Maybe you'll take a few days off this weekend?"

Liam let go of her hand. "Doubtful. I have to work on a presentation for a conference next week. There's a lot riding on how it's received."

And there was a lot riding on how well she would be able to divert him from that task. Nuala glanced back down at the brilliant blooms between them. "May I ask...why did you choose yellow?"

"It's her favorite color."

Nuala brushed a finger over the tips of the fragile petals. "But it's also the color of friendship."

Liam's brow creased. "It is?"

She nodded. "You didn't know that?"

Liam shook his head. "Do all women know that?"

She lifted a slender shoulder. "I don't know. But maybe it's good that a white one found its way in here."

"Why? What does white mean?"

"White can mean anything you want it to."

Liam arched a brow. "That's a powerful rose."

"It is." Nuala smiled, shifting the bouquet so the fragrance filled the air between them. Perhaps he would embrace this change. This chance. This *opportunity*. "What do you want this one to mean?"

"I don't know." Liam looked thoughtfully at the single white rose. "I guess I'd have to think about that."

Nuala's gaze dropped to that lovely-shaped mouth. She couldn't help it. It was impossible *not* to look. How long had it been since a man's lips brushed against hers? She wanted to know how they tasted, how *he* tasted. What it felt like to kiss a man like Liam O'Sullivan. Her fingers itched to reach up and touch that silky black hair.

But she swallowed the urge. For years she had lived in the shadows. Cut off from everyone, every*thing* she had ever known. When she made the trade, she hadn't counted on the loneliness. The sorrow that would eat at her like a salty tide ate at the shoreline. Rubbing against the fine broken rocks until there was nothing left but dust.

But she had served her time. They would have to accept her back now. They would not turn her away when she brought back her prize. "Is it new, then?" Her eyes lifted, meeting his. "This relationship with the woman you're having dinner with tonight?"

Liam nodded slowly. "You could say that."

"Then maybe it means new beginnings," she offered.

"New beginnings." Liam tested the words as they rolled off his tongue. "That sounds right."

Nuala gazed back out at the water. "New beginnings can be wonderful." Through the mists, a sprinkling of whitewashed cottages dotting a rocky hillside came into view. Lamplights burned in the windows and smoke curled from the squat chimneys of the homes leading up to the cliffs. The scent of peat-smoke burned her throat and she swallowed the urge to choke, burying her face in the fragrant roses.

Three days. Nuala's hands squeezed the tissue-covered stems. Three days and the new beginning she'd wanted for ten years would finally be hers.

Liam pushed off the railing and waved to the captain sheltered behind the protective plastic covering, signaling that he would take care of the bow line. "Do you mind holding onto those while I help Finn with the lines?" Liam gestured to the roses, already gathering up the thick wet rope in his strong arms.

Still clutching the flowers, Nuala watched Liam swing one leg over the railing, ready to jump down to the pier as they motored up beside it. A second rope lay coiled in a loose circle around his other foot still resting inside the railing. It was now or never. She pushed the pointed toe of her heeled boot underneath it, nudging it up and over his ankle.

The motor made a loud grinding sound, pulling at the water to slow the heavy vessel. She almost missed the sharp intake of breath from her son. Clinging to the opening in the cabin, his black hair mussed from sleep, Owen stood frozen, staring at her boot. Nuala glanced over her shoulder, meeting her son's panicked eyes and, with one last flick of her ankle, caught Liam's foot in the other rope.

Dark shapes slid from the rocks in the harbor. The seals, usually numb to the comings and goings of the ferry, shrank back from the boat, slipping soundlessly into the sea. Nuala watched Liam push off the edge and, holding her arm out over the water, she opened her fingers and let the roses, all of them white now, drop into the sea.

CHAPTER TWO

*D*odging the village, Caitlin veered onto the rocky cliff path leading down to the harbor. If Liam was still at the docks chatting with Finn, she was going to let him have it! She didn't care who heard her give him a piece of her mind. She spied *O'Sullivan's* pub, where all her friends and neighbors would be gathered around the crackling fire, telling tales over a pint and a warm bowl of stew.

Which is where she should be, too—in a comfortable pair of jeans and a sweatshirt—not tromping around in these toe-pinching heels. The faint squeak of a weathervane faded behind her and she was almost past the outskirts of the village when the door to the pub swung open and voices spilled out into the night. She heard an American accent shout, "Dom, get my med kit!"

Med kit? Caitlin whirled, spotting Tara O'Sullivan break into a run, heading for the harbor. More footsteps pounded on the cracked pavement. The frantic murmurings of her friends and neighbors flowed into the street. She reached down, jerking off her soiled heels. A man's footsteps, heavier and faster, followed and she spied Dominic running after his wife, her bag tucked under his arm.

A thick mist slid over the cliffs, dripping liquid silver over the jagged edges. Struggling to see through the fog, Caitlin started after them. She saw a flash of white light. Was that a runner light from the ferry? Her bare feet slipped on the wet earth as the trail curved sharply, connecting with the single road leading down to the docks. Another beam of light swept over the harbor, illuminating the body of a man lying motionless on the pier.

Liam! Caitlin raced down to the docks. Finn's voice echoed over the water, shouting to Dominic. She spotted Tara through the fog, dropping to her knees in front of the man lying on the pier. "What happened?" Caitlin skidded to a stop, grabbing Dominic's arm.

"I don't know." Dominic's gray eyes were wild with worry as he passed the bag to his wife. "We just got the call from Finn."

"Did he fall in the water?" Caitlin asked, frantic. "He's soaking wet."

Finn's knuckles were white as he gripped his wool cap. "He lost his footing stepping off the boat."

"This is all my fault," an unfamiliar female voice hitched.

Caitlin started, noticing the woman kneeling beside Liam for the first time. Her sleeves and hair were dripping wet. She was wrapped in one of the captain's blankets and a small boy—his face hidden under a black hood—huddled behind her.

"His foot caught in one of the ropes," she explained. "I tried to reach him before he fell, but I wasn't fast enough."

"Finn, get the boat ready to leave again," Tara ordered, leaning down to breathe air into Liam's water-clogged lungs.

Caitlin sank to her knees, wrapping Liam's cold hand in both of hers. This wasn't happening. This couldn't be happening.

Dominic knelt beside her. "Liam!" His voice was rough with

panic, his fingers digging into his brother's shoulder. "Liam, wake up!"

Tara scooted down to his side, interlacing her fingers and pumping the heel of her palms against Liam's chest.

"Liam," Caitlin whispered. "You have to wake up."

LIGHT PIERCED the insides of Liam's eyes. Searing pain filled his lungs. He sucked in a breath, but it lodged in his throat. He choked, rolling onto his side. Familiar voices echoed through the ringing in his ears as he coughed seawater out of his lungs. He held himself up on arms that ached. Every muscle in his body felt like it was on fire.

Where was he? He tried to push himself up to a sitting position, but the dark surface of the water blurred with the edge of the pier. He squeezed his eyes shut as the ground began to spin.

"Liam, can you hear me?" A familiar voice—*Tara's* voice—rang out in the night. What was Tara doing here? His head throbbed but he blinked, struggling to focus. He dragged a spoonful of air into his lungs. Moist, wet air. Cold air. It tasted of salt. His fingers curled around the edge of the pier, his palms rubbing on something gritty, like sand.

"Liam, it's Tara. Can you hear me?"

The wind snatched at her words, bit into his wet clothes. He clenched his teeth to keep them from chattering. Why was it so cold? His eyes flickered open, focusing on the rings forming in the sea. The dark shapes moving in frantic circles just under the surface.

"He's waking up," another voice whispered, this one only vaguely familiar. But there was something about it. Something that pulled to him. He turned, his gaze locking on a mysterious blonde. Seawater dripped from her long pale locks. She was wrapped in a thick gray blanket. But the heavy material had slipped off one slender shoulder, revealing a deep v-neck sweater soaking wet and clinging to her lush figure.

"Where am I?" he breathed.

She reached for his hand, her sleeves dripping cold water onto his wrist, her palm curling soft and cool around his. She smiled hesitantly and he caught the first faint chords of a song, drifting like whispered words over the waves. He pushed himself up onto his elbows, unable to tear his eyes from that glorious face. "What happened?"

"You fell off the deck of the ferry," Tara answered from behind him. "Finn and another passenger pulled you out of the water, but you have a head wound that's still bleeding. I need you to stay flat on your back until I can stop it."

Liam brought a hand up to his head, felt something sticky and warm running down his forehead. He pulled his fingers away. They were coated in blood. "I fell?"

Finn's weathered hands worried over the frayed plaid of his cap. "I'm so sorry, Liam. If it weren't for the lass here..."

"I'm teaching you to swim, Finn," Tara cut in, pressing a fresh wad of gauze to the wound. "As soon as it's warm enough."

Liam's gaze drifted back to the blonde, inhaling the scent of wet wool and saltwater. "You pulled me from the water?"

The woman squeezed his hand. "The captain said he couldn't swim... I just dove in."

That voice. Those words. Where had he heard them before? Lost, he continued to gaze into those lovely almond-shaped eyes until he felt warm, insistent fingers curl around his other forearm.

"Liam," a familiar female voice asked from his other side. "Do you feel okay?"

Reluctantly, he pulled his gaze from the mesmerizing blonde. His brow creased as he focused on the other woman's face. *Caitlin?* Her red curls were tamed into soft waves. Her smoky blue eyes were filled with raw concern. The hem of her fitted dress had ridden up her thighs, revealing a pair of dark lace stockings. Since when did Caitlin wear stockings? Liam's gaze flickered up to her face, then back down at the dress hugging her generous curves. "You look...different."

Caitlin's eyes clouded with confusion.

Liam's gaze dropped to the muddy heels discarded on the pier beside her. "Why are you dressed like that?"

"Why?" Caitlin lowered her voice, her gaze darting over to Dominic. "You know why."

"I do?"

From the corner of his eye, Liam saw Tara put her hand on her husband's arm. "Dom, why don't you let the rest of the islanders know that Liam's okay and I'll finish up here?"

Rocking back on his heels, Dominic looked back and forth between Caitlin and his brother. "I think I'd like to hear the answer to this question first."

"Liam." Caitlin tugged the hem of her dress further down her legs, looking at him strangely. "You were coming over for dinner tonight."

Liam squeezed his eyes shut and opened them again. "Were you having a party?"

"Not exactly."

"Then...why was I coming over?"

Caitlin's gaze fell to where the blonde still clutched Liam's hand in her lap. "You don't...remember?"

"Remember *what*?" Dominic pressed.

Fog slithered over the pier and the water churned beneath them, lapping against the pilings. "We had a...date."

Liam pushed himself up to a sitting position. "A...date?"

Caitlin nodded.

The wet air curled around his limbs like witches' fingers. The faint scent of honeysuckle and cloves drifted toward him and he stared at Caitlin. Was she wearing perfume? For a date? With him? "But...why would we have a date?"

Caitlin dropped his hand as if she'd been burned.

Dominic grabbed him by the shoulders, shaking him. "You had a date with Caitlin? And you *forgot* about it?"

"Dominic," Tara cut in sharply. "This isn't helping." She pried her husband's hands off Liam's shoulders.

Liam caught the sudden movement under the surface of the water. There were more of them now—dozens of distressed seals swimming in frantic circles around the pilings. Somewhere, in the village, a sheep dog began to howl.

"Liam, it's possible you're suffering a slight trauma from your head injury." Tara glanced over at Dominic, warning him to back off. "Why don't you start by telling us what you *do* remember?"

Liam looked back at Caitlin's hurt face. His gaze lingered on her rosebud mouth, tinted a darker shade than normal. Christ. She was wearing lipstick. Surely, it was all a misunderstanding. He'd remember if he was coming home for a date with Caitlin. He glanced over at his brother, who was glaring at him like he wanted to throw him back into the water. His gaze drifted back over to Nuala. Nuala the songwriter from Limerick. Nuala the woman who pulled him from the water.

"Nuala," he said, the syllables rolling off his tongue like the quiet rhythm of waves curling over the sand.

She squeezed his hand. "You remember."

He nodded, sitting up and ignoring the pain that shot through his head. How could he forget? "We spoke on the ferry."

She nodded.

His gaze lingered on those captivating ice-blue eyes. "You're a writer. A songwriter."

Tara's eyes caught Nuala's over Liam's head, and Nuala nodded. "It's true."

"What else do you remember?" Tara pressed.

Liam glanced up at Finn. "I remember reaching for the lines, and letting Finn know I'd take care of the bow."

Finn nodded. "That's right."

Liam's gaze dropped to the wooden planks of the pier. "I'm not sure what happened after that."

"That's okay," Tara soothed. "Do you remember what you did earlier today?"

Liam nodded. "I went to the office this morning. Worked on a presentation I'm giving at a conference next week. I printed out the draft to bring with me to work on. I went home, packed, and drove to Sheridan. I stopped..." He trailed off.

"You stopped?" Tara asked.

Liam stared at a long, thin crack in one of the boards. "I think I stopped somewhere along the way, but I can't remember where." The faint scent of roses drifted through the misty air and he shook his head. Why couldn't he remember the rest?

"Don't worry about every detail," Tara coaxed. "Just focus on what you can remember. Do you remember anything from the rest of your drive to Sheridan?"

Liam thought back to the drive up the winding seaside roads of Connemara. He had his briefcase on the seat beside him. He remembered because he kept shoving his hand in it for a pen and paper to jot notes down while he was driving, a habit he was still trying to break. But there was something else on the seat beside him.

He could smell them again, the roses. But he pushed the thought away, trying to focus. "I remember driving into Sheridan, parking and walking down to the docks. I chatted with Finn for a while and we talked about fishing." He glanced up at Finn and the captain nodded. "I remember boarding the ferry and seeing Nuala and a child." Liam looked back at the blonde and noticed the child huddled behind her for the first time, his face hidden under a dark hood. "I remember thinking it was odd that they'd be coming to the island in the winter. But tourism has picked up since this summer, so I didn't really give it that much thought."

"Go on," Tara urged.

He ran a hand through his wet hair, struggling to focus. Why was this so hard? "They went into the cabin and I rode up on the deck. We were almost to the island when Nuala came out and we started talking."

"What else do you remember about the ferry ride?"

"I caught up with Finn for a while and then wandered up to the bow. I like to see the island come into view. I was thinking about..." A searing pain shot into his eyes. He squeezed them shut, waiting for it to pass. The scent of roses, sweet and feminine and seductive, rolled through him again and he felt sick. Sitting up, he pressed the heels of his palms to his eyes. "I can't remember."

"Come on." Dominic grabbed him by his jacket and hauled him to his feet. "Let's get you inside."

Gathering up her medical kit, Tara offered Nuala a hand. "Are you staying at the O'Neils' B&B?"

"I haven't figured out where I'll be staying yet."

Tara's eyes cut to the small child, huddling behind his mother. "You didn't think to book ahead?"

"It was a spur of the moment trip." Nuala's arm curved around her son. "We didn't have much time for planning."

Liam watched Dominic and Tara exchange glances. "I'm sure the O'Neils can take you in," he said, reading the question in Tara's eyes.

Dominic shook his head. "The O'Neils are booked this weekend. Their family is in town from Dublin."

Liam's gaze shifted to Caitlin. She was gathering up her heels. The bottoms of her stockings were covered in mud. A long tear ran up one leg. She couldn't have gotten dressed up for him.

He would have remembered if he had a date with Caitlin. "Are you still fixing up the McFlaherty's old place?"

"Yes."

"Could Nuala stay there?"

Caitlin shook her head. "It's not finished."

"But it's livable, right?"

"It's only for three days," Nuala appealed, her heeled boots clicking against the pier as she walked up to stand beside Liam. "You'll never even know we were here."

CHAPTER THREE

Sunlight streamed in her bedroom window and Caitlin blinked, squinting against the bright morning light. What time was it? Her hand pushed out from under the tangle of covers, fumbling over her cluttered night table for the clock and stilled when her gaze landed on the dress and stockings balled in the corner by the door. The dress and stockings she was supposed to wear on her first date with Liam.

She squeezed her eyes shut. How could she have been so stupid? How could she have actually believed things had changed between them? When nothing ever changed? Kicking at the covers, she swung her feet to the cold wood floor. Well, guess what? She was done with Liam O'Sullivan. If he didn't want her —if he couldn't so much as *remember* their date—then he didn't deserve her!

She marched to her closet, tugging an old cardboard box from the top shelf and digging through the contents for a pair of battered sneakers. How dare he lead her on? How dare he call her every night for the past three months and stay up talking until midnight? How dare he get her hopes up like that and then cast her aside as if she was just another one of his women?

She should have known better! She pulled on a sweatshirt and sweatpants, caught her hair back into a ponytail and spied her reflection in the mirror. *Nice, Caitlin. Really nice.* She shook her head, turning away from the mirror. What was she thinking getting all dressed up and making a fancy dinner last night? Liam didn't want a relationship. He'd never wanted a relationship. He dated women for mindless, no-strings sex. He dated women who looked like *Nuala.*

Nuala. With her perfect blond hair and perfect blue eyes. Caitlin stalked to the front door and swung it open, letting the bitter winter winds rush into the cottage. Nuala, who could pull a grown man from the freezing November waters without even shivering afterwards. Like she was some damn mermaid.

She slammed the door behind her and broke into a jog, ignoring the stares of her neighbors. It was time she made some changes—*drastic* changes. She picked up her pace through the village, her sneakers pounding on the cracked pavement. When the door to the pub swung open and Dominic stepped out with a broom, she groaned. Great. Just what she needed.

"Caitlin?" Dominic stammered.

She pretended not to hear him, pumping her arms and running faster. She rolled her eyes up to the sky when she heard the broom drop with a clatter and his heavy footsteps start after her.

"*What* are you doing?" Dominic called, catching up to her.

"What does it look like?" Caitlin dragged air deep into her lungs. She wasn't having any trouble breathing. She could do this all day long.

"It looks like you're running." Dominic matched her pace when she tried to pull ahead. They passed the market. Sarah

Dooley was writing up the day's specials on the board outside the shop, but she paused, her jaw falling open as she caught sight of them. "But *why* are you running?"

"Cause I want to get in shape," Caitlin snapped.

"Since when?"

"Since now!"

"Cait." Dominic blew out a frustrated breath. "Stop. Talk to me."

The road forked and she veered onto the path leading up to the east side of the island, bypassing the pier and a reminder of the events of last night. The boats rocked in the harbor, the wind pushing them into the pilings. White caps churned over the surface of the glittering sea. "I really don't want to hear what you have to say right now, Dom."

"Tara's going to talk Liam into seeing a specialist today."

"Go away."

"She thinks there's something wrong with his memory. He's forgetful, but he wouldn't have forgotten a date with you."

"I'm not talking about this with you."

"Caitlin, you're my best friend, and Liam's my brother. If there's something going on between you, I want to know."

"Too bad," she retorted. "Not everything that happens in my life is your business."

"It's my business if you get hurt."

Her eyes flashed as she jerked to a stop. "Because I could only get hurt, right? Liam would never get involved with someone like me."

Dominic stopped running, his breath coming out in puffs in the cold air. "Caitlin, that's not what I meant."

"It's exactly what you meant. Because it's true, isn't it?"

He stared at her, too stunned to speak.

Caitlin spun on her heel and broke into a sprint, running

until Dominic was only a dot in the distance behind her. Her lungs burned and the wind stung the sweat on her cheeks as she slowed. The gentle sloping fields of Brennan Lockley's sheep farm stretched out to the ocean. She leaned against one of the walls, catching her breath.

How was she going to face all her friends and neighbors now that everyone knew the truth? That she'd actually thought something was starting between her and Liam. That she'd actually believed she might finally get the whole package—marriage, kids, family—with Liam. What a fool she was.

The sharp click of a woman's heeled boots on the pavement snapped her head up. She spotted Glenna McClure walking up the path from Brennan's cottage with a pile of books in her arms. Caitlin caught the worried look on her friend's face and she lifted her foot, propping her heel against the wall and pretending to stretch.

Glenna stared at Caitlin. "Are you *exercising?*"

"Yes," Caitlin answered, like it was the most natural thing in the world.

Glenna walked up to her and pinched the baggy sleeve of her torn sweatshirt between her thumb and forefinger. "Where did *this* come from?"

Caitlin tugged her arm away. "It's a sweatshirt. It's not supposed to be stylish."

Glenna angled her head at Caitlin's defensiveness. "Since when do you run?"

"Since today." She started to push past her. "Look, I have a lot on my mind right now. And I'd rather keep going."

Glenna turned, watching Caitlin stalk away. "I know you're hurt."

"I don't want to talk about it."

"I respect that," Glenna called after her. "But you're going about it all wrong."

"Oh, really?" Caitlin spun around, her eyes narrowing. "How *should* I be going about it?"

Glenna took in Caitlin's oversized sweatshirt and baggy sweatpants. She shook her head, clucking her tongue against her cheek. "You're never going to get Liam back looking like that."

Caitlin's hands balled at her sides. "I'm done with Liam O'Sullivan."

"Really?" Glenna raised a brow. "I've never known you to be someone who gives up so easily."

"There's nothing to give up," Caitlin retorted. "He was never mine in the first place."

"He's always been yours, Caitlin. He's just...distracted at the moment."

"*Distracted?*" Caitlin echoed. "Sure, Glenna, he's distracted." She turned, starting back on her run. "I'd like to know what you'd do if the love of your life got distracted?"

"I know I wouldn't be running around this island in ugly sweats feeling sorry for myself," Glenna shouted after her. "I'd be fighting to win him back."

WHAT DID GLENNA KNOW? She wouldn't go out on more than three dates with a man for fear of getting attached and, God forbid, falling in love. She probably didn't even know what love felt like. Caitlin's calf muscles burned, but she kept running, putting more distance between her and the village.

She ran until her lungs ached and she had to slow to a walk, clutching at the sudden cramp in her side. Dominic's words floated back to her. *'Tara's going to talk Liam into seeing a specialist. She thinks there's something wrong with his memory.'*

There wasn't anything wrong with Liam's memory. He remembered everything else about the day—driving to Sheridan, chatting with Finn, meeting Nuala, even helping the captain with the lines before the accident. He remembered everything *but* their date.

A mare raised her head from a neighboring pasture and Caitlin reached out, brushing a hand over the horse's soft whiskered muzzle. But then how did that explain their kiss at Tara and Dominic's wedding? It was an epic kiss—the kind of kiss that made your toes curl and your arms tingle.

Surely the kiss had meant something to him, too. But if it had, then what changed? She let her arm fall back to her side, circling back on the single road leading north to the bogs. Was there a shift in their conversations she hadn't picked up on? Or was Tara's concern justified? Was it possible a head injury could erase only a single strand of memories?

Icy winds whipped over the barren landscape, cutting through her sweaty shirtsleeves. No. That was ridiculous. Memories could be lost over a block of time—a day, a week, even a month before an accident. But not memories of a *single person*.

She picked her way over the stone-and-boulder footpath, pausing when she spied a fresh set of footprints in the grass. They were small, belonging to a child. Curious, she followed them along the edge of the bogs until she spotted a boy kneeling alone outside the crumbling ruins of a stone cottage. His back was to her and he was studying something on the ground.

Caitlin shaded her eyes from the sun. "Hello, there."

The child shot to his feet, shoving his hands in his pockets.

"It's okay," Caitlin said. A pair of ocean blue eyes stared back at her warily. She recognized him from last night; he'd ridden the ferry in with Liam. "No one lives here." She glanced around for the child's mother—the absolute *last* person she wanted to see. "You can poke around all you want."

The boy stepped back from the cottage as she came closer,

but his gaze drifted back to the spot on the ground where he'd been kneeling.

Caitlin's gaze fell to where a single white rose had bloomed overnight in the dead of winter, ice water dripping from its frozen petals.

CHAPTER FOUR

Tara popped the stethoscope out of her ears. "Everything seems fine." She used a penlight to follow the movements of Liam's eyes. "How does your head feel?"

"I've a headache, but nothing a bit of whiskey can't cure." He smiled devilishly up at Tara and she shook her head, popping the penlight back in her pocket. Liam and Dominic were so different in personality, but when he smiled like that it was hard not to recognize that impossible-to-resist O'Sullivan charm.

Liam scooped his glasses off the night table and slipped them on. Tara noted the scratches in the glass, the bent frames. His raven black hair was still mussed from sleep and he had ink all over his fingers. She glanced down at the sheets. Sure enough, there were blue ink stains all over the pillows.

She shook her head. Absent-minded, yes, but he still had the same long lean muscles as his older brother. And when you combined a brilliant imagination and sharp mind with that hard Irish body tucked into a simple white T-shirt and jeans, it was easy to see why women sometimes got tongue-tied around him.

"Keep me posted on how you feel throughout the day," she

said, slipping supplies back into her medical kit. "I want to know if anything changes."

He caught her hand before she turned. "I could use your help with something else."

Tara paused. The scent of boiled ham and roasted tomatoes drifted up from the kitchen where Fiona was preparing breakfast for a small group of regulars. "What is it?"

"Do I owe Caitlin an apology?"

A murmur of voices floated up from the barroom. The sound of chairs scraping against the wooden floor, being pulled out from tables as neighbors and friends called out a morning greeting to each other. Tara bit her lip. He seemed so innocent, looking up at her with those troubled eyes. "I think she's confused."

"Because she thought we had a date?"

Tara slid a hip back onto the bed. The mattress squeaked under her weight. "From what I heard, you did."

"What exactly did you hear?"

"That you two were talking on the phone several times a week. That you were taking things slowly, but things were certainly...progressing."

Liam stared at her for a long moment. "Caitlin and I were talking on the phone *several times a week?*"

"You don't remember?"

Liam shook his head. "What were we talking about?"

Tara started to zip up her bag. "I think you better ask Caitlin that."

Pressing his palms to his eyes, Liam leaned his head back. "What else?"

"What else what?"

"What else am I not remembering?" He opened his eyes, the worry in them stilling Tara's hands. "Is there...more?"

Tara felt a pang of sympathy for Liam. If there was one thing Liam couldn't afford to lose, it was his mind. "I don't know," she admitted. "Caitlin doesn't tell me everything. She's kept most of this to herself, but I did stop by one night when she was on the phone with you and she told me you two had been talking. That something happened at the wedding." She put her hand on his. "I examined your vitals and you seem perfectly fine. You're telling me you feel okay. But I'm worried that you don't remember this. I really think you should consider seeing a specialist. Sooner rather than later."

"What kind of...specialist?"

"A neurologist. I can recommend someone in Galway."

"No." Liam shook his head. "No. I'm fine. I'll be fine. I'll go talk to Caitlin and straighten this out." He stood, and Tara frowned when she saw him shift unsteadily.

"Will you at least give it some thought?"

Liam crossed the room to the window, his hands resting on the edge of an aged walnut bookshelf overflowing with volumes of Irish folklore and worn university textbooks. Paperbacks were stacked beside it, teetering in knee-high piles. "I'll give it some thought."

Wondering if she should push harder, Tara lingered, watching his gaze focus on something outside in the street. Straightening, Liam turned away from the window. "I think I'll have a word with Caitlin now."

"Good." Tara stood. "I think that's best." She watched him turn, pull on the wool sweater from the day before and run a hand through his unruly black hair.

He smiled at her, reaching out and squeezing her shoulder reassuringly. "Everything's going to be fine."

He breezed past her, trotting down the steps two at a time. Wasn't that supposed to be her line? Tara heard him shout, 'good morning' to Dominic and the squeak of the heavy oak door as it opened and slammed shut behind him. He was in far too good spirits all of a sudden. Suspicious, she walked to the window and looked out into the street.

The woman from last night was down there. Nuala. The one who saved his life. She was turning at the sound of Liam's greeting behind her. She paused, waiting for him to catch up to her, and they smiled at each other for a long moment before they began to walk, side-by-side, right past Caitlin's cottage and up toward the cliffs.

Frustrated, Tara started to turn away from the window. But a shimmer of pale silver drew her eye back out to the street. Nuala's long cloak rippled in the wind, billowing out behind her and Tara blinked when a faint ice-blue shimmer skimmed down the fabric like waves. Rubbing her eyes, she waited for them to refocus, but the last thing she saw was the blinding white tail of Nuala's cloak as the pair turned, disappearing behind a stone wall.

CAITLIN TOOK a step closer to the rose and the child edged away. The wind whistled through the cracks in the crumbling stone cottage. The sweet fragrance of the flower, its fragile stem clinging to the frozen earth, tangled with the raw scent of the sea and the bogs.

"Why is there only one of them?" the child asked.

"I don't know." Caitlin shook her head slowly. The last time wild roses grew out of season on this island, it was a sign of trouble to come. But this rose didn't look foreboding. Not like the blood red roses climbing up the walls of Tara's cottage earlier this year. This one just looked lonely. "I've never seen a rose bloom here before."

The child hunched his shoulders against the bitter winds. "What's that underneath it?"

Caitlin's gaze fell to the moss-covered stone under the rose bush. "It's a memorial."

The child took a tentative step closer. "What do those markings mean?"

The wind tugged a curl from Caitlin's ponytail. It whipped into her eyes and she pushed it away. How many times had she come here to escape to the isolation of the bogs and trace the faint engravings on that stone, wishing things hadn't turned out the way they did? "They're initials," she explained quietly. "The first letters of someone's name."

"Who?"

The waves rolled over the northern shore, playing their solemn melody. "Someone who passed away a long time ago."

The child took another step closer. "Maybe the rose grew for her."

"*Him*," Caitlin murmured, tucking the memories back where they belonged.

Kneeling, the child reached out to touch one of the petals. "It's cold," he whispered. "Like it froze that way."

Caitlin saw the tips of the child's exposed fingers turning blue. "Like you will if you stay out here much longer." She turned her back on the rose, facing the child. "What are you doing out here alone anyway? Where is your mother?"

The child lifted his shoulders in a shrug. "Don't know."

"Won't she be looking for you?"

"No."

"She lets you wander off like this?"

He nodded.

"Somehow, I doubt that," Caitlin murmured, but she really didn't want to be discussing the woman who saved Liam's life right now. She turned her attention back to the child, noting there were circles under his eyes like he hadn't slept well. "How are you settling into the cottage?"

"It's nice." The child slipped his hands back in the pockets of his sweatshirts. "I like the seashells."

"The seashells?"

"The ones in the bowls."

"Oh, right." Caitlin scrubbed her hands up the sides of her arms to warm them. He was probably just having trouble adjusting. Lots of kids had trouble sleeping in unfamiliar places. "On the window ledge."

He nodded, pulling a handful of the pretty polished shells from his pocket. "Where did you find them?"

Caitlin stared at the shells. He was carrying them around with him? "On the beach."

"The beach," he repeated, moving his fingers so they caught the sunlight sparkling over their shiny surfaces. "Will you show me?"

"Right now?"

He nodded, and Caitlin crossed her arms over her chest. "How about if we find your mother first, and the three of us go?" Yeah, that's exactly how she wanted to spend the rest of her morning.

"No," he said quickly, slipping the seashell back in his pocket. "Never mind."

Caitlin narrowed her eyes. Why didn't he want to find his mother? "I don't think I caught your name last night...?"

"It's Owen."

"I'm Caitlin." She held out her hand and he stared at it, finally putting his hand in hers and shaking it stiffly, like he wasn't sure what to do. "Where are you from, Owen?"

He looked down, avoiding her eyes.

"Dublin?"

He scuffed the toe of his sneaker into the earth, scrubbing it back and forth.

"Galway?"

He lifted a shoulder, still refusing to look at her. Puzzled, Caitlin thought back to his mother's words the night before when Tara asked why she hadn't thought to book a room on the island ahead of time. *'It was a spur of the moment trip. We didn't have much time for planning.'*

What were they trying to get away from in such a hurry? Caitlin peered down at his worn sneakers, noting for the first time they were soaking wet. The hem of his pants was drenched, too, like he'd been out wading in the surf. "Have you been down to the beach already this morning?"

"No."

"Then how did your clothes get all wet?"

He shrugged. "I don't know."

He didn't know? The hood of his sweatshirt was still pulled up over his face, but the black curls that peeked out were damp and his hollow cheeks were far too thin for a child's. "Owen," Caitlin asked slowly, "have you had breakfast?"

He shook his head, still avoiding her eyes.

"Fiona O'Sullivan makes the best porridge in Ireland." She nodded toward the pub, where smoke curled invitingly from the squat chimney. "It's piping hot and full of brown sugar." She smiled. "How about it? Want to join me?"

His wary gaze flickered up to hers.

"If we ask nicely," she added, wiggling her eyebrows. "She might add a swirl of cinnamon."

Owen's stomach growled and he looked back down at the ground and nodded.

"Come on, then," Caitlin said, turning toward the path leading back to the pub. But she took one last glance over her shoulder at the rose, shimmering in the bright sunlight, its petals coated in ice.

~

"I found a neurologist in Galway," Tara said without looking up from the computer screen. "He wasn't taking any new patients, but I convinced him to squeeze Liam in tomorrow." She glanced up when Caitlin cleared her throat. "Caitlin!" She rose, snapping the laptop shut guiltily. "I thought you were Dominic."

Caitlin's eyes filled with worry. "You think Liam needs to see a neurologist?"

Tara crossed the room quickly to her friend. She took Caitlin's cold hands in hers. "It's just a precaution."

"But...something must be really wrong if you're sending him to a specialist."

"I just want him to have a few tests done." She squeezed Caitlin's hand. "I'm sure it's nothing, but I'll feel better after I see the results."

Caitlin searched Tara's face. "You promise?"

Tara took a deep breath. From the corner of her eye, she could see her daughter, Kelsey, watching her. She lowered her voice. "Okay, I admit. I'm worried." How could she not be worried after examining Liam this morning? How could he forget this one thing, but remember everything else? "But I'm not jumping to any conclusions until I have the data to back it up. Now come inside and warm up by the fire. Your hands are freezing."

Tara ushered Caitlin into the room, pausing when she spotted the child lingering in the doorway. Wasn't that Nuala's child?

His gray-blue eyes lifted and Tara took a step back. Why did those eyes look so familiar? "Are you Fiona O'Sullivan?"

Tara shook her head. "She's in the kitchen. Do you want me to get her?"

"It's okay," Caitlin said, pushing the child's hood back from his face and ruffling his hair. "You can ask Tara."

He looked down at the ground, shifting from one foot to

another. "May I please have a bowl of porridge with extra brown sugar and cinnamon?"

Tara looked down at the child, then back at Caitlin. What was Caitlin doing with Nuala's son?

"I'll have one, too," Caitlin said, pulling off her damp sweatshirt and hanging it over the back of a chair.

"Of course," Tara said slowly. Walking around the bar and popping her head into the kitchen, she put in the order with Dominic's grandmother and then came back out, smiling down at the child. "Why don't you join my daughter by the fire and warm up while you wait."

He looked uncertainly at the blonde curled up on a blanket reading a book. Kelsey scooted over, patting the blanket beside her. "Do you like fairy tales?"

"I guess," he said, shuffling over to her and lowering himself to the very edge of the blanket.

As soon as he was out of earshot, Tara turned to Caitlin. "Where's his mother, Caitlin?"

"I don't know," Caitlin admitted, walking with Tara over to the bar. "I found him wandering alone by the bogs. His clothes were wet like he'd been wading in the surf."

"I saw her walk by earlier—Nuala, I mean," Tara said, leaving out the part about Liam following her out into the street. She felt a new stab of frustration with Liam. And what kind of mother let her child wander around a strange island alone in the middle of winter in wet clothes?

"He wouldn't tell me where he was from," Caitlin said, lowering her voice. "I can't help but wonder if something... happened before they came here."

Tara's eyes strayed to where Kelsey was turning the book around to show him the pictures. "Like what?"

"I don't know," Caitlin admitted. "But I have a bad feeling about it."

Tara thought back to what she'd seen out the window this morning. The strange shimmer on Nuala's cloak. "We should talk to Glenna."

"No." Caitlin shook her head. "She'll just think I'm jealous."

"What do you mean?"

"She thinks I'm sulking. I ran into her this morning and she accused me of giving up and letting Nuala win."

"Are you?" Tara asked gently

"I don't know," Caitlin confessed, rubbing her thumb over the polished wood of the bar. "What would you do, if you were me?"

Tara's gaze fell to the spot on the bar Caitlin was picking at. She thought back to what Liam said this morning—that he couldn't remember anything about Caitlin or their relationship, which meant this wasn't going to be easy for Caitlin. But what in life worth having was ever easy?

Tara thought back to everything that happened to her in the past year. She heard the familiar squeak of rusted hinges as the back door of the pub opened, followed by Dominic's deep lilting Irish accent striking up a conversation with his grandmother in the kitchen. She felt the love surge inside her at the sound of his voice. She thought of Kelsey and Fiona and all her friends. And the life she would have lost if she'd kept running from her abusive husband instead of standing and fighting.

She lifted her eyes to Caitlin's. "I'd fight back."

CHAPTER FIVE

Owen gazed at the glossy pages and hard canvas binding of Kelsey's book, mesmerized. "Where did you get this?"

"My uncle gave it to me."

"You said it's a...fairy tale?"

Kelsey nodded, setting the book between them and turning the pages as she read silently to herself.

He angled his head to see the pictures better. She was turning the pages too fast. He reached out, stopping her.

"Sorry," she said. "Are you still reading?"

He stared at the open page. The creatures in the drawing looked so familiar. He traced a finger over the markings at the bottom of the page. "What are these?"

Kelsey looked up at him, puzzled. "The words?"

"I guess."

She stared at him. "That's what makes up the story."

"Oh." He gazed down at the letters. Maybe if he knew what they meant, he would know why these pictures seemed so familiar. "Could you...would you tell me what they say?"

Kelsey's eyes widened. "Can't you read?"

Owen's gaze darted over to where Caitlin and Tara sat at the bar, still deep in conversation. He lowered his voice. "Sure, I can...read."

Kelsey narrowed her eyes. "Then what does this say?" She pointed to a word at the bottom of the page.

He squirmed, trying to make out the letters. Or were they initials? Isn't that what Caitlin had called the markings on the rock under the rose? Frustrated, he buried his hands in the damp material of his sweatshirt. Rocks and roses. Those he could understand. They had rocks and roses where he was from, wherever that was. But he'd never seen a book before. He reached out, touching a finger to the edge of the binding. It was sharp. Like the tip of a starfish.

"Owen?" Kelsey asked.

"Yes?"

"What does this word say?" She tapped the bottom of the page.

Folding his legs up, he wrapped his arms around them, hugging them to his chest.

Kelsey scooted closer, so their shoulders were almost touching, and lowered her voice. "It says, 'selkie.'"

Owen's eyes combed the page, staring at the dark creatures surrounded by silver fish and pink seashells. Like the ones in the cottage. He pushed his hand in his pocket and felt the shells. They were still there. He rolled them around in his hands and the quiet clinking calmed him. "What's a selkie?"

Kelsey pointed to the creature on the page. "A selkie's a seal that can turn into a woman on land."

He picked up the book, looking more closely at the picture. "A seal that can turn into a...woman?"

Kelsey nodded. She reached over his shoulder, flipping through the pages while he held the book. "See," she said when they came to a picture of a beautiful woman with long black hair on a beach, her seal-skin hidden beneath a rock.

"Are there selkies that can turn into a man?"

"I don't know. I've never heard of one."

Owen touched the page where the seal-skin was tucked under a rock. "Why does she hide it?"

"It's complicated." Kelsey smiled, reaching for the book. "Do you want me to read it to you?"

Owen held onto the book, shaking his head and refusing to let it go. Flipping back through the pages to the pictures of the seals deep in the ocean, he tapped a finger against the glossy page. "I've been there."

"Where?"

"To this place."

"You mean...snorkeling?"

"What's snorkeling?"

"You don't know what snorkeling is?"

Owen shook his head.

"It's when you swim around with a mask that has a tube sticking up out of the water so you can breathe."

"I wasn't wearing a mask," Owen murmured. "But I've *been* there before."

Kelsey giggled. "You couldn't have been there."

"Why not?"

"Because humans can't breathe underwater, silly."

Owen stared at the pages. Slowly, he reached out and turned to the next page. Then the next. Then the next. He could taste it —the salt of the sea. The sense of weightlessness as the dark water surrounded him. The feeling of pushing through those cold waters with...he glanced down...something *other than legs*. He started to shiver as the song, an echo of harp strings in the distance, pulsed through that quiet kingdom of green.

Kelsey reached out suddenly, grabbing hold of his shirt.

"You're all wet," she exclaimed, watching him shiver. "Is it raining out?" She pushed up on her knees to see out the window. "No. It's still sunny out. How did you get wet?"

He could hear her voice, could feel her touching him, but he couldn't make out the words. He stared at the picture of the pack of selkies swimming together. "How come all the selkies are black?"

"That's the color of their seal-skin. It's always black." Kelsey tugged at his now-dripping shirt. "How did you get so wet?"

"Are there any white selkies?"

"I don't think so."

He flipped through the pages again, searching for one. "Do you have more?"

"More *what*?"

"More books."

Kelsey sighed. "Yes, but I don't think they have white selkies in them either."

Owen bit his lip, flipping back through the pages. "Have you ever seen one?"

"A selkie?"

Owen nodded, looking at her intently.

Kelsey sat back and smiled. "Sort of."

"What do you mean, 'sort of?'"

"My mum's part selkie." Kelsey nodded at Tara.

Owen's eyes went wide. "Your *mum* can turn into a seal?"

Kelsey giggled and Tara glanced over, smiling at them. "No, silly." She lowered her voice. "But her great-great-great-grand-mother was a selkie... It's a long story."

"Tell me."

Kelsey's brows lifted. "Now?"

He nodded urgently.

"I can't. I'm playing football with Ashling and Ronan soon. You can come play with us if you want."

"Football?"

"It's a game." Kelsey rolled her eyes. "*Where* did you come from?"

He hugged his knees tighter to his chest.

Kelsey lifted her eyebrows. "Well?"

"I don't know," he whispered.

"You don't...know?"

"I can't remember."

Kelsey stared at him, then scrambled to her feet, letting the book fall aside. She held out her hand. "Come on, we need to talk to my mum."

"No!" He shook his head emphatically. "You can't tell anyone."

Kelsey's eyes widened. "But we need to find out where you're from!"

"I'll figure it out. Please." His eyes darted to the door. "Don't tell your mother. Don't tell anyone."

Kelsey sank back down to the blanket. "Why not?"

"Promise me," he said quickly.

Kelsey just stared at him.

His eyes darted around the room again. "If I come back tonight, will you tell me the story?"

Kelsey continued to stare at him when her great-grandmother came out of the kitchen, setting a piping bowl of porridge in front of Owen. "Extra brown sugar and cinnamon, like you asked for."

"Thank you," he said softly, wrapping his hands around the steaming bowl.

As soon as she turned her back, Owen grabbed Kelsey's hand. "*Promise me*," he mouthed.

"Okay," she whispered, pulling her hand away and crossing her arms over her chest. Sitting back, she watched him for several moments with a puzzled expression on her face. "I promise."

He picked up the spoon, bringing the warm sugary bite to his mouth, soothing his hunger. But his eyes strayed back to the pages of the book. He didn't know where he was from. But he knew those creatures—*selkies*—and that world.

He scooped another piping hot bite into his mouth, savoring the sharp taste of the cinnamon on his tongue. He would figure this out. And he would get back to his home. But first he needed to figure out why all these selkies were black, when all he could remember was a cold, blinding white.

"THANK you for showing me around the island," Nuala said, pausing outside the door to her rented cottage and smiling up at Liam. White caps chopped at the surface of the harbor, rocking the fishing boats docked at the pier. Seagulls soared above the rocky coastline, their solemn cries echoing over the water as they dipped and rolled with the wind. "I can see why you come back here so much. It really is beautiful."

"It's the most beautiful place in the world," Liam agreed, dipping his hands in his pockets. "But showing you around is the least I could do after you saved my life."

"Please stop saying that," Nuala said. "Anyone would have done the same thing."

"I'm not sure about that," Liam countered, his eyes holding hers. "And I don't think a walking tour quite repays what you did. Why don't you let me take you and your son out to dinner tonight?"

"I don't know," Nuala said, looking out to the sea.

"What is it?"

"It's Owen." Nuala said softly. "He can be shy around strangers. I wouldn't want him, or you, to get the wrong idea."

"And what idea would that be?"

She lifted her eyes back to his. "I'm only here for a few days."

Liam smiled and little lines fanned out from his eyes, warming them. "It's only dinner, Nuala. Besides, there's only the one place to eat on the island, and it's my family's pub so it's not like it'll just be the two of us. But I *can* ensure you'll get special treatment."

He flashed her a winning smile, and she couldn't help but laugh. "You're very convincing."

"When I see something I want, I usually get my way."

So did she, Nuala thought, holding his gaze. And nothing was going to stop her from getting what she wanted this time. "Let me run it by Owen first. But thank you. It's been a long time since either of us got special treatment. An evening out at an island pub sounds innocent enough."

He held her eyes for a long moment, and *innocent* was the opposite of what she saw deep in those eyes. She looked away, feigning shyness.

"Until then," he said, turning on his heel and strolling back toward the pub.

She watched him walk away, that long, lanky build so easy on the eyes and when she heard him begin to whistle an old Irish tune, she smiled, fishing out her key and letting herself into the cottage. The cottage the redhead—*Caitlin*—had decorated. She laughed as she looked around at the small details. The ridiculous bowls of tiny broken seashells. The mismatched kitchen table chairs. The flimsy curtains that barely offered a hint of privacy.

She hadn't expected Liam to be completely unattached. Men who looked like that didn't go around long without a girlfriend. But she hadn't expected her competition to be so pathetic. It was almost too good to be true.

"Owen," she called out to her son, running her fingers over a worn brass four-leaf clover hanging above the fireplace. "Time to get up."

When she didn't get a response, she walked into his bedroom, and spotted the three rocks stacked on his pillow. So he hadn't forgotten everything after all. She crossed the room, collecting the rocks and dropping them into the pocket of her long white sweater. Owen always left three rocks when he wanted her to know he'd gone out but would be back soon.

Her hands closed around the rocks and she backed out of the room. The wind rattled the windows, pushing the scent of the sea into the house. She closed her eyes, breathing it in, fighting the force that pulled her to it. Three days. She could do this. The sea spray beckoned, crashing up onto the rocky shore below. A small sliver of beach led away from the harbor, curving around the rocky coast leading up to the cliffs.

It would be so easy to run down that worn path, to feel the wet sand beneath her feet, to dive into the salty waves and feel the cold ocean welcome her home. *Home.* She leaned against the frame of the door, breathing in the scent of salt and kelp. She would be there soon enough.

And everything she had ever wanted would be hers again.

She bolted the lock on the door to the cottage, in case Owen was on his way back now, and slipped into her bedroom. She dropped to her knees, cursing those flimsy lace curtains, and reached under the rug, prying the wooden floorboard loose with one of Owen's rocks.

Pulling the carefully folded bundle from its hiding place, she ran an oiled rag lovingly over the soft seal-skin. She tucked the smaller child's pelt back into the corner, and then pulled out a third pelt, letting the silky coat run through her hands. In three days they would return to the water.

And this time, they wouldn't be going alone.

CHAPTER SIX

The man had balls. Either that or Liam O'Sullivan was the stupidest man on the planet. Standing in Caitlin's crowded living room, Glenna took in the gorgeous blonde walking with Liam through the doorway and shook her head. What was he thinking, bringing Nuala to Caitlin's house tonight? Even if it was a fake birthday party, *he* didn't know that. He didn't know they'd already celebrated Glenna's birthday last week and patched together this last minute party to help him get his memory back.

She watched him take Nuala's coat and hang it with his on the hook beside the door. Oh, she wanted to knock some sense into that handsome face of his. She'd been so proud of Caitlin for coming up with the idea. But it was going to take a lot more than creativity to lure Liam away from this blonde. Glenna's fingers curled around the stem of her glass when Nuala smiled up at Liam and whispered something in his ear. *Distracted* didn't begin to describe the way she already had him wrapped around her pretty little finger.

"You don't like her."

Glenna jumped at the sudden voice in her ear. Sam. Just what she needed. He was close enough that she could smell the musk of his soap and the leather of his jacket. His hair was still wet, like he'd just stepped out of the shower. It was getting longer, curling down around the collar of his shirt. Why? Why did that have to make him more attractive? And why did Caitlin insist on inviting him tonight? "No, I don't."

"How come?"

"Just a gut feeling."

"I could ask her to leave," he offered.

She turned to face him, gazing up into those whiskey-colored eyes. "How chivalrous of you."

"What can I say?" He took a sip of bourbon. Ice clicked around in the glass. "You bring out the knight in me."

He smiled and Glenna rolled her eyes. As much as she'd love to take this delicious man home tonight for an entirely different sort of birthday celebration, that was the problem with Sam. She'd need more than that. And then things would get complicated. As Caitlin so bluntly stated this morning, Glenna didn't do complicated. "Thanks," she said. "But I can manage."

He reached out, twisting a finger around one of her long russet locks. Little shivers of pleasure danced along her skin. "You look incredible tonight. As usual."

"And you look like you showered." She smiled pleasantly, taking a sip of her wine. "How *is* life on the farm treating you?"

"Why don't you come down sometime and I'll show you."

She lifted a winged brow. One of the guests brushed past her, jostling her, and she grabbed hold of his upper arm to steady herself. She could feel the rock-solid mass of muscle through his jacket and she drew her hand back quickly, smoothing it down her cashmere sweater. "I was there this morning, actually."

"At Brennan's?"

She nodded.

"Doing what?"

"Oh, just a little research." She flipped her heavy hair back over her shoulder, out of his reach. She couldn't have him rolling it around in his fingers like that. It was driving her crazy. "I needed to borrow some books."

"What books?"

Glenna's lips curved. "Wouldn't you like to know?"

Sam leaned back against the wall. "Maybe I'll just ask Brennan."

"You could," Glenna said slowly. "But I doubt he paid any mind to what I took."

"You enjoy this, don't you?" Sam's eyes held hers, the little flecks of gold in them warming like the first snapping sparks of a fire. "Making me wonder what you're up to."

"I'm always up to something, Sam." She smiled, turning on her heel. "Now if you'll excuse me."

The jumble of conversation ebbed and flowed. Wax candles flickered in tiny glass jars nestled in black sand. More guests streamed through the front door and winter winds swirled into the room in sharp, biting gusts. Sam continued to lean against the wall, watching Glenna saunter away. "Seems like a long way to walk for a couple books when I could have brought them to the pub. Met you halfway."

Glenna looked over her shoulder. That simple statement went way beyond a couple of books. He was trying to get her to open up, to talk to him after she'd been shutting him out for the past few months. But she couldn't. She needed him to live his life so she could live hers. There was so much he didn't know. So much the people on this island still had to go through. And she had to keep her focus. She couldn't afford to slip up. Not once. And certainly not for some man. "I like to walk."

"Then come back tomorrow." Sam pushed off the wall, closing the distance between them.

"For what?"

"To say hello," he said. "What you should have done today."

Glenna lifted a shoulder. "I didn't think of it, at the time."

Sam smiled and Glenna took another sip of wine. Of course they both knew that was a total lie. She could barely be within a mile of this man without sensing him, without feeling his presence and wanting him. But that didn't mean she needed to act on it. She had incredible willpower when it came to men. Especially ones who couldn't be trusted. And there was no doubt in her mind, despite everything that happened this summer, Sam was not to be trusted.

"I'll keep an eye out for you next time," Sam offered, that fire still burning in his eyes. "I'd like to show you around so you can see what I've done."

"I'm sure that would be a riveting tour," Glenna replied, her fingers curling around the stem of her wine glass to keep them from creeping up the folds of that worn leather jacket and tangling into those sun-streaked curls. "Seeing all the fences you've mended."

Sam's lips curved. He held out his hand, and she noted the new calluses forming on his wide palms. "I've got farmer hands now."

Glenna's mouth went dry. God, she wanted those hands on her, on every surface of her.

"You seem flushed," Sam commented after several long moments. "Are you hot?"

"I'm fine," she said quickly.

He fished an ice cube from his drink and cupped it in his palm, holding it out to her. "Maybe this will help."

"What do you want me to do with that?"

He grinned. "I can think of so many things."

Dᴏᴍɪɴɪᴄ ᴛʜʀᴇᴀᴅᴇᴅ his way through the crowd gathered in Caitlin's living room. A cozy peat fire snapped in the hearth and a steady bubble of conversation followed him into the connected kitchen, where he found her peeling the foil off a plate of herbed potatoes. "Can I help with anything?"

She tossed the foil into the trash and carried the steaming plate over to the table where the rest of the food was laid out. "I think I've got it under control." She wiped her hands on a dish towel and folded it back over the handle of the oven. "But thanks."

Dominic leaned back against the counter, taking in the subtle changes throughout the room. Vanilla and cinnamon-scented pillar candles burned in the windowsills, wax dripping down their fat stems. Tea lights flickered over the coffee table, illuminating an impressive collection of fairy tale books laid out with their beautifully-illustrated covers in full display.

"I didn't know you had all those," Dominic commented, watching Kelsey choose one from the table and pull it into her lap. He stiffened when the newcomer's child, Owen, climbed up onto the sofa beside her.

"I've had them for years," Caitlin said, twisting the top off a Harp and handing it to him.

Dominic took the bottle, his hand wrapping around the cold glass, but his gaze lingered on Owen as he edged closer to Kelsey, peering over her shoulder at the pages of the book. A strange, unsettling feeling took root in his gut as he thought back to the brief conversation he'd had with Nuala when she'd walked in with Liam an hour ago.

He'd asked her a few simple questions about Limerick, just to be friendly, even though he was furious with his brother for bringing her to Caitlin's house. But his frustration quickly turned to worry when some of the newcomer's answers didn't add up. It was almost like she hadn't really spent any time in Limerick at all.

Glancing over at his brother, he saw that Nuala was still locked to his side, smiling up at him as he refilled her glass with white wine. He'd seen his brother get moony over a woman before, but he'd never seen anything quite like this. He knew Liam could handle himself—at least, he *hoped* Liam could handle himself—but he was fairly certain now that this woman was hiding something.

His gaze drifted back to where Owen was watching his mother across the room with a strange detached expression on his face, and the worry rooted deeper. Kelsey was reading aloud, oblivious to whether or not Owen was paying attention. If the newcomer was hiding something, as he suspected she was, then he didn't want that boy anywhere near his daughter.

"I've seen that look before." Caitlin lowered her voice. "What's the matter?"

"I'm not sure." Dominic lifted the bottle, taking a long slow pull. There was no need to get Caitlin worried yet. At least, not until he'd had a chance to talk to Tara about it first. "Has Liam noticed anything yet?"

Caitlin shook her head. "Not yet."

"What else did you set out to trigger his memory?"

She tugged at one of her curls. "Little things."

Dominic sighed. He didn't know what any of these things meant or how they were supposed to bring back his brother's memory, but Caitlin must know something he didn't. He was going to have to trust her. He watched her gaze drift back across the room to where Liam and Nuala were chatting with Tara. "About this morning..."

Caitlin picked up a sponge, wiping at a nonexistent crumb on the counter. "Can we please forget about that?"

Dominic dipped his hands in the pockets of his jeans. "No."

"Look," Caitlin said, turning to face him. "I was upset. I didn't mean to snap at you."

"No," Dominic said, turning to face her. "I'm the one who should apologize. I admit...you and Liam? It took me by surprise. But that doesn't mean I'm against it. It just means I have to shift my way of thinking. We've been friends since, well, since forever. I sort of took on that role of looking after you, like you were my own sister. I assumed Liam felt the same way." He lifted his eyes back to hers. "I was wrong. I'm sorry."

Caitlin put down the sponge. "Look, Dom. I don't know what's happening between me and Liam. But if what I want plays out, you're going to have to let go and give us some space. Even if it means I end up getting hurt."

"Is that what you really want?"

"It's what I've wanted for a very long time." Caitlin's gaze drifted across the room when Nuala's laughter floated over the swell of conversation. "And until the accident on the ferry last night, I thought that's what he wanted, too."

OWEN HEARD his mother laugh and caught her eye briefly across the room. She was talking with Kelsey's mother, the woman with the black hair Kelsey said was a 'selkie'. There weren't any selkies in the book Kelsey was reading now. But there were mermaids. And mermaids couldn't wiggle out of their tails like selkies could shed their seal-skin. They had to make some kind of trade with the sea witch first, which seemed like a really bad idea.

Curled up on the sofa with a piece of birthday cake on his lap, Owen waited for his mother's back to turn, then he peered over Kelsey's shoulder at the pages of the new storybook. "The mermaid trades her voice and her *soul* for a chance to live on land for three days?"

Kelsey nodded, breaking off a piece of his cake and popping it in her mouth. "So the prince will fall in love with her."

"But that's crazy!"

"Why is that so crazy?" Kelsey turned the page, revealing a picture of the mermaid swimming up to the surface with legs now, leaving all she'd ever known behind. "She was in love. Nothing should stop two people who are in love from being together."

Reaching across her, Owen flipped the page back to the one before it, gazing down at the mermaid's sparkly tail. "But what if they weren't meant to be together? What if the prince was supposed to be with the princess?"

"Everyone knows the prince is supposed to be with the mermaid."

Pulling the book into his own lap, Owen flipped back to the beginning, starting over and scanning the images of the mermaid gliding up to the surface and watching the massive ship splinter apart in the storm. She carried the drowning prince to shore and waited until the princess found him, only to return to that broken ship lying on the bottom of the ocean. But wasn't that where she was supposed to be? Wasn't that where she belonged?

"Hey," Kelsey said, nudging him. "Don't you like the cake?"

He nodded, only half-listening.

"Then why aren't you eating it?"

He turned the pages to where the prince met the mermaid in human form for the first time. Why couldn't he see that she wasn't the one he was supposed to be with?

"Owen?"

"Yes?" he said, still staring at the pages.

"When's *your* birthday?"

His gaze flickered up to hers, then drifted back down to the pages.

Kelsey lowered her voice. "Do you know?"

Owen shook his head.

Flipping back to the earlier pages, she pointed to the scene of the mermaid swimming around the shipwrecked boat lying at the bottom of the ocean, its broken hull covered in barnacles. "Have you been there?"

Owen glanced up. His mother was still across the room chatting with Kelsey's mother. Her back was to them, but he lowered his voice to a whisper anyway. "I think so."

"You still don't remember anything?"

He shook his head.

"Does your mum...remember anything?"

"I don't know."

"Have you asked her?"

"No."

"Maybe you should." Kelsey stared at his profile for a long time, finally pulling the book from his hands and setting it on the table. "Here," she said, ignoring his protests. "Why don't we read a different story for a while so you can finish your cake?" She looked at him pointedly. "It's a really good piece of cake."

Owen bit his lip. He didn't want to go back to that one later. He needed to know how that one ended now.

Fishing another book from the table, Kelsey settled back into the sofa. She showed him the cover. "It's called *Beauty and the Beast*." She pointed at each word as she read it aloud. "I think you'll like this one. It has a talking teacup in it."

Owen stabbed the fork into the cake. He didn't want to read about talking teacups. He wanted to see the pictures of the ocean again. His gaze drifted over to *The Little Mermaid*, lying facedown on the table. His fingers itched to hold it and he gobbled the rest of his cake, hoping to convince Kelsey to go back to it right away. He stuffed the last bite into his mouth, chocolate crumbs spilling all over his lap as he set the plate aside, reaching

for it. But he snatched his hand back when a shadow fell across
the table.

The tall man with the black hair and glasses, the one his
mother had tripped, was eyeing the same book with an odd
expression on his face. Slowly, he bent down and picked it up. He
turned it over carefully, staring at the cover for several long
moments, then wandered over to the fire and started flipping
through the pages.

"Trying to see if you still have the story straight?" Caitlin asked.

Liam almost dropped the book.

"Sorry," Caitlin said wryly, handing him a Guinness. "Didn't
mean to frighten you."

"No." Liam set the book back on the table and ran a shaky
hand through his hair. "I'm sorry. I'm...somewhere else tonight."

"You're always somewhere else."

Liam lifted the pint glass, taking a long swallow. That was
true. And any other night he might have laughed at her jab about
him living most of his life with his head stuck in the clouds. But
not tonight. Not when he'd spent the entire afternoon trying to
dig up the file he'd been working on for the past three months.
Not after he'd torn his briefcase apart searching for a hard copy
and come up with nothing. When he knew—*knew*—he'd printed
out the pages to bring with him yesterday. But, then, where the
hell had they gone?

What if Tara was right? What if something had happened
when he hit his head on the pier? What if there was something
seriously wrong with his mind? His gaze fell back to the cover of
the book. Something pulled at him, a ghost of a memory floating
back and he struggled to reel it in but it disappeared in a white
blur as quickly as it had taken shape.

"Liam?" Caitlin's brows knitted in concern. "Are you okay?"

"Sure," he lied, taking another sip. "I'm fine." What was it about that book that was so familiar? It was more than that he'd seen it before. It was like it was supposed to mean something to him? But what? Why couldn't he remember?

"So tell me about this new legend you stumbled across."

New legend?

"You know," Caitlin prodded. "The new Irish fairy tale you discovered in Dublin a few weeks ago. At the Trinity College Library. You were going to tell me about it last night."

"Oh...right," Liam nodded. On their *date*. He took another long sip of the dark stout. Wait. Did she just say Dublin? Had he been to Dublin recently? "I...haven't had much chance to work on it lately."

"What are you talking about?" Caitlin angled her head. "That's *all* you've been working on the last few weeks."

"Oh, *that* fairy tale?" Maybe if he kept this going long enough, she'd give him a hint. "I thought you were talking about something else."

"What else would I be talking about? Did you discover another legend since the last time I talked to you?"

"I don't...think so."

Caitlin stared at him oddly. "You were going to present your findings at the conference in Limerick next week. The one the Prime Minister's wife is attending."

Liam's brows shot up. The Prime Minister's wife was attending the conference?

"You said you'd tell me about it when you got here," Caitlin continued, watching him even more closely now. "It was supposed to mean something really big was going to happen to your department if she decided to get behind it. So...what's the big news?"

The big news was that he was losing his freaking mind! The bubble of conversation rose to a fever pitch as more friends and neighbors crowded into the tiny room. The peat fire snapped in the hearth, making the air feel unnaturally warm. Everywhere he looked his friends were huddled in circles chatting and laughing, clinking their glasses together, enjoying themselves.

Why did he feel like he could hardly breathe? He needed to get out of this house, get some air, and figure out what the hell was wrong with him. Setting his glass down, he caught the edge of one of the shallow glass bowls. It toppled off the table, scattering sand onto the rug.

They knelt at the same time, scooping sand into their hands. Their fingers brushed and a jolt, like an electric current, shot up his arm. He caught her hand in his, turning it over and staring at the sparkling sand resting in her palm as snatches of a memory fell into place. "Where did you get this?"

Caitlin held her breath, a flicker of hope igniting deep in her eyes. "Lockley's beach."

"Do you...collect it?"

She nodded.

"Why?"

"It holds a special meaning for me."

It held a special meaning for him, too. But what was it? His fingers curled around her wrist, his wide palm dwarfing her small one. He could feel her pulse beating under the surface of her skin. He skimmed his thumb over her heated flesh. He heard the slight intake of breath as her pulse jumped, and he lifted his gaze to her eyes.

"You used to go there every night," he breathed as a strange tingling sensation spread up his forearm, starting from where her fingers touched his skin. Another memory clicked into place, like slides of a black and white movie. "*We* used to go there."

She nodded, and he rose, pulling him with her. He looked down, lost as those big sapphire eyes glimmered up at him with so much raw hope, so full of expectation. The swell of voices and conversation faded as he untangled the collar of her sweater from where it had caught in a button.

"You used to tell me stories," Caitlin whispered. "The ones you came up with during the day. The ones you refused to write down."

"I remember," Liam murmured, his fingers lingering in the soft hand-knit wool of her sweater. "You believed in them."

"I believed in *you*."

Her rich, red waves cascaded around her pale skin, brushing against her shoulders. How had he never noticed how full and soft her hair was? "You told me this was magic sand," he said, reeling each piece of the memory in like a fish struggling at the end of a line. His gaze fell back to the dark sand in her palm. "Dust from the selkies' pelts when they came up to the beach to dance. You said the beach was enchanted."

"I used to think it was."

"But you don't anymore?"

Caitlin shook her head.

"Why not?" When she said nothing, he searched her eyes. There was a flicker of sadness in them now and he felt a sudden urge to comfort her. "You wanted to build a cottage there," he murmured as bits and pieces of their moonlight conversations floated back to him. "So you could feel their magic. So you could see them at night from your bedroom window."

When she bit her lip, his gaze dropped to where her teeth caught the soft pink flesh. He wanted to brush his thumb over that spot, lower his mouth to hers, and drink in the taste of her. But...it was almost like he already knew what her lips felt like melting against his. "Why haven't you built that house, Caitlin?"

"I haven't...gotten around to it."

"But you still want to?" Why was this so important to him? Why couldn't he remember the rest? "Caitlin, I..." He trailed off as cold fingers wrapped around his forearm. They snaked like ropes, cutting off his air, scrambling those first snatches of memories into dust.

Caitlin's eyes clouded as her gaze shifted to Nuala.

"Thank you for inviting us tonight," Nuala said, her voice as rhythmic and lyrical as the melody of the waves. "But it's time for Owen and me to go."

Caitlin pried her hand free from Liam's grip and leaned down to pick up the dish from the floor. There was still a teaspoon of black sand in it and she cradled it in her hands, like it was the most precious thing in the world. "How's the cottage working out for you?"

The surf pounded in Liam's ears. Seawater clogged his throat. He was frozen, unable to move or speak as the sea surrounded him, filling his lungs with ice-water.

Nuala handed him her empty glass and he took it, numb. Her fingers squeezed his arm as he struggled to breathe over the icy water choking him. "I had some trouble with the heater this morning. I was hoping Liam could show me how to use it."

"Of course." Caitlin's grip on the sand tightened. "He knows how to work it."

Nuala smiled. "I hope you don't mind if I pull him away early."

"Not at all." Caitlin gritted her teeth. "I guess I'll see you both tomorrow."

It was green and quiet. A world of ice and silence. Liam watched Caitlin turn and walk away, and he set the glass down. His fingers stuck to the stem and he pried them off one by one. But when he pulled his hand away, a crystallized seal of ice coated the glass and his gaze fell to his hand where a faint shimmer of blue was slowly spreading over his skin. A sudden movement on the couch caught his eye and he glanced up as Nuala's son stood.

Owen took one look at the glass and Liam's frozen hand, and he flipped up his hood to cover his face. The hood was coated in that same crystallized pattern of ice. He slipped out of the room as black and silent as a ray, a trail of water dripping in his wake.

CHAPTER SEVEN

$\mathcal{C}$aitlin lit a fire to ward off the morning chill. Rain smacked against the windows, streaming down the glass like cold, silver tears. She'd forgotten to bring in the wind chimes and they spun around in frantic circles, their strings tangling in the wind. Glancing out her window at the white caps chopping over the surface of the ocean, she frowned. There was no way the ferry was going to be able to make the crossing in this weather. Which meant Liam wasn't going to be able to make it to his appointment with the neurologist.

He might have thought he fooled her last night, but she knew better. He'd forgotten more than just their date. He'd forgotten the details of his latest research project. And that wasn't like Liam. She started to put away the dishes from last night. Plates and glasses clicked against each other as she fit them back into the tightly packed shelves above the sink.

There was nothing Liam took more seriously than his research. He could overlook trivial things—the leaking pen in his pocket, the screw slipping out of his glasses, the tie he was supposed to bring to a presentation—but he wouldn't forget the details of a research project. Especially one he'd hinted at so often in their recent phone conversations. Caitlin paused in the middle of putting a bowl away. How odd that he would forget *both* of those things.

The wind howled, rattling the windows, and she lifted up on her toes to prop the bowl up on the tallest shelf. No, that was ridiculous. What Liam needed was to get to a neurologist. Not have his friends throw him a party and set out trinkets to help him remember. She'd thought for a second she caught a glimmer of recognition in his eyes after he spilled the sand, but maybe she'd been kidding herself.

At the knock on the door, she tossed the dishrag in the sink and crossed the room. She pulled the door open and stepped back, surprised. "Owen?" He was soaked through, not wearing a raincoat or carrying an umbrella. "Come in, come in." She ushered him inside. "What are you doing out in this mess without a rain jacket?"

He stepped into the warmth of her cottage, dripping all over the floor. "I haven't got a rain jacket."

She grabbed a bath towel and handed it to him. She watched him ball it up awkwardly, patting his arms and, sighing, she took it back and scrubbed it over his wet hair and dried his face and neck. "Where's your mother?"

"She's home."

"She lets you wander off in a storm like this?"

"She's writing a song. She always wants me gone when she's writing a song."

"I see," Caitlin said, taking the towel back and hanging it over the shower. But she didn't see. What kind of mother let her child run off in the rain in the dead of winter? "Come over and sit by the fire. I'll make you some tea."

He crossed the room, drifting over to the bookshelves and poking his fingers into some of the books. He frowned as he slid them back in place. Caitlin watched him curiously as she set the kettle of water on the stove to boil. "What brings you around this morning?"

He slipped his hands in his pockets, guiltily. "I wanted to see the story again. The one Kelsey showed me last night. The one about the mermaids."

"*The Little Mermaid?*"

He nodded.

"Why?"

"I wanted to look at it again. I liked it."

Caitlin slipped into her bedroom and pulled the story out of the top drawer of her bedside table, the drawer where she kept her most special things. She walked back out into the living room and handed it to him. "There was another boy who favored this story a long time ago. When he was about your age."

Owen took it from her hands and settled into the chair closest to the fire. He opened the book, flipping through the pages and savoring the pictures. "Was it the man I rode the ferry in with? The one with the black hair who was here last night?"

Caitlin lifted a brow as the tea kettle started to hiss. "Yes. How did you know that?"

"I saw him looking at it last night."

"Did you?" Caitlin asked, studying him curiously. She noticed the similarities again, the black hair and blue eyes. If you looked, *really* looked, there was a bizarre similarity in some of their facial features, too. Shaking off the unsettling feeling, she watched him pop out of his chair and head back to the shelf, sliding several titles out until he found what he was looking for.

Caitlin lifted a brow. "*Beauty and the Beast?*"

Owen carried it back to the table, sliding it under *The Little Mermaid.* "I just wanted to look at the pictures again."

The copper kettle started to rattle and whistle. Caitlin poured two steaming mugs of Tara's rose petal tea, adding a scoop of sugar to each and setting them on the table. When Owen ignored his and continued to stare at the storybook, a troubled expression swept over his face, eerily similar to Liam's last night when she caught him reading the same story. "What is it?"

Owen glanced up, snapping the book shut. "Nothing." He reached for the mug, yelping when he burned his fingers on the chipped pottery. Hot water splashed out of the mug.

Caitlin dashed back into the kitchen, wetting a dishcloth with cold water.

"I'm sorry," he whispered, staring at the spot where the liquid was seeping into the tablecloth.

"It's okay," Caitlin soothed, hurrying back over and wrapping the cloth around his fingers. "You don't need to be sorry. Here," she said, turning the mug around so the handle faced him. "Hold it here."

She showed him how to curl his fingers gingerly around the handle and then settled slowly back into her chair. Didn't he know how to hold a mug? She watched him blow on the steam and the color rise to his pale cheeks, his gaze drifting back to the books. "So," Caitlin began, careful to keep her voice neutral. "How long does this songwriting usually take?"

Owen lifted the mug, slurping a small sip of sugary tea into his mouth. "A while."

"An hour? A couple of hours?"

"I don't know," Owen said, taking another sip. "This is really good."

Caitlin stared at him. "So...what? You're just expected to get lost?"

He slurped loudly, nodding.

Unbelievable. Caitlin pushed at the sleeves of her sweater. She didn't care how much artistic *space* a person needed. You didn't toss a child out to fend for himself in the rain. "You seemed to be getting along with Kelsey last night. Have you thought of checking in with her? She's probably playing a game with the other children in the pub."

Owen set down his mug and picked at a tear in the peach-colored fabric. "That's okay."

Caitlin's brow knitted in concern. He'd rather hang out with her than with the other kids? Rain battered the windows and Caitlin's gaze dropped to her mug, watching the tea leaves settle into a pattern on the bottom of the cup. She stared at the outline of an infant curled up in a ball. What the...? She swirled the warm liquid around again and her eyes widened as the same shaped re formed.

She set the mug down with a clatter. Owen glanced up, those too-familiar eyes meeting hers intensely. She needed to get out of this house. And she needed to get away from this kid. Now *she* was starting to lose it! "I'm going out," she said, pushing back from the table. "Feel free to stay as long as you want. There's tons of food in the fridge. Make yourself at home."

Owen stood. "Where are you going?"

"Out."

"But it's raining."

"I have work to do."

"Can I help?"

Caitlin's jaw dropped. "Wouldn't you rather hang out with the kids in the pub? And do...kid things?"

"I'd rather come with you."

"Why?"

"Because." He swallowed, looking at his feet. "You're nice."

Of course. She was nice. And look how far that had gotten her. She was babysitting the kid of the woman who was stealing the love of her life away from her! She felt like stomping her foot, but when she looked at that sweet, vulnerable face, what could she do? "Okay," she said, sighing. "You can come with me."

His whole face lit up. "Can I bring the books?"

"There's no light or heat where we're going," she warned.

"That's okay," Owen said quickly, already scooping them up and clutching them in his arms.

Caitlin eyed his still-wet clothes. "Come on, I'll loan you a slicker." She fished two rubber jackets from her hallway closet, one for each of them. He slipped into his, and it fell to his knees. He looked so young and innocent, taking such care to tuck the books safely into the big inside pocket. The ache it left in her chest almost stole her breath away.

Swallowing that desperate yearning for a child of her own, she looked down at Owen's feet. His socks were still drenched, leaving little wet prints on the tiles. She ducked into her room and came back out with a pair of thick wool socks. "Here," she said, handing them to him. "These'll be too big but at least they'll keep your feet warm."

She watched a sudden shadow of fear pass over his eyes. "That's okay," he said, trying to hand them back to her.

Caitlin crossed her arms over her chest. If Owen was her responsibility then she was responsible for making sure he didn't catch a cold. She might not like how his mother was treating her but a mother's actions weren't the fault of the child. "We're not leaving until you put them on."

He shifted his feet nervously, curling his toes under to hide them.

"Come on," Caitlin held out her hand. "Off with the wet ones. I'll hang them in the shower to dry."

His eyes darted around the room, but finding no way out he finally sulked over to the couch, turning his back to her and slipping his wet socks off.

Caitlin shook her head. *Boys*, she thought, rolling her eyes and sliding her feet into her sneakers, then walking into the living room to grab the wet ones before he changed his mind. But she froze mid-step when she caught a glimpse of his bare foot, and the translucent webbing between his toes.

CAITLIN BACKED out of the room, careful not to make a sound. Webbed feet? Her wide-eyed gaze dropped to the puddle his sneakers had made on the floor.

"I'm ready," he said cheerfully, hopping off the couch and handing his wet socks to her. She took them, forcing a bright smile and bit back the questions lodged in her throat. He slipped his feet, covered now in warm fuzzy wool socks, into his wet sneakers. "So where are we going?"

Caitlin swallowed. Surely it wasn't normal for a child to have webbed feet. "Do you remember that cottage where we found the rose yesterday?"

He nodded.

Caitlin opened the door. A blast of cold wind swirled into the house. "That's where we're going."

Owen stepped out into the street, blinking as the rain stung his eyes. "What are we doing there?"

Caitlin pulled the door shut behind them and they headed out into the biting winds, leaning forward to keep their balance. Across the street, the Dooley's sheep dog pressed his paws against the window, barking at them from behind the glass. "I need to decide what to do with it."

"The rose?" Owen asked, jogging to keep up with her.

"No," Caitlin answered, veering off the main road and onto the muddy moss-covered path leading north to the bogs. "The cottage. It's going to take a lot of work to get it livable again. But someone, someday..." Her voice turned wistful and the rubber flaps of her jacket smacked up and down in the wind. "Someone will either spend a holiday in it or call it a home."

"Is that what you do?" Owen asked. "Make old things pretty again?"

Caitlin glanced down at him. "You could say that."

"Is that what you did to the cottage I'm staying in?"

"Yes."

"But you said you weren't finished."

He remembered that? From the first night on the dock? "That's right. I'm not finished."

"What's left?"

"Little things. My friend Glenna is finishing up a few paintings for the walls. I want to get a different comforter for the master bedroom and the window"—she paused, looking down at him—"in *your* bedroom still sticks."

He nodded, like he knew.

"Have you tried to open it?"

"Once," he admitted.

"Isn't it a little cold to be opening windows?"

He lifted a shoulder. "I couldn't hear the ocean."

He couldn't hear the ocean?

"Look!" He broke into a jog as the cottage came into view. "It's still there." His voice caught in the wind, drifting back to her in snippets. He disappeared into the wall of rain, dropping to his knees in front of the rose. "One of the petals fell off," he called back to her.

Caitlin caught up to him, rainwater dripping down her nose and into her mouth. She heard a faint bell-like sound over the thundering ocean and her gaze dropped to the rose, where the rain tinkered over the frozen petals, like water on glass.

Owen picked up the petal carefully, cradling it in his palm. "Look, it must have just fallen."

It was so white, almost like it glowed. There wasn't a smudge of dirt on it, even though Owen had snatched it up off the ground. The wind tugged Caitlin's hood back from her face and she grabbed it, holding it in place. "Come on, Owen. Let's get inside."

"Wait," Owen fished around inside his jacket pocket, pulling out one of the fairy tale books. Rainwater rushed from the roof, splashing onto the pages as he flipped through them. When he found what he was looking for, he held up the picture to her. "It's just like in the story. When the last rose petal falls, the Beast's time is up."

Caitlin felt a cold chill race up her spine.

The rain poured down, hammering against the glass windows of the cottage. Sea spray exploded along the rocky coastline to the north. Owen lifted his eyes to her. "Is someone's time on the island running out?"

"It's just a fairy tale," Caitlin shouted over the howl of the wind. "Come inside."

But Owen reached out, touching the rose still planted in the ground. And slowly, one by one, his fingers turned blue and a thin layer of crystallized ice coated his skin, freezing his hand in place.

CHAPTER EIGHT

"Can you say that again, James? Sorry. The service is spotty." Liam dumped the contents of his briefcase onto his desk, fishing around the crumpled papers, balled receipts, and sticky candy bar wrappers for a clue. The scent of frying cod and malt vinegar drifted up from the kitchen of the pub, where his grandmother was already filling orders for lunch. "This storm's a lot worse than we thought it would be."

"Is your internet still working?"

Liam double-checked. "For the time being, yes."

"Just send me what you have, then. We need to have it submitted by tomorrow and I want a copy in case you lose power."

"Sure. I'll do that." How? How was he going to do that when he couldn't find the document?

"This is going to be huge for the University. And specifically for the department. If this goes as well as I think it will, you'll finally have a term to work on that precious island of yours."

"A sabbatical?" Liam's fingers flew over the keyboard, only half-listening as he searched for the document. It had to be here somewhere. "Since when does the University of Ireland offer sabbaticals?"

The dean laughed, a rich booming baritone through the crackly phone wires. "Very funny, O'Sullivan. You've only been hounding me about a no-teaching term since August. And you're probably going to get it because you're the best researcher we have on staff—even if all your research is grounded in folklore. We all know how seriously Ireland takes its fairy tales. But..." His voice lowered in confidentiality. "You can say it's research all you want, but we all know it's probably about some girl. In the end, it's always about a girl, isn't it?"

A girl. On the island. Liam's fingers stilled on the keyboard as Caitlin's shocked face floated back to him from that first night on the dock. Then the sand, sifting through his fingers last night, and that horrifying feeling of being swept out to sea.

"You haven't told anyone about it, right?"

Liam swallowed. Told anyone about what? "No."

"Good. The historical society's going to eat this up and I want it to be a surprise. To think..." His voice went wistful. "We had no idea they even existed until now."

"*They* being...?"

The dean laughed again. "Don't be daft, O'Sullivan." Then his tone turned serious. "I know your family owns a pub so don't go tapping into the single malt before this file's sent off. And speaking of." Liam heard the sound of a chair squeaking faintly as the dean leaned forward to check his inbox. "Have you sent it yet? I haven't received it on my end."

"Internet's a bit slow out here. It should come through in the next few minutes." He scanned file after file. It had to be here somewhere.

"Did you see the *Times* this morning?"

"Not yet."

"There was an article about the Prime Minister's wife talking about wanting to expand government funding for more research into Ireland's myths and legends. She thinks magic will help bring back the tourist trade." He chuckled. "You've got to love this woman, really. But…I'm thinking big here, but if—and that's a big if—you could crack this new legend like you did with your sister-in-law's, it *could* mean creating a new department dedicated exclusively to Irish fairy tales and legends at the University." He paused. "With you running it."

Liam sat back slowly. A new department dedicated exclusively to Irish fairy tales and legends? "Do you happen to have any suggestions on how I might solve it?" Maybe if he got a sense of how it was supposed to end, it might trigger a memory of the beginning.

"Now let's not go getting ahead of ourselves. One thing at a time. Let's present our findings first, *then* you can spend the next term figuring out how to solve it."

"Right." Liam's hands went back to the keyboard. "I wonder…if you'd given any thought to the title of the presentation?"

"The one we came up with last week is fine."

Liam ground his teeth. *Come on, James. Give me something.* "You don't think we need something catchier?"

"The one we have's catchy enough. And, Liam, I still don't have it. Can you try sending it again?"

"Sure. Maybe if I hang up it'll go through faster."

"Right. I'll give it a read-through as soon as I get it and send my edits back this afternoon."

"Thanks," Liam said, hanging up the phone and dropping his head onto the desk. What was he going to do? He couldn't remember anything about going to the Trinity Library, let alone *being* in Dublin. Rain pounded against the windows, streaking down the glass. How was he supposed to present his findings to the Prime Minister's wife next week if he couldn't even remember what he was working on?

He shoved back from the desk. A bubble of cheerful conversation drifted up the steps from the dining room and he turned away from the tempting scent of frying bacon and pipe smoke, strolling over to the bookshelf by the window. Outside, the heavy wooden Guinness sign swung back and forth on rusted metal chains, squeaking eerily in the storm.

Scanning the volumes lining the shelf, his gaze landed on the anthology of folktales he'd compiled this summer. He snagged it from the shelf and started flipping through the collection of island legends, including Seal Island's own legend, which Tara played a large part in this summer. His fingers parted the pages, lingering on the words of this updated edition which now included the ending. His gaze drifted to the sketch of the selkie ghost, Tara's ancestor, who'd needed her help to break the curse so she could return to the sea.

"Reading your own words again?" Dominic joked, good-naturedly, from the doorway.

Liam snapped the book shut. He hadn't even heard his brother walk up the steps.

"Here," Dominic said, holding out a steaming cup of coffee. "Thought you might need this as you haven't come down for breakfast and it's nearly noon." Strolling into the room, he eyed the scribbled notes on the desk. "Thought you'd be working hard on a new story, not trying to remind yourself of your skill as a writer."

Liam dropped the book onto the desk and took the coffee, swallowing a scalding sip. "Thanks," he said, not even noticing when the hot coffee burned his tongue. His gaze drifted back to the blank computer screen.

"Hey," Dominic asked, concern knitting his dark brows when Liam didn't even crack a smile. "Everything all right?"

"Sure." Liam forced a smile, but it didn't quite meet his eyes. "Just stuck on a bit of research is all."

"Might help if you eat something," Dominic suggested.

"Fair enough."

Dominic pushed away from the desk. "You'd tell me if something was up, right?"

"Of course." Liam lifted his mug, downing another sip, and then brushed past him on his way out the door. "Just a bit of writer's block. It'll pass."

Dominic turned. "Since when do you believe in writer's block?"

"Since today."

A sea of white surrounded him, pulling him under. The echo of waves shattering over a rocky coastline faded as Owen fought to breathe, seawater rushing into his lungs. He struggled against the strings of cold, white pearls snaking up his wrists, tugging him deeper.

The silent, lonely kingdom rose to greet him. He kicked, fast and hard in the other direction at the first sight of the white corral turrets, the soaring towers of broken oyster shells and white-walled paths lined with ice-colored roses.

"Owen!" Caitlin dropped to her knees, pulling him into her arms.

A shaft of light streamed down from the surface. A hollow female voice called out to him and he struggled against the rush of panic, reaching for that fleeting beam of light. Warm arms came around him, hauling him away from that empty kingdom. Clawing his way to the surface through schools of darting silverfish and sleek black rays, he clung to the hands pulling him to safety.

"Let go!" Caitlin shouted over the pounding rain. "Owen, let go of the rose!"

He choked, coughing seawater from his lungs. He tried to sit up, to suck in those first precious breaths of life-giving air, but his fingers were still stuck to the frozen petals. The same petals he'd seen surrounding the towering gates of the palace. He started to cry, little choking sobs and Caitlin grabbed his hand.

"It's okay," Caitlin said, rocking him as she pried his rigid fingers free from the petals one by one. "It's okay. I'm here."

When his last finger uncurled from the rose, he scrambled back, away from the flower, crawling into her lap and sucking air into his burning lungs.

"It's okay," Caitlin soothed, wrapping her arms around him as his fingers dug into the sleeves of her rubber raincoat. He clung to her as the rain poured down around them, soaking streams of rivers into the muddy earth. "You're safe now," she whispered, holding him until he stopped shaking.

And when he finally lifted his head from her shoulder, tears streaked down his face and those big blue eyes blinked up at her through the rain in wonder, as if seeing her for the first time. Slowly, he raised a shaky hand to her cheek. "Mum?"

Mum? "No," Caitlin shook her head, quickly. "No. Owen, I'm not your mother."

"Then...who are you?"

Reaching for the hand still touching her cheek, she brought it down and gasped when she saw the ice coating his fingers. She chipped away at it, rubbing his freezing hand frantically in both of her own. His fingers were as rigid as stones and she struggled to contain her growing panic. "I'm not your mother, Owen.

You're in shock. I'm going to take you to see a doctor. It's going to be all right."

"Wh-what happened? Where are we?"

"You're on Seal Island. Your mother is renting a cottage here for the weekend." She stood, scooping him up. "We're going to find her and get you to the doctor. Now!"

"Wait!" He scrambled out of her arms, catching sight of the book lying in the mud.

"Owen, leave it!" Caitlin's voice was edged with panic as she fought to keep her footing in the gusting wind.

He grabbed for it, wiping the mud off the spine. "I..." He trailed off, cradling the book in his good hand. "I...remember." He looked up at her, rain streaming down his hood and into his eyes. "I remember!" he shouted over the crash of the sea. "This is why we came here." He lifted the book up, waving it at her.

"That's not why we came here!" Caitlin shouted back. "We came here to fix up the cottage!"

Owen shook his head. "No." He fumbled with the pages, flipping through them and then pulling *The Little Mermaid* book out of his coat. "We came here to talk about the sea witch who comes on land to steal the prince away from his true love!"

"*What?*" Caitlin shoved at the wet locks of hair plastered to her face. "Owen, *what* are you talking about?"

"It's right here," he cried, tapping the soaked pages with his frozen fingers. "She steals him away from the girl he's supposed to be with!"

"Please, Owen." Caitlin held out her hand. "That's only a fairy tale. We need to see Tara, *now*."

"No." He shook his head, hugging the book to his chest. "You can't tell her. You can't tell anyone!" Owen froze when a voice calling his name over the wind reached him. He shoved the books into his pocket, stuffing them away as fast as he could, visibly shaking as his mother ran up the path toward them.

"Owen, I've been looking everywhere for you!"

Caitlin spat rainwater out of her mouth and stared at Nuala in a long white hooded cloak, swirling around her ankles, not a splash of dirt or mud on the hem. She ran to her son, snatching him up into her arms. "Where have you been? I've been worried sick about you!"

Owen held Caitlin's gaze over his mother's shoulder, his eyes pleading with her not to say anything.

Nuala set Owen back down, clutching him to her side and taking a minute to catch her breath. She glanced over at Caitlin. "Has he been with you the whole time?"

Caitlin nodded.

"He said he was going to the market and he'd be right back." Nuala shook her head. "I've been all over this island searching for him." She let out a long breath, pressing a hand to her chest. "Owen, please." She looked down at her son. "Please, don't ever do that again."

"I won't," he mumbled, gripping the front of his jacket and stuffing the books deeper into the folds.

"He needs to see a doctor," Caitlin called through the rain.

"What?" Nuala's eyes snapped up, her voice panicked. "Why? What's the matter?" She bent down, cradling Owen's face in her hands. "What happened?"

"Nothing," he said, edging away from her. "I'm fine."

Caitlin opened her mouth to protest, but the wind whipped her hood back from her face and rainwater soaked down the back of her neck. Planting her feet against the wind, she fumbled with the twisted rubber material, yanking it back over her face. Her gaze dropped to Owen's hand and she stared as the faint shimmer of blue faded and he began to wiggle his fingers.

How? How was that possible? She lifted her eyes to Owen's. He shook his head, small snaps from side to side, his eyes pleading up at her not to say anything.

The sea surged, black waves crashing against the rocky coast to the north, spraying white foam into the air. Caitlin swallowed. Why didn't he want his mother to know about the book? Or the rose? "I heard him cough a few times. I thought he should see Tara and make sure it's nothing serious."

Nuala's eyes narrowed, her arm curling around her son's shoulders, protectively. "I think I'll decide what my son needs or doesn't need."

Caitlin's mouth fell open. "I didn't mean..."

"What are you doing out in this storm, anyway?"

"Looking after one of my cottages," Caitlin explained, raising her voice over the howl of the wind.

Nuala eyed the crumbling cottage in disgust. She took Owen's hand and started to lead him back toward the village. "Next time, don't bring my son with you."

"Excuse me?" Caitlin marched after them. Her sneakers filled with rainwater and squished into the soggy blanket of moss with each step. "Owen *followed* me out here. I didn't put him up to this."

Nuala glanced over her shoulder. "He's only a child. He doesn't know any better."

"He *told* me he couldn't go home," Caitlin shouted. "That you wanted to be alone to write."

Nuala stopped and turned to face her. "Children can come up with the most *imaginative* stories, can't they?"

The rain pelted the back of Caitlin's legs, soaking into her jeans. "You're saying it was a lie?"

"Of course it was a lie. I would never throw my child out of my home so I could write." Nuala's eyes were like ice. "I apologize if he was bothering you. It won't happen again."

Caitlin's hands curled at her sides. "Owen's never...a bother."

Nuala pinched the drooping sleeve of Owen's bright yellow rain jacket. "I assume this is yours."

"It is."

"I'll come by later to return it."

"Keep it," Caitlin said through clenched teeth. "Let him use it through the weekend and leave it in the cottage when you go. I'll pick it up later."

"How kind of you," Nuala said, her voice dripping with derision. "But he has his own. He just refuses to wear it."

Caitlin looked down at Owen, but he wouldn't meet her eyes.

"Owen," Nuala said, frowning when she saw Owen rustling around in his pocket. "What do you have in your jacket?"

"Nothing."

"Let me see," she said, reaching for the buttons.

"It's okay," Caitlin cut in. "It's just a book. I told him he could borrow it."

Nuala shook her head. "Owen, give Ms. Conner back her book."

Owen swallowed and with shaky hands he withdrew *Beauty and the Beast*, and held it out to Caitlin. "I'm sorry I got it wet," he whispered.

"That's okay," Caitlin said, tucking it into the crook in her arm. "I'll get another. It's just a book. It doesn't matter."

"Let's go, Owen." Nuala scooped up her son's hand, gripping it tightly in her own as she glanced back up at Caitlin. "I'll be by this afternoon to return your things."

Caitlin nodded, numb as the mother and child turned, disappearing into the curtain of rain. But just before they faded, Owen looked back at her over his shoulder, helplessly. Caitlin stared at their silhouettes until they were nothing but ghosts in a gray landscape and her gaze fell to the book still clutched in her arm.

OWEN DUCKED into the shelter of the cottage, but the chill

followed him inside and he stood in the damp living room, shivering. He flinched when his mother shut the door behind them and locked it.

She swept back her hood, shedding her cloak and draping it over the hook behind the door. "Give me your jacket."

Owen clutched at the rubber folds. "It's got dirt all over it."

She held out her hand.

"I could take it into the bath and rinse it off," he offered.

"Give me the jacket, Owen."

Trembling, he slipped it off, sleeve by sleeve. Rainwater dripped from the hood onto the floor. He bundled it up, wrapping the thick rubber around the book still tucked in the inside pocket and handed it to his mother.

She took it and frowned at the weight. "What else do you have in here?"

"Nothing." Owen's eyes darted to the pocket. "I don't have anything."

His mother shook out the bundle, the wet rubber squeaking in protest. Dipping her hand into the pocket, she fished out *The Little Mermaid*. Her eyes met his. Her voice was cold and quiet. "Did you think I wouldn't find it?"

Owen swallowed the lump in his throat. "I just...wanted to look at the pictures again."

"Owen, listen to me. Listen very carefully. You are not to spend time with Ms. Conner again. You are not to look at books written for children half your age."

He opened his mouth, but she held up a hand, silencing him. "You are not to sneak out of the house unless you tell me where you are going."

"But I told you where I was going," Owen protested.

"You *told* me you were going to the market."

"I did go to the market. And then I...kept walking."

"To Ms. Conner's house."

Owen nodded.

"Why?"

Owen looked down at the ground, scrubbing the toe of his sneaker over the muddy tiles. "Because."

Nuala sighed. "Do you think Ms. Conner wanted you tagging along with her for the day?"

"She likes having me around."

"Does she?" His mother arched a pale brow. "Did she tell you this herself?"

Owen lifted his chin. "She said I could stay as long as I wanted."

Nuala's lips curved into a thin smile. "What did you expect her to say?"

Owen's gaze dropped back to the puddle of water, at the mud streaking across the pretty white tiles. His mother's white cloak hung on the back of the door, spotless and already bone dry. His toes curled inside his shoes, the only part of his body still warm clad in Caitlin's fuzzy wool socks. He remembered how warm and safe he'd felt with Caitlin after the terrible dream. The image of the underwater palace floated into his mind, and he started to shiver again. "Why can't I remember where I'm from?"

Tucking the book into her arm, Nuala looped Owen's jacket over the other hook on the door, careful to not let it touch her own spotless coat. "It's better this way."

"Why?"

Nuala turned, taking a deep breath. "Because we're not going to be here that long." Slowly, she dropped down to one knee and took Owen's hands in hers. "Once we're back home, you'll remember everything. And everything you've ever wanted will be yours."

"But what if I want to stay here?"

Heat flashed behind his mother's eyes but the grip on his hands stayed calm and steady. "That's not possible, Owen."

"Won't you at least tell me what we're doing here?"

"I promise," she said, smoothing his wet curls back from his forehead. "All will be clear in time."

He shivered when he felt her fingertips brush his skin, cold as ice. Just like the rose by the cottage. Just like the roses in his dream. His whole body started to tremble when he remembered the picture of the rose in the storybook. And what happened to the Beast when the last petal fell.

What if the rose by the cottage was *his* ticking clock, representing *his* time on this island. What was going to happen to him when that last petal fell?

CHAPTER NINE

Caitlin's teeth chattered as she fished out the key to her cottage. Her fingers felt numb and useless and she couldn't remember the last time she'd been this cold, or this confused. She fit the key into the lock and stepped back, surprised when the knob turned easily and the door swung open.

Had she forgotten to lock it?

The hair on the back of her arms stood up as she stepped into the dark hallway. The curtains in the living room were drawn and the wind howled through the street behind her. She stifled a scream when she spotted the man sitting in the armchair by the fire.

"Liam!" Caitlin's hand flew to her heart. "You scared me to death!" She fumbled for the light switch.

"Don't bother," he said quietly. "We've lost power."

Caitlin lowered her arm. "How long have you been here?"

He continued to gaze into the dying embers in the hearth. A glass of whiskey, nearly drained, rested on the arm of the chair. "A while."

Letting out a shaky breath, Caitlin stripped off her dripping jacket. "How did you get in here?"

Liam jingled the spare keys she left in the pub for Dominic. "Since when do you lock up?"

"I got in the habit after everything that happened this summer."

Liam lifted the glass and took a long swallow. Ice clinked against the bottom as he set it down and pushed to his feet. Shadows danced over the contours of his striking face as he turned. A dark layer of stubble was growing along the hard line of his jaw, making him look dangerous in the dim light of the cottage. "I wanted to talk to you about that."

"About what happened this summer?"

Liam crossed the room with slow purposeful strides, his gaze penetrating. "About what happened after."

Caitlin's pulse quickened. "After…?"

He paused only when he was right in front of her, reaching up and tucking a wet lock of hair behind her ear. "Between us."

Caitlin felt a surge of hope. "You…remember?"

Liam shook his head, his gaze never leaving hers. "I need you to help me."

Caitlin swallowed when his hand lingered in her hair, his fingers trailing down the side of her neck and sending warm shivers over her skin. "How?"

Liam lowered his mouth to hers, those sensual lips brushing over hers lightly at first, like the first whispered words between two lovers. "The same way they do in fairy tales," he murmured against her lips, his voice low and seductive. "With a kiss."

A warm desperate yearning grew inside her when his mouth stayed on hers, nibbling, tasting, savoring the flavor of her. But there was still so much they needed to talk about. Pressing her palms to the hard muscles of his chest, she could feel his heart beating through the thin cotton of his shirt. She inched back, looking up into those intense blue-gray eyes. "But this isn't a fairy tale. This is real life."

"Is it?" He tugged her closer, fitting her curves to the hard planes of his chest. "Prove it." He caught her mouth in a searing kiss. Rain pounded against the roof of the cottage. The wind caught the tangled chimes, forcing them into a crazy, chaotic song.

It was a test, she realized, sensing his insistence, his urgency. A test to find out how much he remembered. She could make him remember. She pressed her soft mouth to his, her lips parting when his hands twisted in the back of her sweater, yanking her against him.

CAITLIN. He drank in the taste of her, the warmth of her. A soft sound escaped from somewhere deep in her throat and he felt something stir, a ghost of a memory. He molded his hands over her curves, fitting her closer. The images unraveled, one by one, like white thread dripping from a spinning spool.

Caitlin. Something snapped, coming alive inside him, and the memories, *their* memories came flooding back. He pulled her to him, claiming her mouth in a smoldering kiss. He heard her sharp intake of breath, felt her whole body stiffen.

His lips moved insistently over hers. He was sick of uncertainty. The only thing he was certain of was he wanted her. Now. A low primitive thrumming in his blood grew louder until she started to melt. Until she let out a helpless sigh and her hands inched up his arms, curling around the back of his neck, kneading into the muscles of his shoulders.

He inhaled the scent of vanilla and peat smoke, heard the sizzle and pop from the fire in the next room. He needed more of her. All of her. His fingers dug into her hips, guiding her back, step by step, until her back met the wall, until the soft swell of her breasts pressed into his chest. He wanted his hands on them. On every glorious inch of them.

The rain pounded against the roof. The wind howled through the streets. A soft moan escaped from somewhere deep in her throat and it set off something inside him. Something primal. He'd come for answers. But now that he saw her, all he wanted was release. Sweet, desperate release.

He caught her small wrists in one hand, caging her against the wall. A desperate, pagan need to mate drummed through him and he filled his palm with her throbbing breast. The traitorous tip hardened, pebbling with desire through the thin fabric of her shirt. He groaned, all the blood rushing from his head as he grasped her thighs, yanking her legs up so they caught around his waist.

She hooked her legs around him, clinging to him. His heart pounded in his ears. He could feel the heat radiating out from her. His hands molded the soft curve of her hips. His teeth scraped over her bottom lip and the taste of her shot into him like a drug.

The fire snapped as she peeled the dripping raincoat off his shoulders, pushing it down his arms. It fell with a soft splat on the wet floor and he pulled her off the wall. Caitlin's hands reached out blindly, grabbing for the doorway as they stumbled through it, bringing a chair crashing to the floor with them as they tumbled to the rug in front of the fire.

He dragged her shirt over her head. He needed her naked. Under him. Now. He unhooked the clasp of her bra, drawing the stretchy waistband of her black cotton pants down her hips in one swift motion. He had her undressed before she could reach for his zipper. Rain smacked against the glass, a breathless steady rhythm. A growl tore from his throat as her fingers fumbled with the buttons of his jeans, as her small hands worked the denim down over his hips and he kicked off his boots, shook off his pants and the boxers that went with them.

He tugged his own wet shirt over his head with one hand, his silver claddagh cross dropping between them, pooling over her breasts. He followed the trail of the silver chain down, dipping his mouth to her swollen bud. She moaned, arching to meet him.

He slid the last thin scrap of material down her legs, circling the taut bud of her nipple with his tongue, separating her legs with his knee and sliding between them. Her breathing grew shallow. The furnace inside him flamed to life. Now. He needed her now.

She reached for him, pulling his mouth back up to hers. The kiss grew desperate. Needy. Her fingernails bit into his back as she moved her hips up to meet him. *Home*, he thought, blindly as he pushed himself inside her in one long desperate stroke.

He swallowed the gasp of pleasure that tore from her throat, covering her mouth with his, claiming her with a blistering, burning kiss as he buried himself deeper inside her. Her wet heat surrounded him, closing around him like a fist.

She shuddered, her head falling back, those rich red curls splaying out over the carpet as he started to move. Long deep strokes all the way in, and all the way out of her. The wind whipped against the cottage in frantic, furious lashes. Outside, the chimes spun wildly. The sound of something tearing, followed by a loud smack and splintering of wood rushed into the room.

She clung to him as the flames licked up the sides of the hearth. The fire grew, heating their tangled limbs as he moved in and out of her. She met him with every stroke, giving herself to him, every soft glorious inch of her melting into him, fitting against him like a lost puzzle piece locking into place.

Caitlin.

He felt the wave crest and build, gathering force as the rain battered the cottage. He moved faster, harder inside her. She clenched under him, her breath catching in needy gasps. "Liam," she breathed when he stroked his palm over her aching breast, skimming it up over that spot at the base of her throat where her pulse hammered.

Her eyes fluttered open, a sea of emotions swimming into those sapphire pools. His hand curled around the back of her neck, dragged her mouth up to his as the wave crashed, pulling them both under in glorious, splendid release.

A RESTLESS RAIN drummed against the roof of the cottage. The scent of roses, sweet and seductive, drifted into the room. Caitlin stirred. Her limbs felt tingly, her body warm and sated despite the cold draft curling down from the chimney. The soft thump of the log breaking and sliding through the grate had her stretching like a cat. Luxuriating in the feel of a warm naked man wrapped around her, oblivious to the scratchy carpet rubbing against her skin.

Carpet? Caitlin's eyes flew open. Naked man? Her entire body tensed. She tried to sit up. Liam's arm, resting under the curve of her breasts, tightened around her possessively. No! Her heart pounded in her ears. She had not let this happen again.

She fumbled for her clothes strewn across the floor. She knew better. She'd been down this road before. She caught the hem of her stretchy black pants and clutched onto the damp material like a lifeline. Two years. She'd been avoiding him for two years so this exact situation would not happen. When his lazy hand reached out, catching hers and prying her fingers from the material, she squeezed her eyes shut. How? How could she have let this happen?

"Shhhh," he murmured, covering her hand in his and

tucking it back under them, nestling her back against him. Caitlin's pulse raced. She stared at the broken log in the hearth. It was the same thing, every time. It was always like this between them. They'd stay up late talking, not even noticing when everyone else went to bed. But as soon as they realized they were alone one thing would lead to another and wham-oh! Can't-rip-your-clothes-off-fast-enough, can't-make-it-to-the-bedroom, drag-you-to-the-floor-because-I'll-die-if-I-can't-have-you-*right-now* sex.

Once. Just *once* in her life she wanted to make it into the bedroom with him. Was it really that much to ask? She untangled her legs from his, lifting his heavy arm and tossing it off her. He sat up, rubbing his eyes. He looked so damn cute like that, with his hair mussed and his eyes all blue and after-sex dreamy. She glared at him, covering her bare breasts with her arm as she scanned the floor for her shirt. Not that it mattered. Not like he hadn't seen them before. He'd seen them *plenty* of times.

She spied her shirt and crawled over him, snatching it off the floor. He grunted when her knee met his stomach. Good. She hoped it hurt. She'd had sex with other men over the years. A few of them were even pretty good at it. And *they* didn't have trouble making it into the bedroom. It was only Liam. It was like the second his mouth met hers something happened to both of them and they lost all grip on reality.

She spotted her bra and grabbed it, shoving her arms through the straps. She didn't want to lose her grip on reality anymore. She wanted more than this. She *needed* more than this. She thought he'd changed. That Dominic and Tara settling down had affected him. That maybe he wanted to settle down, too.

But he hadn't changed. Nothing had changed! She jammed the clasp together behind her back, pulling the straps up and reaching for her shirt. "That was a mistake."

"Was it?" Liam asked quietly. He sat up, watching her closely

—his eyes a quiet pensive gray now rimmed in ocean blue. "I wouldn't call it that."

"Oh, really?" Caitlin shoved her arms into her shirt sleeves, jerking it over her head. "Because you make it a practice of rolling around on the floor with women in the middle of the day?"

"Caitlin."

"I'm not just another one of your women."

"My...women?"

"The ones you bring to the island," Caitlin snapped. "A different woman every summer. Sometimes a different woman every weekend." They were always the same. Skinny city bimbos who fawned over him. Who sat at the pub all night drinking fruity wine and flirting with the dreamy professor.

Slowly, Liam rose. He snagged the waistband of his jeans, dragging them up over his hips and watching her carefully. "I didn't know you cared about that."

Caitlin huffed out a frustrated breath. "Of course I care."

"Those women mean nothing to me."

"I know." She stuffed her feet into her pant legs. "That's why I don't want to be one of them." She jerked the waistband up. "That"—she gestured back to the floor—"should never have happened."

"It's not the first time," Liam said quietly.

Caitlin's hands stilled on the drawstring. She lifted her eyes to his. She saw the raw emotion in them and she took a step back. "You remember."

He nodded.

"How much?" Her hands fell to her sides. "How much do you remember?"

"I remember that you're the one who broke things off between us. And I'm having a hard time understanding why you're so angry right now."

Caitlin felt her breath whoosh out of her lungs. He remembered. "What else? What else do you remember?"

"I remember that we had a bit of a scare when we were younger. And I offered to stay here with you. To be with you. But when that scare turned out to be nothing, you said you didn't have feelings for me. That I should go to university and forget what happened between us."

His cross winked in the flickering candlelight, illuminating the long scars that seared into the taut muscles of his shoulders and chest. Scars from an awful childhood growing up with an abusive father. A childhood he and Dominic had escaped when they were only boys, when they'd run to this island to seek shelter with their grandparents.

Liam bent down, scooping his shirt off the floor and flipping it right-side out. "I left not too long after that. We *both* left if I remember correctly. But I'm still a little fuzzy on where *you* went." He tugged the shirt over his head, dipping his hands in his pockets and watching her from across the room. "Care to fill in the gaps?"

"So..." Caitlin swallowed. "You're only remembering bits and pieces?"

He nodded. "I still can't remember what happened at the wedding this summer. Or anything about the date. But something happened before that, Caitlin. Something happened between us to make you angry. What was it?"

She lifted her hand slowly, touching her lips where she could still taste him and feel his desire. But it wasn't real. None of it would be real until he got his memory back. "You need to see a doctor, Liam."

"I don't need to see a doctor." He closed the distance between them. "I need you to tell me what happened." He reached up, threading his fingers through her hair. "The only time I remember anything is when I'm with you."

CHAPTER TEN

*L*iam remembered his feelings for her. How much he cared—*still* cared—for her. He didn't have all the pieces yet, but the puzzle was starting to take shape. And every time a piece of that puzzle clicked into place he was certain of one thing. He wanted more of her.

The hiss and spark of the match igniting was the only sound in the cottage save the rain smacking against the windows. Liam watched her work her way through the dark room, cupping her palm around the match to protect the flame. She'd changed into dry clothes and towel dried her hair. But the cream colored sweater and fitted jeans hugged her curves, and those fiery curls tumbled around her pale face wild and unruly now. His fingers itched to touch her again. He knew what she felt like now, what she tasted like. What she'd tasted like when they were only teenagers.

How had he forgotten that?

Lighting the last of the candles, Caitlin waved the match to snuff it out. The black smoke curled into the air between them and he noticed how she lingered on the other side of the room, like she didn't trust herself to come any closer. Tossing the match into the sink, Caitlin took a deep breath. "If I answer your questions, do you promise to see the neurologist Tara recommended on Monday?"

Liam nodded, adding a fresh brick of peat to the fire. He knelt beside the hearth, lighting a piece of magazine paper to train the smoke back up the chimney when it drifted into the house. "What happened when you left the island?"

"My parents sent me to live with an aunt in Donegal. She was a teacher at St. Stephen's—an all girls' high school. She was able to get me a place in the school and it didn't cost them much. They thought I was safer there. After what happened..."

"Between us," Liam finished, dropping the paper into the fire when the flames reached his fingertips.

Caitlin nodded.

Liam chose a knotted piece of driftwood from the weathered wooden crate, watching the flames flicker over the pale wood. "You weren't the first girl to sleep with your boyfriend at sixteen."

"True," Caitlin said slowly. "But you weren't exactly my boyfriend."

Liam met her eyes across the room. "That's debatable."

Caitlin sent him a long look. "It was one night. And there was a rather large bottle of whiskey involved."

"It might have turned into more than that."

Caitlin turned, pulling two tumblers from the shelf above the sink. But he could have sworn he saw her fingers falter. "This is hardly the point. My parents were—and still are—very Catholic." She set the glasses on the counter. "And as the oldest of eight children, I was supposed to set an example. *Not* wind up pregnant while my youngest sister was still in diapers."

Liam winced. "But you didn't. End up pregnant, I mean. It was all a mistake."

"Right." Caitlin looked away and Liam felt a sharp stab of

guilt. She hadn't known any better. She'd panicked when her period was two weeks late. Understandably. She was only sixteen. He'd only been eighteen at the time—a couple years older and heading off to university in the fall, but still just a kid as well. He pushed at the peat with the stick, watching the flames lick up the sides of the log. He hated knowing he'd played a role in having her sent away from her family. Her friends. Her home. "I'm having a hard time imagining you at an all girls' school."

Caitlin opened the freezer, scooping out a handful of ice. "Let's just say I wasn't voted class president."

He glanced up, expecting to see at least a hint of joke in her eyes. But her gaze had drifted to the rain-streaked window, a somber expression darkening her features. "How long were you gone?"

"Less than two years. Just long enough to finish high school."

Liam moved the log a fraction of an inch, sending sparks shooting up into the hearth. "Did you ever consider staying on the mainland? Going to university?"

"No."

"Why not?"

"I didn't want to stay on the mainland." She turned back to the cabinets, pulling out a bottle of Bailey's. "I didn't like it there." She untwisted the cap, setting it on the counter. "This is my home. This is where I belong."

Liam pushed to his feet, letting that soak in. His job was on the mainland. His career was at the University. The dean's words floated back. *'If this goes as well as I think it will, you'll finally have a term to work on that precious island of yours.'* Had he asked for a term on the island to be with Caitlin? The faint scent of roses drifted back to him, just as they had that first night on the dock. He looked around her house, but there weren't any roses anywhere. "Last night..." he began. "You mentioned we'd been talking on the phone."

She nodded. "You don't remember any of the conversations?" He shook his head.

She sighed. "Mostly you talked about the fairy tale you recently discovered in Dublin. You wouldn't tell me the story, but you were really excited about it. You said it was a game-changer. That you would never even have found it if you hadn't stumbled across your mother's name on the registry list when you were researching something else."

Liam took a step back. "My *mother*?"

"Apparently, she'd borrowed it. I know," she said, watching him. "The Trinity Library doesn't let just anyone check out a book. She must have had a special relationship with them...like you do."

Liam stared at her, stunned. His mother had left him and Dominic when they were only children. But he'd found her name connected with a story in the Trinity Library? "When did she borrow it? It would have had to have been..."

Caitlin nodded. "It was only a few weeks before she...left." She let the words hang and watched Liam's mouth fall open. "Apparently it was re-shelved somewhere else in the library, and the librarian had to spend all weekend hunting it down for you."

"My mother...hid it? On purpose?"

Caitlin nodded. "That's what I gathered. But you wouldn't tell me anything else."

"Why would my mother hide an Irish fairy tale in the Trinity Library? Weeks before she ran away?"

"You don't know where she is, right?"

Liam shook his head, looking out the window. "I don't have a clue where she is."

"Have you ever thought about trying to find her?"

"She left us, Cait. She made her decision. If she wanted to be found, she'd come to us." The scent of roses drifted into the room again and he frowned. "Do you smell that?"

She let the ice drop into the tumblers, clinking like bells against the glass. "Smell what?"

"Roses."

Caitlin looked at him strangely as she poured a splash of the creamy liquor into each glass. Crossing the room, she handed him the glass, careful not to let their fingers touch. Picking up a small bowl of pottery off the mantle, she held it out to him. "Is this what you smell?"

Liam gazed down into the dried red rose petals. "Are those Tara's?"

Caitlin nodded. "What's left of them, yes."

"Why do you keep them?"

"To remind me." She took the bowl back from him, setting it carefully on the mantle beside the jars of black sand, the salt-weathered driftwood, the colorful seashells, and sprinkling of beach pebbles. "I hold onto things, Liam. I'm sentimental like that."

And he spent his career digging up myths and legends, searching for truth in ancient poems and songs, finding the stories long buried and bringing them back to life. "I guess we have that in common."

She lifted her eyes to his. "We do."

He'd always been fascinated by what came before him, by the people and the stories of Irish history. But he'd never considered his own history, his own past, to have much meaning. He'd blocked out most of the first ten years of his life before moving in with his grandparents and meeting Caitlin. But now there was a connection between his mother and a missing fairy tale he couldn't remember?

"Liam." Caitlin edged back so she could look up into his eyes. "You don't remember what you were working on before you came here, do you?"

He shook his head slowly. "No."

"Don't you think it's a little strange that the only pieces of your memory you lost are me and that fairy tale?"

NUALA DUCKED her head against the rain and wind. The book felt heavy and sharp against her side. She held it clutched inside her cloak with one hand, holding onto her hood with the other. Rainwater gushed through the rutted streets of the village. She stepped over the swirling puddles, her heels clicking on the cracked pavement as she passed O'*Sullivan's* pub. A warm, inviting light glowed from the windows where the villagers were gathered inside weathering the storm.

What would it be like to have a community to depend on in tough times? To have someone to turn to when the storms came? She'd had that once, long ago. But she'd made her choice. She'd turned her back on her family and chosen a different path. But she wasn't going to be alone anymore. She was finally going to have the life and the family she'd always dreamed of.

The wind ripped a wooden board advertising *Fresh Cod* off the door to the market and it went flying into the street, smacking against a stone wall and landing in a puddle. The dog inside the house down the street started to howl—a terrible, wretched sound that made her skin crawl. She gathered up the soft material of her cloak, lifting it out of the puddles as she tucked her head against the gales and strode through the deserted streets of the village.

She'd made a mistake this morning, underestimating the attachment Owen would form with Caitlin. She hadn't been thinking straight about that, but she would make sure they stayed apart from now on. And more importantly, that Liam and Caitlin stayed apart. She hadn't given the redhead much credit until now, but she might have misjudged the power of friendship and memories. She'd seen Liam's face last night when he recognized the sand. And if a simple bowl of spilled sand and this book could spark that forgotten bond in a single evening, who knew what else that woman had up her sleeve.

She made her way to Caitlin's squat white-washed cottage, where a steady stream of smoke curled from the chimney. Rain-water spilled in waterfalls from sunny yellow window boxes filled with nothing but soil and stones. She imagined these boxes bursting with a colorful assortment of flowers in the summer. Flowers that would blossom and fade as quickly as the sun dipped into the sea at night.

Not like her roses. White roses that lived forever. White roses fit for a queen. The wind chimes spun in crazy circles, their strings tangling in the thatch of the roof and she brushed them aside, rapping the gleaming gold claddagh knocker against the door. She heard voices through the walls, footsteps shuffling toward the door.

"Nuala." Liam's tall, broad-shouldered frame filled the door-way. His long, lean body was tucked into a rumpled gray T-shirt and faded jeans. He was barefoot and his hair was mussed, like someone had been running their fingers through it. She gritted her teeth when she saw how comfortable he looked with his hand resting casually against her doorknob, nursing a tumbler of some creamy liquor, like he made a practice of answering Caitlin's door.

Nuala smiled pleasantly, making sure the book was tucked safely inside the rubber rain slicker. A man like Liam needed space—room to roam. He needed an ocean at his disposal. Not the crumbling shores of a minuscule island, or the four walls of a cottage sorely in need of repair. "I came to return Caitlin's things."

Liam's eyes held no warmth or friendliness as he stepped

back, opening the door wider so she could enter. Nuala walked into the candlelit cottage, noting the cozy fire in the hearth, the open bottle of Bailey's on the counter, and the flush staining Caitlin's pale cheeks as the redhead glared at her from across the room. "I hope I'm not interrupting anything," she said sweetly, her eyes drifting up to Liam's. "I ran into Tara on the way over. She said she was looking for you."

Liam made no move to take her jacket, or return her smile. He stood between her and Caitlin. Nuala felt a surge of rage well up inside her. She had underestimated the redhead all right. She had greatly underestimated her influence over this man. But not anymore. It was time to get rid of her. For good.

"Did she say why?"

"The ferry captain—Finn, I think that's his name?"

Liam nodded.

"He wants you to help him secure the boats in the harbor. He's worried the storm's not showing any signs of letting up."

Liam rolled his jaw, glancing over her shoulder at the white caps tearing over the surface of the ocean, at the torrents of rain pouring into the sea.

"Go," Caitlin urged, her voice taking on an edge of exhaustion. "Finn never asks for help unless he really needs it."

Liam looked back at Caitlin and held her eyes. Nuala didn't like the expression that swam into them. She didn't like it at all. "We're not done here."

"I know," Caitlin said quietly. But she walked across the room, slipping his sweater off the back of the chair and holding it out to him.

He watched Caitlin for several long moments, searching her eyes. There were questions in them, questions Nuala couldn't read and her nails bit into the jacket as that swell of rage built inside her. "Are you sure you don't want me to stay?"

Caitlin nodded.

Liam's eyes never left Caitlin's as he took the sweater from her outstretched arms and tugged it over his head. He slid his feet into his boots and reached for his coat. "I'll be back as soon as I can."

Nuala stopped him with a hand on his arm. "I haven't had a chance to say thank you." She lowered her voice, but not so low that Caitlin couldn't hear it. "For last night."

CAITLIN WATCHED Liam pull his arm away, but not before that witch had a chance to sink her claws back into him. She saw the way his eyes shifted, the way his entire expression changed when she touched him. And she could only imagine what happened last night when Liam walked her home to help her *fix her heater*.

Liam glanced over his shoulder as he opened the door and a cold gust blew into the room. But there was something different in his eyes now, something not quite right. He slipped out of the cottage and the wind caught the door behind him, slamming it shut.

Caitlin crossed her arms over her chest. "How convenient that you ran into Tara on your way over."

Nuala unfastened the front of her long white cloak, pulling out the storybook. "I have no idea what you're talking about."

"You don't want Liam around me."

Nuala smiled. "That's the least of my worries." Stepping into the room, she set the book on the coffee table. The candles flickered under her movement and water dripped from her cloak onto the carpet. "I need to talk to you about my son."

"Where *is* Owen?"

"He's in the cottage."

"Alone?"

"He's ten years old. He'll be fine."

"The power's out all over the island."

"I lit a fire before I left."

"You could have brought him into the pub. I'm sure all the kids are there now playing board games."

"Owen's shy."

Caitlin reached for the glass of Bailey's. "Shouldn't children learn to get over their fears?"

"Some children prefer to spend time alone. Owen's life has been...stressful lately." She reached out, letting her fingers rest on the blanket draped over the back of an armchair. "This weekend was supposed to be a chance for him, for *us*, to get away and relax."

"If you want him to relax, why are you taking books away from him?"

"That's what I came to talk to you about."

Caitlin took a sip of Bailey's, letting the sweet liquor cool her fraying nerves. "So...talk."

"My son has a vivid imagination."

"He's a kid." Caitlin grabbed the stick and poked it into the fire. Why was it so cold in here all of a sudden? "He's supposed to have a vivid imagination."

"For most kids, I'd agree. But Owen is different."

Caitlin focused on the flames. "How?"

"A few years ago, I was reading him a story before bed. He started asking questions about it, like it was more truth than fairy tale."

Caitlin paused, the tip of the stick just touching the log of peat. "Which story?"

"*Sleeping Beauty.*"

Sleeping Beauty? He wasn't the first child who'd found truth in that story. Caitlin straightened, glancing at the bowl of Tara's dried rose petals on her mantle. If Kelsey hadn't followed the clues in that fairy tale to lead them to where to find the selkie's pelt and break Tara's ancestor's curse, would Tara still be here with them today? She turned, narrowing her eyes. "I'm listening."

"Owen became obsessed with the story, looking for signs all over Limerick that it was real. He was sure there was a princess trapped in a tower and convinced the other kids on our street that it was true." Nuala took a deep breath. "I didn't take it seriously. I thought they were just being kids and playing pretend."

Nuala started to pace, back and forth across the small living room. "But one night in the spring, when the roses were blooming as tall as the trees, he snuck out of the house with two of the other children to the ruins of King John's Castle."

Caitlin nodded. She knew the famous castle. It was a popular tourist destination during the day, but no one was allowed inside the gates at night.

"They found a way in and started to climb up to the tower. If they'd made it to the top, they might have seen it was nothing more than an empty room and there was no princess lying asleep waiting for her prince."

Nuala gazed out the window, at the rain streaking down the glass. "But on the way up, one of the children climbed out onto the balcony overlooking the river."

Caitlin gripped the thin stick of driftwood. She knew the ending to this story. She remembered hearing about it on the news. "That part of the castle was blocked off to the public because the rocks were coming loose. But the kids didn't know that."

Nuala nodded grimly. "One of the children fell. He died. Because of Owen."

Caitlin's head spun. Of course she remembered this story. Everyone in Ireland remembered this story. It was a terrible tragedy. But...surely it wasn't Owen's fault. "He was only a boy."

"They wouldn't have been there if Owen hadn't convinced them to go."

"But it wasn't his fault the child climbed out onto the ledge." Caitlin did a quick calculation in her head. "A few years ago, Owen would have only been six or seven years old. He couldn't have known any better."

"He didn't know any better, because I didn't take his questions seriously."

"But...how could you have known?" Caitlin dropped the driftwood back into the box with the other sticks. "I'm sorry, Nuala. I can see how this was traumatic for both of you. But you can't separate him from other children and take books away from him when he didn't know any better. Don't you think he's learned his lesson?"

Nuala shook her head. "I can't take that risk. I don't want him reading those sorts of stories."

"What sort of stories do you want him to read? If a child can't read about magic and fairy tales, what's he supposed to read?"

"Stories based on reality. On truth." Nuala pushed back from the chair. "Stories based on what's actually going on in the world."

"But..." Caitlin protested. "You're a *songwriter*. It's your job to spin tales and use your imagination to make beautiful music. You can't take the will to dream and create away from a person."

Nuala smiled sadly. "I'm afraid you can. And since he's my child, and I've seen how those stories affect him, I won't have him reading them anymore and possibly hurting someone."

"Nuala, this is—"

"What's best," Nuala said, cutting her off. "And until you have a child of your own, you might keep your thoughts on mothering to yourself."

Caitlin felt the sting like a slap in the face.

"And furthermore," Nuala said, sweeping her hood back up and over her face. "I'd appreciate it if you stayed away from

Owen for the rest of our visit on the island. He's young and impressionable. And I don't want you influencing him."

"*Influencing* him? I've hardly—"

"Stay away from my son, Caitlin." She walked to the door and pulled it open. A cold wind swirled into the room. "That's all I came to say."

CHAPTER ELEVEN

*S*tay away from my son? Caitlin grabbed the book off the table, squeezing it in her hands to keep from throwing it across the room. Who did she think she was? Telling her to stop influencing Owen with fairy tales? Like she was some kind of a threat! Like she'd lured Owen over here and set out the big, bad fairy tale books as a trap!

They were just *stories*, for God's sake! Stories that might hold some truth now and then, yes. But to take them away from a child altogether? To cut him off from a world of magic and fantasy because his imagination had gotten carried away one night? It wasn't Owen's fault that boy drowned!

Marching across the room, she yanked the phone off the wall. She started to dial the pub, then remembered the lines were dead. What would Liam think if he knew this woman wanted to suppress the imagination of her child? She shoved the phone back into the cradle and froze, her eyes going wide as her gaze dropped to the book. *'It's right here! The sea witch steals the prince away from his true love—the girl he's supposed to be with!'*

It wasn't possible, was it? This couldn't be happening again.

She circled the room, blowing out the candles. She grabbed her raincoat and shoved her arms back into the sleeves. She'd made the mistake before of not listening to a child, of refusing to see the signs of magic all around her until it was almost too late.

She wouldn't make that mistake again. She stalked out into the rain, wading ankle deep in the puddles filling the dips in the road. If Owen thought there was something about this story she needed to know, then she was going to find out what it was. The wind banged the Fosters' teetering metal gate against the broken hinges. She glanced into the pub as she walked by, her mouth falling open when she saw Nuala seated at the bar through the window.

She hadn't even gone straight home to her son? After everything she'd accused Caitlin of? Unbelievable! Her boots splashed through the rising water as she tromped passed the darkened windows of her neighbors' homes toward the cottage at the edge of the village. She knocked on the pale blue door and heard the sound of a child walking toward it and twisting the knob.

He opened the door a crack, peering out, his eyes widening when he spotted Caitlin. "Ms. Conner," he said, opening the door wider. "What are you doing here?"

"I need to talk to you."

He squinted into the curtain of rain. "Does my mum know you're here?"

"No," Caitlin said, pushing into the cottage and stripping off her jacket. The air inside was so cold her breath came out in little icy puffs and her gaze darted to the fireplace, where a poorly made fire was dying in the hearth. She pulled the book, *The Little Mermaid*, out of her jacket pocket and Owen's eyes went wide as she handed it to him, crossing the room to work on the fire.

Taking one last look down the empty street, Owen shut the door, leaning back against it. "She doesn't want me spending time with you."

"I know."

Hugging the book to his chest, he stared at Caitlin. "Did she give this back to you?"

Caitlin knelt to the cold floor, a match sizzling to life in the darkness and she cupped her hand around it to keep it lit as she trailed it along a piece of sod. "She did."

"What did you say?"

"I said if you wanted to read it, you should be able to read it."

Owen's gaze dropped to the cover as Caitlin got the fire started, a warm lick of flames drawing him toward the hearth where he knelt beside her, opening the book and tracing a finger over the pictures on the pages.

"Owen," Caitlin said, watching the flames play shadows over his gaunt face. "I need you to tell me what happened back there. At the cottage."

He snapped the book shut and clasped it back to his chest. "What do you mean?"

"When you touched the rose. What happened?"

He shook his head. "I don't want to talk about that."

"Why not?"

He nudged closer to the fire and Caitlin laid a hand on his shoulder. "Owen," she began, then paused when she felt the damp material under her fingers. Her brows snapped together. "Your clothes are still wet."

He brushed her hand away. "They're fine."

"But you must be freezing." She started to push to her feet but he grabbed the hem of her sweater. "No." He shook his head. "I'm fine."

Caitlin stared at him for several long moments before sinking back to the floor. "Owen, you said something back at the cottage. After you found the white rose. You said the reason we went there was because of the story." She tapped her finger against the faded spine of the storybook. "Because of *this* story. What did you mean?"

Owen lowered the book into his lap, the firelight dancing over the cover. Smoke curled up the chimney, the hollow sound of rain tinkering against the metal flue fading as the fire heated the hearth. Owen's fingers gripped the book and his voice came out in barely more than a whisper. "I think my mother is the evil sea witch."

Caitlin gaped. It was exactly what Nuala said would happen —that Owen would start believing the stories were real. "It's just a story, Owen. It's not real."

Owen shook his head. "It is real. And she put a spell on me so I can't remember anything."

Caitlin swallowed. What if Nuala was telling the truth? What if fairy tales were dangerous to some children? "What... don't you remember?"

"I can't remember anything," Owen whispered. The fire hissed, a coil of black smoke snaking up the chimney when the flames found an air pocket in the log. "Where I'm from. Who my father is. I don't even know what we're doing here."

"You're from Limerick," Caitlin explained. "And you're here on holiday."

"That's what my mum said." Owen lifted his worried eyes to hers. "But it's not true."

Conflicted, Caitlin felt a seed of doubt take root inside her. If Nuala was right, and she let Owen believe this insane theory was true, then could he end up hurting someone on the island? She searched his eyes, looking for something, anything that would help her understand what to believe. But she saw only innocence and truth in those troubled eyes.

If Owen was right, then Nuala was...the evil sea witch in *The Little Mermaid*? Caitlin bit her lip. Everything inside her screamed not to trust Nuala, but an evil sea witch? That was simply taking this too far. "Owen," she said, letting out a long breath. "Have you told your mother you can't remember anything about where you're from?"

Owen nodded, staring into the fire.

"What did she say?"

"She said, 'everything would be clear in time. And when this was all over, everything I ever wanted would be mine.'"

Everything he ever wanted would be his? A gust of wind shook the cottage, rattling the windows. "And you have no idea what that means?"

"No."

Struggling to come up with a reasonable explanation, Caitlin tucked her legs against her side. "Maybe something happened before you came here. Some kind of accident that caused you to forget. Maybe she's hoping you'll...heal here." By leaving him alone in a dark, unheated cottage during a storm? She was grasping at straws, but what else could she do?

Owen clutched the book tightly to his chest, staring into the fire. "I saw her trip him."

"Trip who?"

"The man who came in on the ferry with us."

Caitlin's eyes went wide. "Liam?"

Owen nodded. "She caught the rope around his ankle when he was stepping over the edge. She tripped him and he hit his head and when he woke up he couldn't remember...things. Just like I can't remember things."

Caitlin's gaze dropped to the book still clutched in Owen's arms. It was Nuala who pulled Liam from the freezing November waters. Nuala who sat on the pier beside him, barely shivering afterwards. So exotically beautiful she seemed from another place, or another time. "I want you to tell me everything, Owen." Caitlin reached out, taking his cold hand in hers. "Is there anything...anything at all you can remember from your past?"

Owen shook his head as a faint scent of roses drifted into the room. "The only thing I can remember is water."

TARA ROLLED out the pie crust, setting the wooden pin back on the counter and laying the dough carefully into the glass. A murmur of voices drifted in from the barroom, where most of her friends and neighbors were gathered around the fire, weathering the storm. She wasn't a stranger to storms. She respected the sheer destruction one could leave in its wake.

She'd ridden that wave of destruction less than a year ago, abandoning her car by a Houston bridge as the river rose and swept it away. She'd used that storm to fake her own death as she caught the last flight to Europe and fled an abusive husband, eventually making her way to Ireland and finding a new home and a new life here on Seal Island.

But she'd never forget the terror of that day, and wondering if she'd make it out alive. She pinched the edges of the pie crust together to form a row of neatly spaced ridges. At the knock on the back door, she let out a breath. Dominic and Liam left a half hour ago to help Finn tie down the boats in the harbor. She didn't want them out in this mess. She wanted them inside, safe and warm where she didn't have to worry about them.

She dusted the flour off her hands and headed for the door. She must have thrown the bolt by accident. A gust of wind blew into the kitchen and she stepped back from the rain spitting inside. "Caitlin?" She paused when she spotted Caitlin and Owen huddled under the overhanging roof in matching yellow slickers. "What are you doing here?"

"We're looking for you."

"Come inside." She opened the door wider. "It's freezing out there."

"No." Caitlin shook her head and Owen shrank back from the doorway. "Can we talk to you privately? In your office?"

"What's wrong?"

"Nothing's wrong with either of us," Caitlin explained, keeping her voice carefully neutral. "We just want to talk to you."

"Okay," Tara said slowly, looking back and forth between them. "I'll just give Fiona a head's up and grab my coat."

"Wait," Owen called when she turned, her sneakers squeaking on the wet floor. "Is my mother in there?"

Tara nodded. "She's at the bar. Fiona's fixing up a couple plates for her to bring home to you. Do you want me to get her?"

Owen's eyes darted up to Caitlin's face. "No."

Caitlin squeezed his shoulder. "That's part of what we want to talk to you about, Tara."

Tara heard the ocean, a restless thundering rhythm in the distance. The skin on the back of her neck started to prickle when she noticed for the first time that the shape of Owen's mouth actually mirrored Caitlin's. "You don't want me to tell your mother you're out here?"

Owen shook his head.

"Where does she think you are?"

"At home," Caitlin answered.

Tara swallowed. Some storms left scars you could heal and wounds you could re-patch. Others left paths of destruction so severe you could never recover. And the people left in their wake could do nothing but pick up the broken pieces and hope to find a way to start over as someone else, in some other place.

A river of rain rushed through the alley, bubbling white and swirling through the puddles. She reached for her jacket, stepping out into the street and closing the door behind her. Which kind would this be?

CHAPTER TWELVE

*L*iam knotted the wet rope around the piling, securing the fishing boat rocking in the dark churning waters of the harbor. Loose trawling nets tangled with lobster traps and crashed into cabins. Coolers and storage crates slid across the decks as the waves threw them from side to side. Blood pumped through Liam's veins as he worked, sheets of rain pouring down around the men as they fought to secure the boats tighter to the pier.

"Not bad, professor," Donal shouted over the rain. "Just try not to fall in the water this time."

Liam ignored him, hauling in a seaweed-covered rope and looping it in a tight, steady knot around the metal hook nailed into the pier. His mind was just now beginning to clear, the terrible feeling of being swept out to sea fading and in its place a slow burning frustration over the afternoon he'd spent with Caitlin. An afternoon that had brought back more than one memory.

Donal trotted down the slippery pier, catching the line Liam threw to him and wrapping it around the piling. "There's no beautiful blonde down here to pull you from the waters tonight."

"Shut up, Donal," Dominic barked, shoving him aside and pointing up at Finn clambering onto the ferry. "Give him a hand. I've got this."

Liam watched Donal step onto the ferry and help Finn cart supplies down into the cabin. Grabbing the cold metal railing of the nearest fishing boat, Liam lowered himself down to the deck. Seawater spilled into the rocking vessel, sloshing into the overturned coolers and storage crates. He went to work securing the loose supplies sliding around the deck, looping lines and tying the tight, steady knots he'd learned as a child.

He caught his brother's eye through the rain. Dominic was working his way down the long, narrow pier, tethering the boats to the pilings. It was so typically Dominic, always one foot rooted to the earth, not nearly as comfortable with the imbalance and unpredictability of the sea. Liam glanced down, where his feet were firmly planted on the rocking boat's deck. He was as comfortable on the water as Dom was behind the bar.

It would have been his trade if he hadn't gone to university. He spent his childhood summers on the island learning to fish, apprenticing with Finn. He'd been climbing around these boats since before he was a teenager. How, then, had he tripped stepping down from the ferry the other night? Had he been so distracted by the woman who rescued him? Liam's hands stilled on the ropes. *'Don't you think it's a little strange that the only pieces of your memory you lost are me and that fairy tale?'*

Rain lashed at the pier. The wind tore over the harbor, snatching at the raised voices of Finn and Donal. "You have to admit," Donal called, reaching for the railing to catch his balance as a swell slammed into the boat. "She's a strangeness to her."

"Aye," Finn said, gathering up the nets and making his way

slowly across the slippery deck to the cabin to stow them. "Can't recall I've ever seen eyes or hair as fair as Nuala's."

"I asked her if she knew the O'Toole's," Donal added. "The ones who own *The Curragower*. Everyone knows *The Curragower*. It's the oldest pub in Limerick. But she'd never heard of it." Donal handed a lobster crate to Finn, still holding onto the railing as the boat rocked. "And have you taken a good, long look at that boy?"

"Aye," Finn latched the door to the cabin, testing it to make sure it would hold against the rain and wind. "He's a strange one too, isn't he?"

Donal nodded, gripping the railing as he swung a leg over and jumped back down to the pier. "There's something familiar about him." Donal held out his hand, helping the older man clamber back down to the pier. "But I can't put my finger on it."

Liam stood, pulling himself up to the pier in one fluid motion. The rain sheeted down, dripping from his black hood and he stared at Donal. He wasn't the only one who'd noticed something familiar about Nuala's son?

Donal crossed to the end of the pier, grabbing the line of the smallest fishing boat and tugging it closer. He grinned over his shoulder through the rain. "Strange or no, I wouldn't kick her out of bed."

Finn let out a bark of laughter. "You wouldn't stand a chance."

"No," Donal agreed, knotting the line around the metal clamp. "At least not while the professor here's got his eye on her." He stood, wiping his muddy hands on his wet jeans. "Besides, Nuala's too thin for my tastes. I prefer my women soft..." He grinned up at Liam. "Like Caitlin."

Liam sent Donal a look of warning.

Donal angled his head, rising to the challenge. "Heard you stood her up the other night."

Liam stalked to the edge of the pier, unwinding a knot Dominic had tied in a hurry and rewinding it so it threaded securely around the wood. "Who told you that?"

"Word gets around."

There'd been talk, Liam realized, gazing out at the angry sea. Talk amongst the islanders of what he'd done. He'd hurt Caitlin, not just by standing her up, but by embarrassing her in front of her friends and neighbors.

"Nobody has any secrets here," Donal went on and Liam turned. "And it's no secret she's been carrying a torch for you for years." Donal took the line Finn threw him and looped it around a piling. "But maybe now that you screwed it up..." He shrugged, yanking it tight. "Maybe she'll make herself available." Donal glanced over his shoulder, wiggling his eyebrows. "I definitely wouldn't kick *her* out of bed."

Liam was across the pier in two strides, hooking a fist in Donal's rain gear. He shoved him back against the piling.

"Whoa!" Donal tripped, his feet slipping on the wet wood as Liam held him there.

"Stay the hell away from her," Liam growled, watching the other man's eyes widen as he fought to scramble free.

"Enough," Dominic warned, hauling Liam off Donal. "He got the message."

Donal rubbed his jaw where it had smacked against the wood. "Idiot." He spat out blood from where his tooth bit into his cheek. "If I had a woman like Caitlin in love with me, I wouldn't fuck it up the way you keep doing."

In love with him? Liam took a step back. Since when was Caitlin in love with him? A storm swell slammed into the pier, sea spray splashing the back of his legs. And what the hell did Donal mean, *'keep fucking it up?'* The water flowed over the planks, seeping through the cracks. A sweet, sickening perfume curled into the wet air and his gaze fell to the pier when the sea receded, leaving a single white rose in its wake.

CAITLIN STRIPPED off her raincoat as Tara reached for the light switch automatically, forgetting the power was out. She took Owen's jacket and hung them both on the rose-colored antique coat hanger, ushering Owen over to the pale green sofa in the corner while Tara pulled a battery-powered lamp from the cabinet.

Islanders were wary enough of doctors. The last thing they needed was to walk into a sterile room before getting stuck with a needle. A doctor's office should be a place where you went to heal and feel better, not get poked and prodded and shepherded in and out with clipboards and charts like cattle.

She and Tara had worked hard to make sure the island's first medical practice was a soothing and calming experience. It helped that it was a converted cottage, so it already felt more like a home than an office, but she welcomed the sense of peace that washed over her as Tara switched on the small lamp, placing it on the coffee table filled with magazines and books.

"The kitchen's pretty backed up right now," Tara said, settling into the worn wooden chair across from them. "Everyone brought over what was in their fridge and Fiona's trying to find a way to salvage it. We have at least ten minutes, maybe twenty at the most."

Owen's hand gravitated to the stuffed seal on the table in the corner and he picked it up, squishing it between his fingers. "Is it true?" he asked, glancing up at her. "That you're a selkie?"

Tara lifted a brow. "Who told you that?"

"Kelsey." He set the stuffed seal in his lap, patting its soft fur.

"I see." Tara exchanged a glance with Caitlin. "What else did Kelsey tell you?"

"She said all selkies are black. Is that true?"

Tara crossed her legs, sitting back in her chair. "As far as I know."

"Have you ever seen a white one?"

Tara shook her head. "I haven't."

"Owen," Caitlin said quietly. "We don't have much time. I think Tara might be able to help us, but she needs to understand the situation first." She reached over, smoothing a lock of wet hair out of his eyes. "I saw something this morning that I'd like Tara to see, too."

Owen's hands froze on the stuffed seal. "What did you see?"

"It's nothing to be ashamed of," she soothed. "But would you be willing to show Tara your toes?"

His fingers gripped the fur of the animal. "Why?"

"Because I think it'll help her understand...things."

Owen stared at the floor. "There's nothing wrong with my toes."

"I know that," Caitlin murmured. "But Tara's a doctor. You can trust her."

Owen squeezed the stuffed animal, but he nudged off his sneakers and peeled off one of his socks.

"Your feet are webbed," Tara murmured, noting the thin translucent layer of skin threading between each toe.

"Can I put my sock back on now?" Owen mumbled.

"Of course," Tara said, bending down and slipping off her own sneaker. "But like Caitlin said, it's nothing to be ashamed of." She took off her sock and Caitlin stared at the webbing that attached Tara's last three toes together on her left foot.

"I didn't know..." Caitlin trailed off, embarrassed.

"It's not that noticeable," Tara admitted. "Really, it's much more common than you think."

Owen looked up at her, relief swimming into his eyes. "It is?"

Tara nodded, looking back at Caitlin. "Is that why you came in?"

Caitlin bit her lip. "Not exactly."

"Okay," Tara said, slipping her sock and shoe back on and settling back in her chair. "Now that we've established that Owen has webbed feet and that's perfectly normal, what did you want to talk about?"

Caitlin fished the book out of the sofa cushion she'd tucked it into. She set it on the table between them.

Tara lifted a brow. "*The Little Mermaid?*"

Caitlin nodded. "Owen has a theory about his mother."

"That has to do with *The Little Mermaid?*"

Caitlin wet her lips. It had seemed like a good idea to bring Tara into this at the time. Especially after everything that happened this summer. But now that she was here, in her office, it all felt beyond ridiculous. "Owen thinks his mother is a character in this story."

"Interesting," Tara commented, threading her fingers together over her knee. "Which character?"

Owen hugged the seal to his chest. "The sea witch."

Tara blinked. "I see." Looking out the window, she studied the rain streaking down the glass. "And what makes you think this?"

He told her the story, everything he'd told Caitlin back in his cottage. When he was finished, Tara stood, walking over to the window where a bouquet of lavender hung from the sill. She let her fingers trail over the silver ribbon binding the dried herbs. When she turned back, her face was pale. "Are there any other legends on this island I should be aware of, Caitlin?"

"I-I don't think so," Caitlin stammered. She'd come to Tara for an explanation, a logical, rational explanation to put this theory to rest. Didn't she see how crazy it was?

Tara turned to Owen. "Does your mother know who you think she is?"

He shook his head.

"Good." She looked at her watch. "We might have a few more minutes. I think we should take a quick trip to the beach before getting you home."

"The...beach?" Caitlin stood, shaking her head. "It's crazy out there." She jerked a thumb toward the window at the pounding rain and raging winds. "We can't go down to the beach right now."

"Actually, we can." Tara took Owen's jacket off the coat hanger and held it out to him. "I have a theory of my own I'd like to test out."

CHAPTER THIRTEEN

*H*ey," Caitlin hissed, grabbing Tara's arm on the way out the door. "What's going on?"

"I'll know when we get to the beach." Tara zipped her jacket up to her neck and hunched her shoulders against the wind. "Come on, we don't have much time."

Several steps ahead of them, Owen sloshed through the puddles heading toward the rocky path dipping down to the sea. The ocean surged against the cliff wall and the scent of wet earth mixed with the peat smoke curling from the chimney of the pub.

"Tara," Caitlin called. "Wait."

Tara turned, blinking as cold rain sprayed her face. Caitlin trotted over the soggy earth to catch up to her, lowering her voice so Owen couldn't hear. "Do you believe him?"

Tara let out a long breath. "No."

"Then what are we doing?"

"Taking him to the seals."

Caitlin took a step back. "The seals?"

Tara nodded.

"*That's* your theory? That...what? He's...?

"I don't know," Tara said, cupping her hand over her eyes to shield them from the rain. "Let's just see what happens when he sees them, and they see him."

Caitlin searched her eyes. "What do you *think* is going to happen?"

"Hopefully, nothing." Tara turned, lengthening her stride to catch up to Owen.

"But what if something does happen?" Caitlin called.

"Then I'll know," Tara shouted back over her shoulder.

"Know...*what?*"

Tara slipped her hand through Owen's as he stepped onto the narrow path leading down to the deafening sea. "Hold onto the side of the wall with your free hand," she instructed, positioning herself between him and the edge. She looked back at Caitlin. "After everything that happened this summer, if Owen thinks his mother is a character in a fairy tale, we can't afford not to listen."

Angry clouds rolled in, spitting more rain into the sea and she scanned the churning surface for the seals. Owen's foot slipped on a rock. "Careful," Tara warned, helping him down the slick trail to the sliver of sand. Waves licked hungrily at what was left of the beach, the white sand glowing an eerie silver in the dark storm.

"What's it like to be a selkie?" Owen shouted, staring out at the waves as the sea sucked them back in a giant breath, and then exhaled again. Sea spray pelted their jackets and Tara let go of his hand.

"I'll show you." She strode forward, stripping her jacket and walking into the sea.

"Tara!" Caitlin shouted, scrambling across the sand and grabbing Owen's hand as he started after her. "Stop!"

Tara turned, the icy waves rolling over her waist and in one graceful move, she lowered herself into the sea, disappearing under the surface.

"Where is she going?" Owen cried, struggling to go after her.

Caitlin wrapped her arms around him when Tara reemerged and a black shape materialized in the surf beside her, slowly rising out of the water. It bobbed on the surface, edging closer, tucking its head under Tara's hand, those black eyes staring at Owen.

Tara lifted her other hand and held it out to Owen.

Caitlin's eyes went wide. "No!"

"Let him go, Caitlin."

More seals slid up to the surface, dark sleek shapes surrounding the woman in the sea. "Tara, what are you doing?" Caitlin cried as the ones on the outer edge of the circle started to swim toward the beach. She shrank back from them, pulling Owen back with her. "This is insane!"

"Caitlin, let him go."

Owen tried to pull away and Caitlin locked her arms tighter around him. "He'll freeze!"

"No, he won't."

The seals snorted water out of their noses, shuffling onto the sand. "What's going to happen?" Caitlin cried.

"Let him go."

It was like her own child was being ripped out of her arms and she felt hot irrational tears well up in her eyes as she let go and he scrambled out of her reach, racing into the icy water.

"Be careful," she whispered, her words lost in the wind as she stumbled back, gripping the wet mossy rock wall behind her.

Tara caught Owen's hand in hers and the waves swirled around them, the seals forming a circle. Tara squeezed his hand. "Are you cold?"

"No." Owen shook his head, staring wide-eyed at the seals.

"Neither am I."

The rain poured down around them and Caitlin watched, numb, as the ring parted slightly to let something floating over the surface of the waves inside the circle. She squinted through the curtain of rain, struggling to make out the shape as the seals edged it toward the child.

Owen caught it in his hand, steadying it in the waves.

Caitlin stopped breathing, her hand covering her mouth when she saw what Owen held—an infant's cradle carved from the palest sun-washed driftwood, encrusted with pearls. "Hey," he called, brushing his fingers over the grooves in the wood. "It has the same markings as the rock by the cottage."

Caitlin's fingers curled into the moss. This wasn't happening. This couldn't be happening.

"What rock?" Tara asked.

"The one under the rose." Owen explained, looking over at Caitlin. "What did you call them? Initials? I think they're the same ones."

"What rose?" Tara asked, her voice sharp and hard as glass.

"The white rose," Owen explained, looking up at Tara as Caitlin sank to the sand, the ocean a roar in her ears.

"Caitlin!" Tara shouted as one by one the seals slid under the surface, disappearing back into the waves. "*What rose?*"

GLENNA FELT THE SHIFT, the sudden change in the energy of the air. Alone in her cottage, she closed her eyes, breathing in the scent of the ocean and loosened earth. The candles flickered erratically as a cold wind blew through the house and she stood, walking to the door.

The two women huddled on the other side were soaking wet. She took one look at the matching haunted expressions on Tara and Caitlin's faces and pulled them inside without a word. She ordered Tara straight into the bedroom and made her change into dry clothes. She sent Caitlin to the fire and nestled a copper kettle onto the hook in the hearth, boiling water over the flames.

"Where did you find this?" Glenna asked quietly, nodding to the driftwood cradle.

"The ocean." Caitlin set it on the carpet between them, letting her fingers drift off the soft, weathered wood. "The seals. They pushed it to shore."

"To you?"

"To Owen."

"Nuala's son?"

Caitlin nodded.

"Where is Owen now?"

"We took him back to the cottage," she answered as Tara came out of the bedroom, wearing a pair of Glenna's slacks and one of her sweaters. She handed Caitlin a fresh towel, but Caitlin ignored it, letting it drop to the floor. Her red curls were plastered to her pale face and her fingers were white from the cold, but she couldn't stop staring at the cradle.

Fat pillar candles of jasmine and sandalwood filled the room with a warm, earthy scent. Tara's gaze fell to the intricate encrusting of pearls around the edges, the soft hollow scoop where a child would lay. "The seals sent this to us for a reason."

Caitlin's gaze flickered up, stricken. "Who is he? What is he? What does this *mean*, Tara?"

"I don't know," Tara admitted quietly. She looked at Glenna. "Do you...have you...seen the rose?"

Glenna nodded.

"Three more petals have fallen," Caitlin whispered.

"What does it mean?" Tara asked.

"I don't know yet," Glenna admitted.

Tara searched her eyes. "You'd tell us, wouldn't you? If you knew?"

"Of course." Glenna laid a hand on Tara's shoulder. "I would never let either of you walk into a danger you could not defeat."

Tara swallowed the lump in her throat, remembering how she barely won the battle against her deranged ex-husband. Fear swam into her eyes as she looked over at Caitlin. Glenna squeezed her shoulder, reading her thoughts. She knew how hard it was to be on the sidelines. It was easier being the one it was happening to, the one who needed to do the fighting.

"Is he...safe with her?" Caitlin asked, lifting her troubled eyes to Glenna's.

"Owen, you mean?" Glenna asked. "With Nuala?"

Caitlin nodded. "I'm afraid of him being alone with her."

"What do you think she's going to do to him?" Glenna asked gently.

Tara's gaze drifted back to the cradle. "He thinks she's the sea witch in *The Little Mermaid*."

"Does he, now?" Glenna lifted a brow. "What do you think?"

"I don't know," Tara said, wringing her hands. "But I know she's hiding something."

The fire hissed, the flames licking at the copper kettle. When steam started to leak from the top, Glenna pulled it from the hearth and poured three cups of tea, setting one in front of each of them. She wrapped her hands around the cup, watching Caitlin for a long time as she continued to stare at the cradle. "She's not the only one hiding something."

Caitlin lifted her gaze to Glenna. Her steaming mug sat untouched on the floor in front of her. "What are you talking about?"

Glenna took a sip of her tea, the sharp taste of jasmine floating onto her tongue. "What are *you* hiding, Caitlin?"

"This isn't about me."

"Isn't it?"

"No." A warning sparked behind Caitlin's eyes. "This is about a child who wants to escape from a mother he's afraid of."

"And you want to help Owen out of the goodness of your heart?"

"Yes."

Tara looked back and forth between the two women, confused. "What's going on?"

"I don't know." Glenna set her mug back on the table. "Caitlin, why don't you tell Tara what happened when you left the island ten years ago."

Caitlin stared at Glenna, stunned. "Excuse me?"

"When you left the island," Glenna repeated. "What happened during the time you were away?"

Caitlin's eyes flashed. "You know nothing about that."

"I might know more than you think."

Caitlin pushed to her feet, anger and fear rippling off her in waves. "How?"

"Let's just say I have my ways."

"You're crossing a line," Caitlin warned.

"Caitlin." Glenna rose, gazing across the candlelit room at her friend. "That line was crossed the moment Nuala and Owen arrived on this island."

Caitlin's voice was strained as her hands clenched at her sides. "I don't know what you're talking about."

"All you have to do is open your eyes."

CHAPTER FOURTEEN

*C*aitlin slammed the door, shoving her arms into the sleeves of her jacket, not even bothering to zip it. Cold drops of rain splattered her face as she splashed through the mud, heading for the cottage by the bogs, the one place on this island where no one would follow her, where she could be alone.

Open her eyes? What was that supposed to mean? She spotted the white rose and stalked over to it, grabbing it with both hands and trying to yank it out of the soil. The icy petals burned her fingers and she sank to the ground. What was it doing here? Why couldn't she pull it up by the roots and get rid of it?

She wrapped her fingers around the frozen stem and squeezed, the thorns biting into her palms. She closed her eyes, remembering what happened to Owen when he touched it and fell into that terrible trance. She squeezed harder, reaching for that place, trying to see what he'd seen. But all she saw was the image of him wading out into the ocean and taking Tara's hand as the seals surrounded him. She felt the sick pull of protectiveness again, that instinctive fear that only a mother can feel about her own child.

Her hands fell away from the flower, dropping to the ground. The wind snatched a petal loose and it drifted to the surface of a silver pool of rainwater forming around the base of the rose. It caught there, like a floating white shell as cold fingers of frost twisted over the surface, snaking out from the center and the image of a dozen glistening pearls formed in the ice.

Caitlin dug her hands into the earth, all the heartache and anger pouring out of her as the surf pounded against the shoreline. The rain fell, silver ribbons of runoff swirling around her like a tangled web of long-suppressed memories. Memories of a time when she'd been young and stupid enough to believe she could bring a child into this world at sixteen.

How did Glenna know what happened when she left the island? How could she have found out when she'd never told a soul? She pulled herself to her feet and fumbled with the door to the cottage. She crossed the dark room, the rain pounding against the roof and dripping through the rotted thatch onto the gritty floor of the cottage. She pressed her hands to the far wall, feeling blindly for the loose stone and slipping it free, letting it drop to the ground with a loud thud, and catching the dozens of letters that spilled out.

She squeezed them in her hands, rainwater seeping into the paper, bleeding through the ink. Had Glenna found her letters? Had she discovered the rose outside the cottage and read the initials carved into the stone? How else could she know? Warm drops of water splattered onto the letters and she realized she was crying. She clutched the precious words to her chest as a sob caught in her throat.

'All you have to do is open your eyes.'

To what? To the fact that she hadn't been strong enough to carry a child into this world? That sheer love alone hadn't been enough to keep her baby alive? She'd have given her life in exchange for her son to take one single breath. But her child had died while she had lived. And when she'd pushed the empty cradle out into the sea—the cradle she'd carved from the palest driftwood—she'd watched the waves swallow it, and a piece of her drowned in the ocean that day.

But as many months as she'd spent whittling that perfect hollow scoop, sanding smooth the rounded edges and carving her unborn son's initials in the wood, it had never been anything more than a simple crib roughly fashioned from a frightened pregnant teenager's hands.

Where, then, had those pearls come from? Why was this white rose growing over her son's memorial? What happened to Liam's memory? And why was Owen the spitting image of the son they would have had if she hadn't lost their child?

DUCKING his head against the wind howling through the web of stone walls stretching out to the coast, Sam Holt spotted the beam of a flashlight through Brennan's darkened windows. Angling away from his own cottage, he headed toward the main house. It wasn't common for the island to have break-ins, but everyone else was up at the pub keeping warm, including Brennan. It couldn't hurt to have a look.

You could take the man away from the investigation, but you couldn't take the investigator out of the man. Sam shook his head. He knew he was being ridiculous, but he couldn't help it. *Old habits die hard.* Rain sheeted down into the pastures where sheep and pigs picked their way over muddy rivers to the ancient sheds. Hail smacked against the windows of the cottage and one of the hunter green shutters was starting to come loose in the wind. He made a mental note to fix it later.

He'd taken a liking to the old farmer. He was starting to look after him like a son would an aging parent. If someone was up to something while Brennan was away, it was his responsibility to take care of it. And after what happened on the island this summer, he wasn't taking any chances. As he got closer, he noted the front door was cracked. Keeping his guard up, he pushed it open slowly, widening the crack little by little to get a view inside.

When he spotted Liam, he let out a breath. The floorboards squeaked as he stepped into the cottage. The beam shifted, shining into his eyes. Sam held his palm up and Liam lowered the flashlight. The two men stared at each other until Sam closed the door behind him. "Looking for something?"

"Yes." Liam aimed the flashlight back at the rows of bookshelves. "Why aren't you up at the pub with the others?"

"I wanted to look after the animals."

Liam glanced over his shoulder. "You're really getting into this, aren't you?"

"I am." Sam brushed his dripping hood back, taking in Liam's soaking wet hair, his crooked glasses and disheveled clothes. "Does Brennan know you're here?"

"No." Liam strode across the room to the next shelf, shining the light over the spines of the books. He was wearing a black slicker, but his dark gray sweater and jeans were soaked through. Restless frustrated energy poured off him in waves.

"Then maybe you shouldn't be here," Sam suggested.

Liam reached into his pocket and dropped something onto the table. Sam's gaze fell to the white rose. The scent of saltwater and rose petals drifted into the room. "Where did you find that?"

"It washed up on the pier."

Slowly, Sam picked up the flower, letting it roll through his fingers. Liam continued to pace back and forth along the row of shelves, slipping books in and out of the shelves, shoving them back into their places with increasing frustration.

"I know I returned it," Liam murmured. "It has to be here."

"What are you looking for?"

"I'll know it when I see it."

"Does it have something to do with this flower?"

Liam nodded.

Sam's hand stilled on the stem. He remembered his conversation with Glenna at Caitlin's house last night. She'd said she was at Brennan's yesterday, borrowing books to do *'a little research.'*

It couldn't be a coincidence that Liam was here now, searching for a book. The day after Nuala and Owen arrived on the island. The day after, from what he'd heard, he'd lost all recollection of his relationship with Caitlin. Sam set the rose back down on the table. "You might want to know that Glenna borrowed a few of Brennan's books yesterday."

Liam turned, the beam of the flashlight lowering to the faded throw-rug. "Glenna?"

Sam nodded.

Liam's gaze dropped to the flower. "Which books?"

"I don't know." Sam took a step back when he realized he'd seen those troubled eyes somewhere else, on some*one* else recently. "She mentioned it at Caitlin's party last night."

Liam grabbed the rose and stuffed it back in his pocket. "I think I'll have a word with Glenna."

LIAM'S BOOTS squished into a thick cover of lichens as he cut through the fields, following a muddy path through stone walls and patchwork pastures. A sheep bleated from a nearby field, calling out to his mother as Glenna's cottage came into view. The stone walkway was submerged in three inches of rainwater. The hardy rosemary plants flanking her crimson door twisted madly as thick stalks cracked off, swirling into the muddy streams of soil rushing from her raised garden beds.

If his instincts were right, then the fairy tale he'd found wasn't just hidden in the dusty back shelves of the Trinity Library in Dublin. It was hidden somewhere on this island as well. Banging on her door, he stepped back. It wasn't the first time she'd kept secrets from the islanders. And he wasn't leaving until he found out the truth.

He banged on the door again, surprised when the knob turned easily. "Glenna," he called, pushing the door open and stepping into the cottage. The sitting room was dark and full of shadows. The heavy burgundy curtains were drawn and a cold draft blew through the room. There was a fire dying in the hearth, but no sign of Glenna.

"Glenna?" he called again, in case she was in her bedroom, but there was no answer and the door was wide open. Screw privacy, he thought, striding into her room. Dozens of ruby pillar candles were scattered throughout the room. They were burnt down to an inch, sandalwood-scented wax suspended in mid-melt, pooling into bronze plates as if they'd been burning all day and she'd blown them out in a hurry.

The shelves that lined the walls above her ornately-carved cherry headboard were packed with books. Books of spells and magic. Herbs and witchery. Celtic legends and forgotten Irish myths. He crossed the room to the books, scanning the collection of worn canvas volumes. How had he not known she had all these?

He spotted the one he was looking for, tucked back behind the others, only visible because of its height. He pushed the others aside, reaching for the heavy volume, his fingertips brushing the worn corners of the canvas, faded now to a pale yellowish-green.

He slid it out carefully, running a hand over the dusty cover. The faded gold lettering was worn so thin only a few of the letters were still legible. The edges of the pages curled and he traced the fraying golden ribbon threading through the middle, opening to the story it marked.

He spotted the ragged edges along the seam, the tear in the precious pages where the story should have been. He snapped the book shut, a cloud of dust shooting up into the air as black spots formed in his vision. It was a small island. He would find her. And when he did, she would explain exactly what kind of game she was playing.

Stalking out of the room, he was almost to the door when a bulky object tucked under the antique drawing table caught his eye. He spotted a curve of pale wood peeking out of a bundled quilt. Bending down, he lifted the corner of the quilt and froze when he saw the sanded driftwood, the line of pearls, the hollow scoop where a baby would lay.

CHAPTER FIFTEEN

*N*uala stood at the window of her bedroom, facing the sea. Tracing a finger along the glass, she followed the line of the horizon, leaving a trail of frost in her wake. The sky was pewter gray, the rain a relentless tap dance of silver slippers on ice. Below, the surf curled over a strand of pearl-white beach. Sea spray shot into the air as the waves pummeled the jetty, swallowing the pathetic barrier of jagged rocks meant to shelter the harbor.

One more day. One more day on this wretched island and everything she'd ever wanted would be hers. She heard the shuffle of Owen's footsteps and she turned. Her son stood in the doorway, watching her warily. Her hand fell away from the window and she crossed the room, sighing when he shrank back from her. She reached out, catching his chin in her hand, turning his face from side to side.

His skin was holding its color better than she'd expected. She drew her thumb over a faint discoloration on his cheekbone, watching the shimmer of blue settle into the darker pigment, transforming it back to alabaster white. As soon as they got back to the ocean, the last layer would heal. She reached for his hand, wanting to see if the marks from where he'd touched the rose by the cottage had faded. But he pulled away from her, hiding his hand behind his back.

Nuala drummed her fingers over the windowsill. Maybe it would be easier if he knew. Maybe it was a mistake erasing his memories. If he could remember the life they had run from, and understand what was at stake in these final hours on land, maybe she could regain his trust. Maybe he could even help her. Help *them* get what they needed to build the life they deserved when they returned to the sea.

It was a risk. But it might be the only way to have him back on her side. To keep him from causing any more trouble. She opened her mouth, closing it when she spotted a movement outside her window. She parted the lace curtain, recognizing the brunette from the other night at Caitlin's house. *Glenna.* The artist who'd moved to the island a few years ago from Dublin. Her gaze dropped to the bulky object balanced in the woman's arms. Brushing past Owen, Nuala opened the door to a rush of wind and rain.

"Hi." Glenna smiled warmly, stepping around an overflowing pothole. "I hope you don't mind me popping over like this." She juggled the object wrapped in cellophane. "Caitlin asked me to finish this painting for over the fireplace ages ago. Do you mind if I hang it? I'll just be a minute and then get right out of your way."

Nuala stepped aside uncertainly.

"Thanks," Glenna said, walking into the dimly lit cottage. Her long coat dripped rainwater onto the floor, already slick from the spray shooting in the door. She took a moment to scan the simple furnishings. A wheat-colored sofa and matching arm chairs circled a throw rug in creams and pale blues. A wooden rocker sat in the corner by the far window with a view of the harbor. An antique dining table nestled close to the hearth, separating the tiny kitchen from the sitting room. "It's rather cozy, isn't it?"

"It is," Nuala lied. She wanted nothing more than to leave this place and return to her home.

Glenna smiled down at Owen, still huddled in the corner of the room. "It's nice to see you again, Owen."

"You too," he mumbled, looking down at his feet.

Glenna wandered into the sitting room, setting the heavy object down and turning her attention back to Nuala. "How are you enjoying your stay on the island?"

"It's a lovely place." What was it about this woman that set her on edge?

"It is," Glenna agreed. "I'm sorry the storm is keeping you from exploring more of the island. The views from the cliffs are breathtaking. On a clear day you can see as far south as the Cliffs of Moher."

"We'll have to make a trip back one day." Out of the corner of her eye, Nuala caught her son's head snap up. "But we're making the best of our stay. And we're glad to be away from the mainland for a few days." She looked pointedly at her son. "Aren't we, Owen?"

"Yes," he mumbled, his gaze drifting over to the wrapped object.

"I'm glad to hear it," Glenna said. "Maybe when you return, we'll have a few cottages for you to choose from." She strolled to the window, dipping her fingers into the bowl of seashells. "This is our second renovation. Mine and Caitlin's. That's what we do on the island."

"I thought you were an artist?"

"I am." Glenna glanced over her shoulder. "But I never pass up a lucrative business opportunity." She selected a silver shell from the bowl and held it up to the dim light streaming in through the window. "Caitlin designs and manages the properties and I fund the purchase of the homes. We hope to have a string of holiday homes on the island one day to bump up the tourist trade to compete with the more popular islands."

Nuala gritted her teeth. She didn't care about holiday homes or tourist trades. And she didn't have time for social calls. Why was this woman still here anyway? She better not expect her to offer to make tea. It wasn't happening.

Owen took a step toward the painting. "Can I see it?"

Glenna smiled down at Owen as she set the shell back in the bowl and walked over to the painting. "Do you like to paint?"

He stared at the murky white wrapping, taking another hesitant step closer. "I don't know."

Glenna slipped a nail into the tape, sliding it through the holds. She looked up at Nuala. "You should bring him by my studio later. I'd be happy to set him up with some paint and an old canvas."

"Thank you, but we have plans later."

Glenna lifted a shoulder, snapping the second piece of tape. "Maybe next time."

Owen inched closer, his fingers brushing the top of the bubble wrap.

"Go ahead," Glenna urged. "Tear it off." She lifted knowing eyes to Nuala's. "I guess it's almost like unwrapping a present."

Owen tore the wrapping away from the painting and Nuala's breath caught in her throat when she saw the white coral towers, the soaring marble gates, the sparkling beds of oyster shells around shimmering roses made of ice.

Glenna lifted the painting into her arms, carrying it over to the fireplace. "Might as well set it up on the mantle and see how it looks."

"Owen." Nuala struggled to find her voice. How? How could this woman know what her palace looked like? How could anyone know exactly what it looked like unless they'd seen it? "Go to your room."

"But the painting," Owen stuttered. "I've…"

"Go to your room," Nuala snapped, her voice cracking through the damp air in the cottage like a whip.

Glenna turned, her smile fading at the change in Nuala's tone. "Is everything all right?"

"Everything's fine," Nuala said as soon as her son was out of earshot.

Glenna wandered away from the fireplace, studying the painting from a few different angles to make sure it was straight. "I heard you were a songwriter." She walked back up to the wall, edging the left corner up a half an inch. "I'd love to see some of your songs." She stepped back, scrutinizing the position, keeping her tone light and friendly. "If you ever feel like sharing."

Nuala's fingers curled into her palms, her nails biting into the skin. "I never show anyone my work until it's completely finished."

Glenna angled her head, a powerful flame burning deep in those amber eyes. "Never?"

"You must understand that vulnerability," Nuala quipped. "You're an artist."

"Of course," Glenna said, nodding. "But maybe you'd let me see one that's finished?"

"Unfortunately, I left my song books at home."

"That is unfortunate." Glenna trailed a hand along the back of the sofa. "I guess I should be going. Bye, Owen," she called loud enough so the boy could hear.

Owen ran out of the bedroom, his wet socks skidding across the slick floor. "Wait. Where are you going?"

"She's going home," Nuala said tightly.

Glenna's lips curved as she brushed past Nuala.

"But the roses," Owen stammered. "Look!" He stood on his

toes, pointing to the line of roses leading up to the palace gates. "She knows exactly where all the roses go!"

Nuala's hand shot out, closing over Glenna's wrist. "What did you come here for?"

"To hang a painting for a friend." Glenna looked back at her work. "I'm rather proud of it, actually. I always imagined this is what an undersea palace would look like." She smiled, her gaze drifting back to Nuala. "Not that I'd know."

Nuala heard the faint sizzling before she felt the burn, before she tore her hand free from Glenna's arm and felt the blistering heat sear into her skin. She swallowed the cry of pain as Glenna brushed past her, stepping out into the curtain of rain and sweeping the hood of her honey-colored raincoat over her head.

"Who are you?" Nuala hissed.

Glenna looked over her shoulder and smiled. "I'm just an artist from Dublin. And you're just a songwriter from Limerick."

CHAPTER SIXTEEN

*S*am scooped up a pile of manure with his pitchfork and plopped it into the ancient metal wheelbarrow. Steam rose up from the muck, drifting into the cold air. He turned at the squeak of the barn door sliding open, spotting the silhouette of a woman slipping through the widened crack in the door. "Tara?"

She nodded, closing the door behind her and stepping into the damp barn. Her small frame was dwarfed in an oversized raincoat. One of Dominic's, no doubt. Her short dark hair was wet and plastered to her pale face, her expression guarded.

Sam leaned the pitchfork against the wheelbarrow. "Is everything all right?"

The wind raced over the pastures, an eerie whistling through the web of stone walls. Tara pulled her coat tighter around her shoulders. "I'm not sure."

Sam rolled the wheelbarrow out of the stall, hooking the rope guard behind him. "What's up?"

She glanced over her shoulder, as if she was afraid of being watched. "I probably shouldn't be here." She walked over to where a white pony stretched his neck over the stall. She cupped her hands under his velvety muzzle, letting his whiskers tickle her palms. "I need to ask you something. I...wasn't sure who else to talk to."

Stay out of it, Sam. You're here to slip off the radar. To blend. Just take care of the animals and stay out of it. The sheep pawed restlessly at the hay. An icy wind blew in through the cracks in the rotting barn door.

The pony nickered, nuzzling her hand and Tara took a deep breath. "I think there's something happening again. I don't know what it is. And I can't get my head wrapped around it."

"What do you mean?"

Tara reached up, letting her fingers comb through the pony's gray forelock. "When you came here this summer and first heard the selkie legend, is that what changed your mind? Is that what made you stay?"

He caught the edge in her voice, the way her eyes kept darting back to the door. "It wasn't just the legend. It was that and the roses, seeing you and realizing you weren't the woman Philip said you were...meeting Glenna."

Tara nodded. "But it was the story? The fairy tale? That's what first clued you in?"

"I think so, yes."

"What if there was no legend? What if things just seemed...off?"

Stay out of it, Sam. Just stay out of it. Questions, angles swirled inside his investigator's mind, but he clamped them down. He wasn't that person anymore. He was someone else now. "What are you getting at, Tara?"

"Did you..." Her fingers toyed with a string coming loose on the pony's faded red halter. "Did you believe in magic before coming to this island?"

"No."

"Do you believe in it now?"

He chose his words carefully. "I believe there are some things that can't be explained by logic."

When Tara said nothing, continuing to thread her fingers through the pony's mane, Sam dipped his hands in his pockets. All he wanted to do was work on this farm, care for these animals and keep a low profile. But he could feel Tara's anxiety. He could sense her tension sizzling through the wet air of the barn. It reminded him too much of the mood he'd caught Liam in earlier. "Tara, is this about the book Liam is looking for?"

Tara's hand dropped to her side. "What book?"

"Liam came by Brennan's cottage earlier." Pushing away from the stall door, Sam crossed the narrow passageway to stand on the other side of the pony, propping his shoulder against a wooden beam and looking down at her. "He seemed...troubled."

"What book was Liam looking for?"

"He said he'd know it when he found it. I told him to go to Glenna's. She'd been by the day before to borrow some of Brennan's books."

Tara's gaze drifted to a thin crack in the barn doors. A tangled web of stone walls cut through the stretch of land dipping down to the churning sea. "They're looking for the story."

A ringing, like a warning bell, went off in his head. "A story about a white rose?"

Tara lifted her eyes to his. "You've seen the rose?"

"Liam showed it to me."

"Liam?" Tara's green eyes clouded with confusion. "He had it...with him?"

Sam nodded. "In his pocket. Said it washed up on the pier at his feet."

Tara eyes widened. "There are two of them?"

The ocean played a haunting melody over the shore. If the roses were multiplying... "Where's the other one?"

"Outside the cottage by the bogs," Tara breathed. She pushed a shaky hand through her wet hair and told him about the falling petals. She told him about her conversation with Owen this afternoon, about his webbed feet and taking him down to the beach. She told him how the selkies surrounded him, like they'd surrounded her last summer. "He thinks his mother is the sea witch from *The Little Mermaid*," Tara finished. "But I think he might be part-selkie. But I don't know enough about the island and its legends. Caitlin said there was only one that she knew of. But maybe I'm missing something." She looked up at him, fear swimming in her eyes. "Or maybe I'm going crazy and reading too much into this."

Sam pushed off the wall, pacing back and forth along the narrow barn hallway. "How many petals?"

"How many...?"

"How many petals have fallen?"

"At least half of them," Tara answered.

Sam turned, facing her. "What does Dominic think about all this?"

Tara looked away.

"What?"

She swallowed, looking guilty. "I haven't talked to him about this yet."

Sam's brows shot up. "Why not?"

"I don't know if he can be objective. Whatever we're dealing with, I'm afraid it's connected to Liam and Caitlin. He's still struggling to come to terms with the fact that his little brother was starting a relationship with his best friend. Even though, between you and me, I think something's been going on between them for a lot longer. But until he can accept that, really accept that, I need an outsider's ear. Someone who can tell me if there's any merit to my fears before I get too carried away."

Sam rubbed a hand over the back of his neck. "How's he going to feel about you talking to me about this first?"

"You're a good detective, Sam. I trust you. And Dom will come around someday. You just have to give it time."

Sam lifted his gaze to the leaking roof. "I wouldn't. If I were him."

Tara closed the distance between them, putting a gentle hand on his arm. "You've changed, Sam. I don't blame you for leading Philip here. And I understand what it's like to be running from a terrible past and to just want forgiveness and a clean slate."

As much as those words meant to him, he didn't want to go back down this road again. His investigative skills had done nothing but get him into trouble over the years. Slipping his arm free, he grabbed the wooden handles of the wheelbarrow and rolled it across the hall to the next stall.

"You can't run forever, Sam."

"Maybe not," he conceded, shoveling more hay into the wheelbarrow. "But I can drop off the map for a while."

"Your past will catch up with you. Take it from someone who knows."

His past would catch up with him all right. But at least for now he could breathe. And focus his energy on taking care of something besides himself for a change. He scooted a sheep aside and scooped up another pitchfork full of muck. It was best to take life one day at a time. Keep your expectations low. And wait for the next punch life threw at you. Then decide whether to dodge or fight back. It was nice, at least for now, to be miles from the punches.

"You could have taken the money and run," Tara said softly. "You could have gone anywhere."

"It was a moment of conscience." A stocky bay in the neighboring stall stuck his nose through the metal bars. Sam couldn't resist the urge to feed him a sugar cube and fished one out of his pocket. "I don't have many of them."

"You stayed here, Sam. On *this* island. A place where it was possible no one would accept you after what you'd done."

The horse crunched the sugar cube, bumping his shoulder for another one. "But you do."

"I do. I don't blame you. If you hadn't led Philip here, I might still be running." Tara walked up to the stall, curling her fingers around the top of the door. "This island speaks to you, Sam. I can see it in your eyes. The same way it speaks to me. But if you want to be a part of this island. If you want it to heal you, you have to become a part of it."

"You're a better person than me, Tara."

"I don't believe that."

He paused, gazing at her across the stall.

"I know you want to help, Sam. And I know you're afraid. But you can't keep hiding out on this farm, pretending all the company you need is these animals."

He looked away.

"If you won't do it for me, do it for Glenna."

He lifted his eyes to hers slowly.

"We need you, Sam. *She* needs you. I don't know what's going on yet, but I'm afraid it has more to do with Glenna than Nuala. That it's bigger than any of us realize. And like this past summer, it's going to take all of us."

Sam shoved one last scoop of soiled hay into the barrel, then rested the pitchfork across it. Ambling over to the door, he leaned his arms over the top. "I might have been reading up on a legend or two lately. After everything that happened this summer, I started studying them. As a hobby, I guess. You know Brennan's house is full of them?"

Tara let out a breath, nodding.

"I can't make any promises," he warned. "But I'll tell you what I know."

"Anything," Tara urged. "If you can think of anything at all that would explain Owen's...situation."

"Only one. But it's not really a story, or a legend. It's more of a superstition."

"What is it?"

"Have you ever heard of a changeling?"

Tara shook her head.

"Some cultures believe that magical creatures—fairies, dwarves, trolls—will sneak into homes at night and steal human children, leaving one of their own in its place."

Tara chewed on her lip. "You think someone stole Owen? When he was a child?"

"It usually happens when they're infants, so you can't tell the difference. I know it seems crazy, but it comes up a lot in fairy tales of all different cultures. It's at least worth considering. Are we sure Nuala is his real mother?"

"No," Tara said slowly. "But Owen's convinced he's been living underwater. That's not possible, is it? A human child can't just go underwater."

Sam scratched his fingers over his chin, pondering. "Changelings are stolen by fairies or trolls to live in the woods or underground in caves."

"But that's still on land," Tara argued. "That's still breathing air. We're talking about a kid being stolen and taken *underwater*. We don't have the same breathing mechanisms."

"True," Sam agreed. "Unless...the child had selkie blood in him already."

Tara lifted her eyes to his. "You think...?"

"I don't know what I think." Sam shook his head. "But I'd like to have another look at this child, and maybe ask him a question or two."

CHAPTER SEVENTEEN

*G*lenna snatched the hem of her coat from the rusted nail jutting out of the wooden stile. She clambered over the slippery ladder leading over the stone wall, her red leather boots sinking into the mud as she jumped down, hurrying back to her cottage. She'd done what she set out to do—to shake Nuala up. But she still didn't know who Nuala was, how she'd gotten tangled up with Owen, and what she wanted with Liam.

The only reason she knew to paint that palace was because she saw it in a vision this morning, not long before Caitlin and Tara came to her door. She painted the image furiously by candlelight, but it left her rattled and shaken. She could pretend as well as any woman, but the truth was, she didn't know what they were up against yet.

And something about this whole situation had Moira written all over it. Restless, thundering rain poured down around her, soaking the already saturated pastures. She scrambled over another slick stile, her coat streaming out behind her as she dashed across the open expanse of land. This wasn't Moira's fight. Moira's fight was with Glenna. *Not* Caitlin.

Unless there was something Glenna didn't know. The wind tore over the barren landscape and she gripped the hood of her coat, shielding her face from the stinging rain. She knew that Owen would come one day, that there would be a struggle. But not like this. Nothing like this.

She ducked under the canopy of thatch, her hand grasping the door handle. Whatever they were dealing with, she needed answers. She needed to know what they were up against so no one got hurt. She pushed the door open, letting out a thin scream as a man's strong hand closed over her wrist and yanked her inside.

"Liam," she gasped, stumbling into the dark cottage. "What are you doing here?" She let out a breath when she found her footing.

But his eyes never left hers as he closed the door. "You've some explaining to do, Glenna."

"What do you mean?"

Liam led her into the room, turning her by the shoulders to face the table beside the door. "Why don't you start by telling me where *that* came from?"

Glenna froze. Why hadn't she hidden it better? Liam had pulled the cradle out from under the table. The blanket was tossed aside. She'd been in such a hurry to finish the painting, she'd forgotten to find a better hiding place for it. What was the matter with her? She couldn't afford to fall apart now. They needed her.

"Liam." She tried to shake him off, but his grip tightened around her.

She glanced up at him, meeting those cold, hard eyes. The scent of smoke, of something burning, rushed into the room. "It washed up on the beach yesterday."

"What beach?"

"Liam..."

"*What* beach?"

"The one by Tara's cottage."

"Who found it?"

Glenna tugged again, biting back a curse when he held onto her. "Liam..."

A muscle in Liam's jaw started to tick. "*Who* found it?"

"Caitlin," Glenna breathed.

He spun her around to face him, his strong hands gripping her shoulders. "What the hell kind of game do you think you're playing?"

Glenna stepped back, out of his reach. "I'm not playing games."

Liam grabbed the book off the floor, holding it up. "It's all connected. The rose. The cradle. The missing fairy tale. You knew it all along, didn't you?"

He'd found it. Of course he'd found it. Glenna shook her head, keeping her eyes on him as she backed slowly into the sitting room.

He opened to the story, where the missing pages were torn from the book. "Tell me where you hid the story, Glenna."

"It was gone before I got to it."

"You're lying."

"I went to Brennan's yesterday. I don't know why the story is missing. But it was gone when I got there."

"You expect me to believe that?"

"I'm on your side, Liam."

He stared at her, frustration rippling off him in waves. He was trying to decide whether or not to believe her. She understood that. She wasn't sure she would believe her if the roles were reversed. "Who the hell is she?"

"That's what I'm trying to figure out," Glenna breathed. "Caitlin told me you'd...forgotten things. Have you started to remember?"

"Only pieces." His gaze dropped back to the cradle. "And none of them adds up." Walking slowly back over to the cradle, he stared down at the pearls shimmering in the dim light of the cottage. Pulling the rose out of his pocket, he looked down at the matching iridescent petals. "You said this cradle washed up on the beach today."

Glenna nodded.

"And Caitlin found it."

"Yes."

"She brought it here? To you?"

"Yes."

"What does it mean?"

"I think you better ask Caitlin that question."

GLENNA WATCHED Liam stalk into the storm, his shape fading into the swirling gray mists. As soon as he was out of sight, she turned away from the window, crossing the dark room to the hearth. She built a fire and pulled out the white petal—the single petal that had fallen when Liam shoved the flower back in his pocket on his way out the door. It pressed into her palm, cold and hard as ice.

She closed her eyes and whispered a quiet chant. The faint tingling built. The rush of power flooded down her arms, through her fingers. The snap and crackle of fire burst from the hearth. The flames flared, filling the room with their warmth. She opened her eyes, inhaling a breath of smoke and seawater. Uncurling her fingers, she tossed the petal into the flames.

She saw nothing at first, heard nothing but the faint sizzle of steam as the icy petal turned to vapors and floated up. But as the curl of black smoke began to take shape, she saw the patterns form in the smoke. It could have been anything—the small bundle wrapped in a blanket—until the wisps of white smoke curled around it and the image of a cradle formed. The smoke teased the shape of a mother sitting beside it, rocking the cradle from side to side. The image was of Caitlin, and the child she would have had if he survived.

Glenna edged closer as another shape formed and a hand reached out, snatching the child away from the mother. A cold wind drifted into the hearth, swirling the smoke, and the images faded as quickly as they'd come. Glenna whirled as the terrible sound of something cracking and igniting reared up behind her.

No! She dashed across the room to the cradle, smothering the flames in a blanket. But the fire swallowed the blanket, kicking out into the room. She scrambled back as it licked up the sides of the drawing table, swirling into a blazing fire. Every muscle in her body tensed as the flames took on the shape of a woman.

Black smoke swirled around the woman in the fire, curling into the strawberry blond waves that tumbled down to her slender waist. She wore a gold crown, glittering with rubies. A bracelet snaked up one arm, black volcanic rock braided with burnt coral. The woman smiled, her luminous green-gold eyes glittering. "Playing with fire again, darling?"

Her voice echoed into the room, hollow and foreign, like a voice from the sea. Empty as the sound of the ocean when you hold a shell up to your ear. Glenna felt all the energy, all the power drain out of her. "What do you want?"

Fire licked at the glittering hem of her golden dress, at the amber gemstones dripping from her fingers. A chunk of amber dangling from a glittering gold chain rested between her breasts, sparkling in the firelight at her feet. "Only to pass on a warning."

Glenna fought to breathe over the black smoke filling the cottage. "A...warning?"

A shimmering golden dress draped over one shoulder, the silky material clasped with a chunk of rough-cut topaz. The woman stepped into the room, the thin fabric shifting like waves at sunset. Rich golden waves warmed by the sun. "Stay away from Nuala."

"Who is she?"

"She is not your concern."

"*Who* is she?"

"I told you," the woman hissed, her bracelets jangling as she flicked her wrist toward the other side of the room. "She is not your concern."

A painting—a silver beach bathed in moonlight—burst into flames. Paint melted down her butter-cream walls, the fire crackling over the canvas. Glenna gasped when all at once the flames died as quickly as they'd come. Leaving nothing but charred walls and a pile of pale ash and spilled pearls where the cradle used to be.

CHAPTER EIGHTEEN

$\mathcal{N}$uala flinched at the knock on the door. Hadn't these islanders ever heard of privacy? She tucked her pelt back under the floorboards, folding the slick seal-skin and covering the loosened board with a rug. She stashed the oil behind the night table, and smoothed her hands over the carpet to pat down any wrinkles.

She'd thought she had until sunset tomorrow. But now that Glenna had entered the picture, everything had changed. Caitlin was one thing. Caitlin she could deal with. But until she found out who Glenna was and what she wanted, she would be ready to leave at a moment's notice.

She unlocked her door and stepped into the hallway. Owen's bedroom door was still shut. She'd sent him to his room earlier, after his outburst over the painting. There was no way she was telling him the truth now. Not until she knew who they were up against.

She glanced at the painting of the white palace on the way to the front door. It was still hanging above the fireplace. She'd decided to leave it there in case the woman paid her a second visit. She didn't want to explain why she'd taken it down, or raise any more questions.

She opened the door. Tara stood on the other side with a man she recognized from the gathering at Caitlin's house the other night. A gray wool cap was pulled low over his forehead and his burnished bronze hair tangled around the collar of a faded barn coat.

"Sorry to bother you, Nuala." Rainwater dripped down the hood of Tara's oversized coat. "Do you remember Sam?"

The man held out his hand and a pair of sharp whiskey-colored eyes locked on hers. Nuala nodded. His grip was firm and he smelled faintly of wet animals and sweat. Deep lines from years of working in the sun were etched into his rugged face. "I'm not sure we had much of a chance to talk the other night. It's nice to meet you. Again."

Nuala pulled her hand away and she didn't like the way those assessing eyes moved past her, sweeping through the room.

"Is that one of Glenna's paintings?" Sam asked, nodding to the piece above the fireplace.

Nuala made no move to open the door wider or invite them in. "It is."

"Don't think I've seen that one before."

"She just brought it over today."

"Did she?"

There was an edge to his voice, something in his tone she didn't trust. She'd seen the way this man looked at Glenna, the way he practically followed her around the other night. There was something between the two of them. Which meant he couldn't be trusted. None of them could be trusted.

"Sam and I were on our way back to the pub," Tara explained, shaking the rain off the arms of her jacket. "I was wondering if Owen would like to come over to play with Kelsey?"

Her son wasn't going anywhere. Especially not near this man. "Thank you for the offer, but Owen's sleeping right now."

"I'm not sleeping," Owen spoke up from behind her, and Nuala gritted her teeth. He'd padded silently into the room in his socks. He was standing behind her, peering around the door.

"Owen," she seethed. "Go to your room."

"Hi, Owen." Tara waved and smiled down at him, ignoring Nuala's command. "Did you have a good nap?"

He nodded.

Tara smiled back up at Nuala. "Kelsey's grandmother brought her a new board game and she needs another player for her team. I'll be there all afternoon and so will Dominic. Liam will probably be in and out too, unless of course...he's here with you."

It was impossible to miss the implication behind her words. *'I'll take your son off your hands if you want a few hours alone with Liam.'* But why would Tara want to help her find time alone with Liam. Wasn't she good friends with Caitlin? And Glenna?

"I'm afraid we're all getting a bit stir crazy," Tara continued. "But the children especially don't like to be cooped up inside for so long."

Owen tugged gently on Nuala's shirt sleeve. "Can I go?"

She didn't know who to trust, or what to believe anymore. But she had things to do—things she couldn't do around Owen. If she let him go, it would get him out of her hair. At least for a little while. "I should come with you," Nuala suggested. After the accusations Caitlin threw at her earlier, she couldn't afford to have others suspecting she let her child wander off into the storm alone, or with people who were practically strangers.

"Only if you feel like it," Tara insisted. "I'm happy to watch them. None of us is going anywhere."

Nuala looked back at Sam. His eyes were still trained over her shoulder, still focused on the painting over the fireplace. No,

she didn't like this man. She didn't like him at all. But she needed
this time alone to store up her strength, to prepare for her return
to the sea. It would be easier if Owen was occupied. How much
trouble could he get into at the pub, playing board games with
other children? "I was finishing up the lyrics for a new song...I
could work on it there..."

"Nonsense." Tara waved her off. "Come by when you're
done and we'll fix you up some dinner. The power's still out, but
Dominic's grandmother left a big batch of stew simmering in the
cauldron over the fire. It might not be the best thing you've ever
eaten, but it's warm and it'll satisfy the hunger."

Owen was already shoving his feet into his shoes and slipping
out the door. Tara took Owen's hand and looked sympathetically
up at Nuala. "I'm really sorry your stay happened during this
power outage. I hope you'll come back another time, when the
weather's nicer."

"I'd like that," Nuala said sweetly, her fingers curling around
the door as Tara led Owen out into the flooded streets.

Sam took one last look at the painting and then turned, his
long strides catching up with Tara and Owen. Nuala stood in the
doorway, watching their figures fade into the curtain of rain. As
soon as they rounded the bend into the village, she grabbed her
cloak, fastened it around her neck and set out in the other direction. It was time she paid a visit to Moira. And found out just
how much she had left out of this story when she'd made the
trade.

Dominic glanced up from his ledger when Tara walked into
the kitchen. An oil lamp burned on the counter, a small circle of
light illuminating the columns on the page. Pipe smoke drifted in
from the dining room where Brennan Lockley sat alone at the

candlelit bar reading the paper. Dominic narrowed his eyes when he spotted Sam shrugging out of his jacket and ambling over to join Brennan. "What's *he* doing here?"

"Dom," Tara warned, closing the door behind her. "Sam has a right to come into the pub for a drink now and then."

"I don't like him in here."

Tara rubbed her muddy sneakers on the mat by the back door. "Where's Fiona?"

"She's at the Dooley's. Jack got the generator to work. Most everyone headed over there a little while ago."

Tara glanced through the small window into the bar. "Why didn't Brennan go with them? He could use a bit of warmth." Her brows knitted in concern. "I imagine his arthritis is acting up in this weather."

"You know how Sarah feels about pipe smoke in her house," Dominic answered. "She won't have it."

"And Kelsey?" Tara spied Owen settling onto the blanket beside their daughter. She had a pile of books spread out around her and she picked one up, handing it to Owen.

"Ronan was getting on her nerves." Dominic sent her a knowing look. "You know how he gets when he's stuck inside for too long."

Tara nodded. Ronan O'Kelly was only nine years old, but he could drive them all nuts at times. She didn't blame Kelsey for wanting to hide out in the pub for a while. Her gaze shifted back to the bar as Brennan peeled off a section of the newspaper—at least a day old by now—and handed it to Sam. Plus, it would give Sam a chance to get to know Owen a little without too many distractions. If anyone could get to the bottom of this, it was Sam.

"Dom," she said, turning away from the window and lowering her voice. "Can I ask you something?"

"You can ask me how many ways I'd like to remove Sam Holt from that barstool."

Tara sighed. "Actually, I have a question about Caitlin." If Glenna was right, and the reason Caitlin was so worried about Owen was because she was hiding something, she had a hunch she knew what it was. Almost from the moment Owen set foot on this island, Caitlin had been mothering him. She'd brought him into the pub for breakfast that first day. She'd taken him with her to see the new cottage she was working on. She'd given him books to read and listened when he voiced fears about Nuala. She'd brought him in to see her at her office, worried about his webbed feet. And then she'd clung to him—like only a mother would cling to her own child—almost unable to let him go when he'd tried to follow her into the sea this afternoon.

None of these actions alone would raise suspicion. But when you added them all up, you couldn't help but wonder if there was a reason Caitlin and Owen were forming this unlikely bond—and in only a matter of days. Especially when, if you looked closely, the child held a striking resemblance to both Caitlin *and* Liam.

Tara bit her lip when Dominic wandered over to the stack of boxes he was unloading and tracking in his ledger. "What's on your mind?"

"Glenna mentioned something earlier," Tara began, trying to keep her tone light. "About Caitlin leaving the island when you all were younger..."

Dominic flipped to a new page, grabbing the pen from behind his ear and marking a note down. "We all got off the island now and then."

"No. I mean, for an extended period of time."

He glanced up. "What's this about?"

Tara turned, picking up Fiona's loose recipes and sliding them back into the box in alphabetical order. "I'm just curious about...things."

"What sort of things?"

"Oh, you know..." She smoothed out the corner of one of the

index cards. "I hear things sometimes. And I just want to know that, as the island's only doctor, I'm fully informed about my patients." She squeezed her eyes shut. She was *such* a terrible liar.

Dominic narrowed his eyes. "I don't quite see what one has to do with the other, but since you asked, it's no secret. She got some kind of scholarship her last two years of high school. She went to live with an aunt of hers in Donegal for about eighteen months."

Tara opened her eyes. She turned around to face her husband. "She left the island when she was sixteen?"

He nodded. "I imagine that's about right."

Tara opened her mouth, closed it. She grabbed a dishrag and ran it over the counter. "I guess I'm surprised I never knew that."

"I don't think she talks about it much." The bottles clicked as he rummaged through the boxes, counting each variety and noting the numbers in his ledger. "It was some fancy all girls' school in the south. Not exactly the best fit for Caitlin. But I think she got in because her aunt taught there." He shrugged, like he hadn't ever given it much thought before. "Maybe her parents wanted her to experience something else besides island life for a while."

"I see." Tara stared at the fog clinging to the windows. But she didn't see. Caitlin's father was a fisherman and her mother was a seamstress. They lived in Cork now, with one of Caitlin's sisters, but from everything she'd heard they weren't the kind of parents to dole out special opportunities to their eldest child. They would have preferred to have her around to help with the chores and the rearing of her seven younger brothers and sisters. "I guess I'm still surprised it never came up in any of our conversations."

Dominic smiled, his pencil trailing down a column of numbers, counting at the same time. "I'm sure she hasn't told you all her secrets."

Tara watched him closely. "Is there anything about *your* past you haven't told me?"

Dominic glanced up from the notebook. "Anything in particular you want to know about?"

Tara blew out a breath. "Okay. This is going to sound crazy. But I'm just going to come right out and ask it." She folded the towel over the handle of the stove. "Are you descended from selkies?"

Dominic almost dropped the bottle in his hands. "Not that I know of."

"Did you...have webbed feet when you were a kid?"

He choked out a laugh. "No."

"Did your mother?"

He stared at her, biting back the next laugh when he saw the look on her face. "I don't know, Tara. I don't remember much about my mother. She left us when we were very young."

"And you have no idea where she is?"

Dominic pushed away from the counter and crossed the room to his wife. He cupped her face in his hands, rubbing drops of rainwater off her cheek with his thumb. "Do you want to tell me what all this is about?"

Tara swallowed, looking up into those pensive gray eyes.

When she didn't say anything, a troubled expression darkened his features. "Is this about Nuala and that boy? Should I be worried that Kelsey's taking a liking to him?"

No, Tara thought, shaking her head. If they were cousins it made perfect sense for Kelsey to bond with Owen.

"Then why do you want to know all this?"

"I'm just trying to piece everything together," Tara answered.

"You want to fill me in on the pieces you have?"

"Not yet," she said. "I need some more time to think."

He studied her face for a long time, finally dropping a tender kiss on her lips. "When you want to talk, I'm here."

Tara let out a long breath when he pushed away and turned back to the task of inventory. He trusted her. He believed in her. And he would wait for her to come to him. That was what she loved about him. His kindness. His patience. That they had no secrets between them. But she was about to break that trust for the first time. Because she couldn't talk to him about this. Not when she wasn't completely sure yet herself. And not when it wasn't her truth to tell.

CHAPTER NINETEEN

*O*wen flipped through the pages of the book, confused. It was the same story, *The Little Mermaid*, but the pictures were different—all bubbly and colorful. He traced his finger over a sea crab with big blue eyes and dark eyebrows. Since when did sea crabs have eyebrows? And why did the princess in this book look so cheerful? She was supposed to be frightened, fighting for the love of her prince. He turned back to the cover, pressing his palm against the shiny surface. It didn't even *feel* like the other book. "Is this the same story?"

"It's a different version," Kelsey explained.

"Version?"

Kelsey sent him a look. "You don't know what that means, do you?"

Owen shook his head.

"It's just a different way of telling a story."

"I liked the other one better," Owen muttered.

A shadow fell across the blanket and Owen glanced up, spotting the gold-haired man who'd come with Tara to pick him up this afternoon. "What other one?" Sam asked, reaching for a chair from a nearby table. The legs scraped against the wood floor as he pulled it over, straddling it backwards and leaning his big arms over the top to peer at the title.

He had a glass of something that looked like soda resting in one hand. But it didn't smell like soda. It smelled like something that would taste really bad.

"*The Little Mermaid?*" Sam's eyes shifted to Kelsey. "I thought *Sleeping Beauty* was your favorite."

"It is," she chirped, tucking her legs up and scooting closer to the fire. "But Owen won't let me look at any other fairy tales. He only wants to look at this one."

"Not *this* one," Owen cut in, frustrated. "This one doesn't even look real."

Sam lifted his free hand, rubbing it over his wool cap. His skin had lots of marks and scratches on it, like he'd been building something with rocks. "But the other one does?"

"This is the *Disney* version," Kelsey explained. "It follows the story of the movie." She lowered her voice. "Mrs. Dooley had it special ordered for my birthday. She didn't know any better."

"And the other one...?" Sam asked.

"The other one is the Hans Christian Andersen version."

"Of course it is." Little lines fanned out around Sam's brown eyes when he smiled. "You've been spending too much time with Liam."

"Maybe I have," Kelsey admitted. "But at least he knows what he's talking about."

"So...what's the difference?"

"The main difference is that this one ends happily." Kelsey tapped a finger over the glossy cover. "In the Hans Christian Andersen version, the mermaid turns into foam and the princess wins.

"Like I said," Owen mumbled. "The other one's better."

Sam lifted an eyebrow. "Why do you want the mermaid to turn into foam?"

Owen squirmed. "I don't really want the mermaid to turn into foam. I just want her to go back where she belongs."

"Underwater?"

Owen nodded.

"But what if the mermaid really loved the prince, too?"

"It doesn't matter."

"But..." Sam's gaze shifted to where a row of instruments hung above a cozy booth in the corner. "The mermaid saved the prince's life. Without her, he wouldn't be able to choose either of them."

Owen shook his head. "The prince is supposed to be with the princess."

"I think you're being too hard on the mermaid."

"She should never have made the trade in the first place," Owen argued. "It was a stupid idea."

"The trade with the sea witch?"

Owen nodded.

"But what if she didn't have a choice?"

"She *did* have a choice. She could have stayed in her kingdom and married one of the mermen."

"You know," Sam said thoughtfully. "Sometimes it's harder to stay where you are. Especially when you consider what could be waiting for you on the other side."

Owen narrowed his eyes. "What do *you* think is on the other side?"

"I don't know," Sam admitted. "I've never been there. But I imagine it could be wonderful."

"Well, I have." Owen shoved the book aside and shot to his feet. "And it's not."

"Owen!" Kelsey scrambled up after him. "Wait!" She grabbed his arm before he got to the door.

He whirled. "I can't go back there!"

"Nobody's asking you to go back there!"

"Back where?" Sam stood, crossing the room to join them.

Owen started to tremble. He lifted a finger, pointing at the book. "Back *there.*"

"We still don't know if that's where you're from," Kelsey hissed, trying to keep her voice low enough so Sam couldn't hear. But it was too late. He'd already heard. "You said you can't remember ever even *seeing* a mermaid."

"No," Owen whispered. "But I've seen selkies. And everything else in that book."

Sam dropped to his knee and looked Owen straight in the eye. "These selkies..." he asked gently. "The ones you can remember. What did they look like?"

Hot tears sprang to the backs of Owen's eyes. What if this man turned him into his mother? What if she made him go back to that terrible palace? What if all of the petals from the rose had already fallen? Owen swiped the back of his sleeve across his cheek, mortified as a tear slipped free. "They're white."

Kelsey squeezed Owen's hand and looked at Sam. "That's what he keeps saying. But I've never heard of a white selkie. Is there such a thing?"

"A white selkie?" The barstool squeaked as the lone man at the bar turned. "Now there's a story I haven't heard in a long time."

THE WATER FELT SO COOL, so soothing against her raw skin. Her pale arms lifted, weightless beneath the undulating waves. Her hair drifted around her face like silverfish, dancing with the movement of the sea. The welts were slowly fading, the marks the rain had left on her skin.

How could they live like this? Trapped on this spit of land when all the wonders of the ocean glittered under the surface? A fish brushed against her bare leg and she closed her eyes, relishing in the rough scales sweeping against her skin.

Home. Soon she would be home. Her toes curled into the silky white sand, sinking into the palette of shells sparkling at her feet. All she needed now was her king.

Her hand darted out, catching the fish. It writhed, squirming against her vise-like grip. She'd seen the change in Liam this afternoon. She'd seen the way he had stood between her and Caitlin, like *she* was the one who couldn't be trusted.

The redhead was determined to steal him away from her. Her lips curved. She had no idea who she was dealing with. She opened her mouth, shoved the fish down her throat. She heard the bones break, felt the slimy wriggling as she swallowed it whole. She didn't have time to waste on foolish teenage crushes. Her time was almost up.

She kicked her way up to the surface, the sea sluicing down her long hair as the frosty air surrounded her like a winter kiss. The rain had thinned to a quiet mist. And a thick fog wound through the village, a yellow ribbon dripping over the edges of the cliffs.

She walked out of the crashing waves, gathering her cloak around her shoulders. She felt the itching in her throat, the burning in the backs of her eyes before she smelled the smoke. Before she saw the glow of a tall thin flame in the circle of rocks on the beach.

Nuala paused, ankle deep in the waves, letting the cold water roll over her bare feet. She drew strength from the sea as the woman stepped out of the fire. Moira's strawberry blond hair tumbled around her shoulders, curling in the mists. Those cruel green-gold eyes were as cold and hard as gemstones. The raindrops sizzled as they met the heat of her skin. Steam rose up around her like curls of golden smoke. "You wanted to see me."

"I need your help."

Moira lifted a bejeweled hand, studying her long scarlet nails. "I thought you would work faster than this."

"There's been a...complication."

Moira arched a winged eyebrow. "A complication?"

"There's a woman on the island." Nuala's gaze drifted up to the village. "She says she's an artist from Dublin, but she knows who, or at least, *what* I am."

"You didn't expect that there would be some who would recognize our kind?"

"I thought most of our kind were gone."

"Most. But not all." Moira walked out onto the beach, her dress crackling around her like a driftwood fire. "Glenna is not your problem. The only woman you should be worried about now is Caitlin. Liam is already starting to remember things about her. About how he felt about her before you arrived."

"I can handle Caitlin. I need to know who Glenna is. She painted a picture of my palace today. She brought it over to hang in the cottage I'm renting. She wanted me to see it. She wanted me to know."

"Did she?" Moira's lips curved. "How thoughtful of her."

"Do you know who she is?"

"Of course I know who she is," Moira's voice snapped out into the rain. "But what I don't know is why we're having this conversation. If you can't do this on your own, Nuala, then let me take Owen off your hands for a while. He's getting in your way."

Nuala narrowed her eyes. "What do you want with Owen?"

"What do I ever want with anyone?" Moira's eyes gleamed. "Leverage. It's all I live for, darling. You could learn from me. I'm never in debt to anyone. But many people owe me many things." She smiled. "Including you."

Nuala took several long, deep breaths. "I can do this on my own. I *will* do this, but I want this to be Liam's decision, too. I don't want to take him until he's ready. Until he wants to go."

"You stole his memory," Moira reminded her, angling her head. "Suddenly you're developing a conscience?"

"It'll be easier this way. If he wants to be there. If he sees it as a chance, an opportunity to continue his research, it'll be easier to get back into the kingdom."

Moira laughed, a low hollow sound that made Nuala's skin crawl. "You didn't really believe that? When I told you they'd let you back in?"

Nuala staggered back into the ocean. "Of course they will. I've paid my penance. I've suffered long enough. They'll accept Liam."

"They'll never let you back in. Not after what you did."

"But this is all they've ever *wanted* me to do." She shook her head. "I don't understand."

"Oh, my dear. It's not Liam you should be worried about. It's Owen. What you did to him was unimaginable."

"Unimaginable?" Nuala stammered. "I did the best I could."

"You stole Owen from his mother and locked him away in an ivory palace."

"To protect him!"

"I'm not sure that Caitlin would see it that way."

"I thought it would be easier to take a child! Stealing a grown man from his home and his family is wrong."

"And, yet, that's exactly what you are doing right now."

"Because I have no choice!"

"There's always a choice." Moira picked up a glittering seashell, tucking it into her hair. "You were the one who chose this path so many years ago."

"I was eighteen. I didn't know any better. I was in love!"

"What is love, but a weak emotion to make us all suffer? Where is your precious Rowan now?"

Nuala looked away, blind with rage. Rowan had been her husband—her *selkie* husband. He was her first love, her only *true* love. At eighteen, she'd turned her back on her fate, refusing to accept her role as the new white selkie. A white selkie was supposed to find a land-man and bring him into the sea. The man she chose was destined to be king. Together, they would rule the ocean. And with this man's connection to the land, they would maintain the peace between their two worlds.

But instead of bringing a land-man into the ocean, she fell in love with one of her own kind. She eloped with Rowan and they had a child, a sweet selkie child she'd loved more than anything in this whole world. But Rowan and her son were killed in an accident, when two boats collided on the surface of the sea where they liked to play.

In her grief, she blamed the selkie kingdom and their backward traditions for her loss. She should have done then what she was doing now. She should have chosen a land-man—*any* land-man—and taken him with her into the sea. But she vowed one final rebellion against the selkie kingdom.

Instead of choosing a land-man, she went to Moira. She asked the sea witch to help her find a suitable child, a boy who could rule beside her as her son. She knew no man would ever replace her Rowan, but maybe in time she could learn to love this boy the same way she had loved her son. Moira assured her she knew the perfect child, and Owen would hardly be missed.

Panic lodged like a stone in Nuala's throat. Had she lied about that, too? Had she lied about everything? She had never meant to hurt anybody. All she had ever wanted was a family. But because of what she'd done, she was cast out of her kingdom, exiled from her home.

For years all she'd had was Owen. She had tried to love him.

She had tried to raise him as her own. But he had never filled the hole inside her. And the loneliness had eaten at them both until she knew the only way forward would be to accept her fate and find the land-man who would be their key back into the selkie kingdom.

Nuala struggled to breathe. She had gone back to Moira then. And Moira had led her to Liam. She could never have done this alone. White selkies were linked too closely to the sea, their pelts more fragile, more delicate than regular selkies' pelts. The longer her seal-skin was exposed to the air, the weaker it became. Even these three short days were a risk. But she had taken it. She had made the trade.

Moira smoothed a hand down her dress, her bracelets glittering in the firelight. "You weren't seeing clearly when you came to me the first time. And you're not seeing clearly now. You could have chosen a suitable mate, and surrendered to your fate. You chose this path, Nuala. Not me."

"You knew," Nuala whispered. She had foolishly traded her powers to the sea witch in exchange for this time on land. She had thought Moira *wanted* to help her. But all Moira had ever wanted was power. "You knew the whole time that they wouldn't accept Owen? That they would send us away?"

"Of course I knew. Just like I knew that Owen would never be enough. Nothing is ever enough." Moira walked back to the circle of rocks, the flames bursting out of the sand. "The only thing certain in this world, is that everyone wants more."

CHAPTER TWENTY

*I*f there was ever a time in her life when she needed to turn on a light, this would be it. Caitlin sat in her candlelit cottage, the rain thrumming against the walls like witch's fingers, tapping an impatient rhythm, beating against the thick layers of paint for the truth. *The truth.*

What *was* the truth? She didn't even know anymore. Her last log was burning down in the hearth and she scooted closer to the dying flames, tugging a blanket tighter around her shoulders. There had to be a reasonable, logical explanation for all of this. She hadn't been thinking straight since the moment Nuala and Owen had arrived. She'd been letting her twisted emotions string her along, but it was time she got control of them. There was no way what Glenna was suggesting was possible. It simply wasn't possible.

But why, then, couldn't she sleep? Why couldn't she stop running all these crazy possibilities over and over in her mind? What *if* her baby hadn't died? What *if* Owen was in some kind of danger? What *if* Nuala was a sea witch? What *if* that was what the selkies were trying to tell her when they pushed her baby's cradle into Owen's arms?

She jumped at the sudden knock on her door. It was probably one of her neighbors coming to check on her, to see if she needed anything. If she didn't answer the door they'd poke their head in anyway, to make sure everything was all right. Dropping the blanket, she rose and walked to the door. She pulled it open and the scent of saltwater and kelp rushed in from the ocean, colliding with the dizzying scent of loosened earth.

Liam's cobalt eyes seared into hers. Caitlin felt a sudden rushing, like rivers of rainwater sucking her under. His long black coat flapped around him like wings in the wind. He strode into the cottage, sweeping back his dark hood. His thick black hair glistened with drops of water. The shadow along his jaw was even darker now. His wet shirt clung to his broad shoulders and chest, the thin dark gray cotton plastered to the hard outline of muscles. His eyes never left hers as he closed the door. "I think we should finish that conversation we started earlier."

The sharp snap of the lock clicking shut set off a warning somewhere deep inside her. His eyes were so blue, so beautifully blue, and so much like Owen's, she started to tremble. "What conversation?"

Liam dug a crumpled object from his pocket, holding it out to her. "The one about the fairy tale."

Caitlin reached for the rose, her fingers brushing the smooth green stem. It was bent and twisted, but the petals were snow white and perfectly shaped—glowing iridescent in the candlelit cottage. "Where did you get this?"

"It washed up on the pier."

"The...pier?"

"You were right." Liam took a step closer. She had to tilt her head to look up at him. The wind whistled through the strings of the chimes, a restless chorus of caution singing in the storm. "What you said earlier. It's all connected."

"I'm not sure about that anymore," Caitlin whispered. Because things were getting too close now. They were stepping over that line she never wanted to cross. If all of it was connected, she wasn't ready for it. Not now, maybe not ever. "Do you... remember anything else?"

"I remember you." He lifted a hand to her cheek. Her skin warmed under his touch. She could feel the calluses as he skimmed a thumb over her cheekbone, could smell the sea on his rough palm. "I remember this."

Caitlin placed a shaky hand on his chest. She could not let this happen now. Not after everything that happened today. "Liam." One of them had to be rational. One of them had to keep both feet on the ground. The scent of the rose swirled into the air between them, deliriously, intoxicatingly sweet. "If this rose has something to do with the fairy tale you can't remember, do you know what it means?"

"No." His strong hand curved around the back of her neck. "But I think you do."

Icy shivers danced over her skin. "What do you mean?"

"I heard you went down to the beach today." His other hand settled on the curve of her waist, drawing her against him. "Care to explain what you found?"

"It was...nothing," she stammered. "Just a piece of driftwood..."

"I've seen it, Caitlin. It's not *nothing*." Something like sadness flickered deep in Liam's eyes. "What happened?" The sickening sweet scent of the rose grew stronger. "You're the one who turned *me* on to fairy tales and magic. What happened to make you stop believing?"

"That was a long time ago." Caitlin's fingers curled around

the stem. "We were children." She winced as a thorn bit into her thumb.

"And isn't it always the children who seem to know the truth, when we're all too blind to see it?" Flames crackled in the hearth. The rain pounded against the roof. "There's a reason this flower washed up at my feet today."

And there was a reason the sea sent that cradle to her and Owen. A reason that white rose was growing on her son's memorial. A reason it pulled Owen into a trance when he'd touched its frozen petals. A reason why when he'd come out of it, he'd called her 'mum.' Caitlin felt her throat constrict. "Maybe someone ordered them from the mainland. Maybe…"

A spark, a flame hissing to life, smoldered deep in his eyes. "You can't explain your way out of this one."

"But…"

He let out a low growl as he pulled her against him. She felt those coils of frustration snap as he crushed his mouth to hers. He tasted of sea salt and rainwater. The scent of him—soap, salt, male—tangled with the scent of the rose and she melted against him.

The hungry kiss stole her breath. Her lips parted, their tongues tangling. Those last shreds of resistance started to slip. He yanked her against him. The rose dropped from her hand. The petals spilled onto the floor at their feet, shimmering like glass. Like silver moonlight. Until one by one, the shells of ice softened and turned to liquid gold.

KELSEY GRABBED Owen's wet shirtsleeve, dragging him back into the barroom. His sneakers scuffed over the worn wooden floorboards, leaving a trail of water in their wake. "You mean, they do exist?"

"Aye." Brennan Lockley nodded. "Though I haven't heard tell of it since I was a child. It's not a story that comes around often."

Kelsey sank into the chair closest to Brennan, pulling Owen down into the one beside her. "Why not?"

"Because a white selkie only comes to land once every hundred years or so. And she's never here for long. She only has three days to get what she came here for. And there are few who remember ever seeing her at all."

"What does she come here for?" Owen asked.

"To find a husband. A land-man, they call it."

"Why does she want to find a husband?" Kelsey's gaze darted to Owen. "Why can't she marry a selkie-man?"

"Because that's not her fate." Brennan settled back into the bar stool, the legs squeaking under his weight. "A white selkie is the most powerful of all the selkies. She lives an unnaturally long life. And she's the only selkie who can turn a land-man into one of her own kind."

"She can turn a human man into a selkie?" Kelsey's eyes went wide. "Why would she want to do that?"

"When a white selkie takes a land-man back with her into the sea, they become king and queen. Together, they rule the ocean. And it is with this man and his connection to the land that she can watch over the safe passage of ships. To make sure the fishermen always have fish in their nets. To shelter the harbors and protect the islands from the worst of the storms. Together, they maintain the peace between us."

"It's a sacrifice," Sam murmured.

"Aye." Brennan nodded. "You could call it that. But it benefits all of us."

"But..." Owen stammered. "What if the land-man doesn't want to go?"

"It's not a question of want. No man can resist a white selkie's spell. Once her enchantment is cast, he will lose all memories of his home and his family. Of the ones he may have loved who came before her."

"But what if he's meant to be with someone else?"

Brennan smiled sadly. "I'm afraid that's not her concern."

Owen shot up, out of his chair. "But there must be a way to stop her!"

"Why would you want to? Her failure means terrible storms. Coastal towns wiped out. Island villages decimated. Ships sinking. Fisherman losing their jobs."

Kelsey leapt up when Owen ran for the door. "Owen, wait!"

He wrenched the door open, running out into the storm. Kelsey dashed after him, bracing herself against the wind tearing over the cliffs. "Owen!"

He whirled. Rain spat into his eyes. "I was wrong!"

She splashed through the puddles, closing the distance between them. "About what?"

"My mother's not the sea witch from *The Little Mermaid*. She's a white selkie!"

Kelsey searched his frightened eyes. "We don't know that yet. Come back inside. Let's talk to my mum. She'll know what to do."

"Don't you see?" Owen cried. "She's going to take your uncle!"

Uncle Liam?

"That's what she came here for! It all makes sense now!"

"*What* all makes sense?"

"The palace! The painting! The petals falling off the white rose!"

"What palace? What painting? What *rose*?"

He told her about the rose, what he saw when he touched the frozen petals, how Glenna had brought over a painting of the exact same palace this morning. "I was wrong. The petals aren't marking my time on the island. They're marking *his* time! But what's going to happen to *me* when the last petal falls?"

"Come on." Kelsey grabbed the sleeve of his jacket, pulling him back toward the pub. "We're going to tell my mum, now!"

"No!" He snatched his arm away. "You can't tell her. You can't tell anyone!"

"Why not?"

"Because if they don't believe us, they'll tell her! They'll bring her into it!" His eyes were wild with fear as they darted over his shoulder to the cottage at the edge of the village. "I don't know what she'll do to me if she thinks I know!"

"But what if that's the only way to stop her? We can't let her *take* Uncle Liam!"

"There has to be another way!"

Kelsey's eyes went wide. "You said there was a rose? Growing out at the cottage by the bogs?"

Owen nodded.

"Last summer, we found the selkie ghost's pelt hidden under the roses. Maybe your mum's pelt is hidden under *this* rose. Maybe if we could find it, we could stop her."

"Come on!" Owen grabbed her hand, starting to lead her to the cottage.

"Wait." Kelsey ground her heels into the pavement. "We can't go now. She could see us!"

Owen dropped her hand.

"I'll come for you tonight," Kelsey whispered when the door to the pub opened and Sam stuck his head out. "After dark."

CHAPTER TWENTY-ONE

$\mathcal{M}$oira was lying. She had to be. The sea lashed the back of Nuala's legs. The rain fell harder, splattering over the white sand like shattering crystals, dowsing what was left of the fire in the circle of rocks. She would never have dreamed of trading her powers if Moira hadn't promised this would work!

She lifted her eyes to the swift-moving clouds. She'd been a pawn since the day she was born. Her fate decided for her. Her life nothing more than a trap. When would it end? When would it *ever* end?

Would it go on like this forever?

Cold tears spilled from her eyes, mixing with the rain. She sank to her knees as the wave of grief crashed over her. She pictured her lover—her Rowan. She hadn't even been allowed to choose her own love. Or grieve the child they lost. And when she had done the one thing she thought they wanted—bringing a human into the sea, they'd punished her.

Because she'd brought a child instead of a husband. A boy with no memories. With almost no family who would miss him.

From the arms of a mother who was far too young to care for him. But they hadn't understood her mercy. They'd sent her away, casting her out of her own kingdom, forcing her to fend for herself. With nothing but instincts and fear to guide her.

Her hands closed over the wet sand. But she'd found her way. She'd made a new home for them, deep in the arctic seas. She'd found a deserted palace of bone-white coral fit for a queen, planted a garden of roses carved from ice to match the color of her heart. She'd taught Owen how to catch fish. How to swim as fast as a ray. How to watch for a polar bear's claw, and listen for the distant call of a whale.

They had survived. And they would survive this. She pulled herself up, her heels sinking into the sand. Her skin began to glow, like the first twinkling lights of a ship lit up at night. The surf swirled around her ankles as she walked out of the sea. And closing her eyes, she started to sing.

"I REMEMBER," Liam whispered, his breath warm against Caitlin's skin. "The rose. It must have come from the flowers I brought you." He inched back, his eyes widened as his gaze fell to their feet and he spotted the golden petals. "Yellow roses," he breathed, bending down and scooping up a handful. "I brought you yellow roses. For our date." He looked up at her, the memories swimming in his eyes. "You said they were your favorite."

Caitlin stared at the yellow petals in his palm, her heart pounding in her ears. "The petals...they were white only moments ago."

His arms tightened around her. The wind outside howled through the village streets. "I had them with me on the ferry. I asked Nuala to hold them when I went to help Finn with the lines. But something must have happened to them during the accident."

"Liam," Caitlin breathed, gazing up into those intense blue-gray eyes. "What if your fall wasn't an accident?"

"It wasn't." His fingers closed over the petals. "It couldn't have been. I've been working on those boats since I was a child. I would never have lost my footing that way." He stepped back suddenly, his hand falling to his side. "Do you hear that?"

"Hear what?" Caitlin watched his fingers open, the petals spilling back to the floor.

"That voice. It sounds like..." He turned, reaching the door. "It's coming from outside."

Caitlin shook her head. "I don't hear anything." Her breath caught in her throat when his hand closed over the knob and she saw the faint blue shimmer dancing over his skin. "Liam!" She grabbed his hand, trying to pry his fingers from the knob, letting out a small cry when she felt how cold it was.

His gaze drifted down to her, but all the color had faded from his eyes. She moved between him and the door, but he pushed her aside easily. His mouth was set in a thin line, the rim of his lips turning blue. "Liam? What's wrong? What's happening?"

His pupils dilated when he turned the knob. The storm swirled into the cottage, the ocean a thundering roar below the cliffs. He stepped into the curtain of rain, and Caitlin ran out after him. "Liam! Wait! Come back!"

He turned, as if seeing her for the first time. His eyes were as pale and cold as broken glass. The water sluicing down his coat took on a silver shimmer, and then froze like that, a web of ice snaking over his clothes, down to his legs, over his shoes. His teeth chattered as he looked back at her. "I have to go."

"Liam, come back inside!" The rain stung her face, the wind whipping it into her eyes. "Please, come back inside and warm up by the fire!"

Ice chips formed in his hair, dripping from his frozen locks. He pulled the hood of his coat up, covered in frost, and turned, striding toward the cliffs.

SAM STEPPED BACK from the doorway as Kelsey ran across the street, ducking back into the shelter of the pub. She shook rainwater off the sleeves of her sweater, dripping all over the polished floor. "Is everything all right?"

"Of course." She rung out her hair and then started across the room to the kitchen. "Why wouldn't it be?"

"Where's Owen?"

She paused with her hand on the door, glancing over her shoulder, her expression unreadable. "He went home."

Sam dipped his hands in his pockets. "I thought something about the story might have upset him?"

"Oh, don't worry about that." She rolled her eyes. "Owen's always upset about something."

Sam lifted an eyebrow.

"It's true. He's a bit of a worry wart, that one." She pushed into the kitchen, her blond curls bouncing as she let the door slap shut behind her.

Brennan glanced up from the barstool. "He *is* a bit strange, isn't he?"

Sam nodded and Brennan swiveled on his stool, going back to reading the newspaper he had open in front of him. Sam wandered over to the edge of the bar, turning the sports section toward him and pretending to scan the headlines as he strained to hear the muffled voices through the door.

"Dad," Kelsey said. "Can I spend the night at Ashling's tonight?"

Bottles clinked in the kitchen. "I don't see why not."

"Great!" Her wet sneakers squeaked on the kitchen tiles and Sam straightened as her footsteps headed back his way.

"Wait a minute." Tara's softer voice drifted through the small window adjoining the bar and the kitchen. "I'm not sure that's such a good idea."

"Why not?" Dominic asked, surprised.

Sam moved closer to the window, straining to hear Tara's voice. "I'd feel better if Kelsey stayed with us tonight."

"Why?" Dominic asked. There was a low scuffing—heavy boxes scraping against the floor. "What do you think is going to happen?"

"Nothing," Tara said quickly. "I'm just a little shaken up by this storm. I'd rather we all stick together tonight."

Kelsey walked back over to her father. "But Ashling's mum was going to teach us how to make beeswax candles."

"Beeswax candles?" Dominic echoed. "Now there's a useful idea. We're all going to need more candles if this storm doesn't let up soon."

"Can I go, then?" Kelsey pressed.

"I don't see any reason why you should have to stay here with us when you could be making candles with Ashling. But I agree with your mother about spending the night. We'll pick you up on our way home."

"But I can stay past dinner, right? So we can test the candles after dark?"

"Sure."

"Thanks, Dad!" Kelsey dashed back toward the door, pushing it open and smiling far too cheerfully up at Sam. "I'm going to learn how to make candles."

"How nice." Sam looked over at Brennan. "Isn't that nice, Brennan?"

Brennan turned the page of the paper. It crinkled as he folded it up. "We could use a few more candles up at the farm."

"I'll bring some by tomorrow," Kelsey sang, dancing over to the front door and grabbing her jacket.

Sam narrowed his eyes as Kelsey breezed out the door. "I'll meet you back at the farm later, Brennan." He crossed the barroom, shrugging into his own jacket, and followed Kelsey out into the rain. He watched her skip through the puddles as she ran across the street to Ashling's. She glanced over her shoulder when she got to the door. She hesitated for a split second when their eyes met, then waved like it was the most natural thing in the world, and slipped into the cottage.

He had to hand it to her. She was a clever kid. But not as clever as he was. He flipped up the collar of his jacket, shielding the back of his neck from the icy rain and set off through the alley toward the path leading north to Glenna's cottage. He had a pretty good idea what Kelsey had in mind and when she was planning on doing it. But there was someone he needed to talk to first before he decided to stop her.

Caitlin spotted Sam disappearing into the alley behind the pub as she raced through the streets of the village. Sam! He might be able to help her! She tried to call out to him but her voice caught in her throat. What if no one believed her? What if they thought she was crazy? She splashed through the puddles, wrenching open the heavy door to the pub. She knew what she'd seen. She knew now that Liam was caught in some terrible spell.

She stopped short in the doorway, her gaze darting around the near empty room. Where was everyone? She caught Brennan's eye as he glanced up from his paper. Forget it. She didn't have time to worry about everyone else. Racing to the stairwell, she bounded up the steps two at a time. Her clogs clacked over the worn floorboards, echoing through the hallway as she rushed to Liam's bedroom.

If Liam's fall wasn't an accident, if he was starting to remember things, if the roses were changing from white back to yellow, maybe she could find the document he lost. Her wet hands fumbled with the knob, her fingers slipping on the handle as she twisted it. Maybe she could find the fairy tale and put the missing pieces together. She stumbled through the door, letting it fly open and smack against the bookcase. If she could find the story, maybe she'd know what she was dealing with.

"Caitlin?" Tara's voice called up the stairs.

She grabbed Liam's leather briefcase, turning it over on the bed and shaking it. When only a few pens and crumpled pieces of paper fell out, she dipped her hand inside, searching the hidden flaps and zippered pockets for clues. She heard footsteps on the staircase. *Tara.*

"Caitlin? Is that you?"

She tossed the briefcase onto the floor, grabbing the pile of folders on the bed. She flipped through the handwritten notes. The corners broke off in her fingers as she turned the pages frantically, scanning the words for something, anything that would explain how a grown man could fall under a spell.

How many times had he sifted through these pages in the last two days? How many hours had he spent trying to dig up the same document? The other night on the pier, after the accident, he said he printed out the paper he was working on for the conference next week. He said he brought it home to the island to work on over the weekend. It was all he'd talked about in the weeks leading up to their date.

"Caitlin?" Tara's eyes went wide as she stepped into the room. "What's going on?"

It has to be here. She threw the worthless pages back on the bed, pushed past Tara and sank into Liam's desk chair. Running her fingers along the sides of his laptop, she found the power button and switched it on. Please let it have enough juice left in the battery. The screen blinked and flashed, and she held her breath as the files on the screen lit up.

She scanned the titles of each folder, searching for something that had to do with a fairy tale. Her heart skipped a beat when she spotted the folder titled, *'Limerick Conference.'* She heard the hiss of a match igniting as Tara lit a candle and set it on the desk beside her. She put her hand on the back of Caitlin's chair, peering over her shoulder as Caitlin double-clicked on the folder.

What if Owen was right? What if his mother was a mermaid? What if Liam had discovered some new tale about a mermaid in the Trinity Library? And she had come on land to steal it away from him? But there was only one file inside the folder. A single document titled, *'The White Selkie.'*

"The White Selkie?" Tara whispered. "Is this...?"

"It has to be," Caitlin breathed, her hand shaking as she clicked on the file and Liam's words filled the screen. The wind howled through the streets, rattling the windows of the pub. The rusted chain holding the Guinness sign snapped, sending the sign flying and the loose chain cracking through the night like a whip. The image on the screen wavered, the words blurring together like wet ink.

"What's happening?" Tara breathed, reaching over Caitlin's shoulder to adjust the light on the laptop. But her hand froze on the dial as the cursor began to move backwards on its own, deleting word after word, sentence after sentence, paragraph after paragraph. Until there was nothing but an empty white document and the sound of the rain beating against the windows.

THE SIREN'S song threaded into Liam's mind. Her words twisted into his soul as he stumbled down the rocky cliff path. The ocean curled like fingers over piano keys, playing a haunting melody over the sliver of white sand far below. That voice. That song. Where had he heard it before?

Rocks slipped over the edge of the muddy footpath, tumbling into the sea. His hands brushed over the wet moss clinging to the cliff wall. Wherever she was. Whoever she was. He would find her. He would follow her.

He lifted his gaze to the water. And in the waves he saw her. Her white dress clinging to her curves. Her pale hair streaming to her waist. Her skin as fair as a winter moon. He staggered onto the beach, his shoes catching in the soft sand. He kicked them off, drunk with a desperate need to be near this woman, to touch this woman.

Nuala's eyes were closed, her arms lifted, consumed in her song. His bare feet crunched over a trail of silver seashells. "Nuala," he whispered her name, like a spell on his lips. Like a longing unearthed deep inside him. He held out his hand to her, over the spray of the sea. Over the restless thundering of the waves. Rainwater dripped from his hood, into his eyes. The rain tasted of sea salt, of rosewater, of *her*.

She opened her eyes as the wind caught the final notes of her song. As her words drifted up, fading into the night. She watched him, her eyes as cold and pale as the petals of the rose that had washed up at his feet.

"Nuala."

Her skin shimmered as she walked out of the ocean, as the waves guided her toward him. Her dress moved with the swell of the sea, the thin translucent material clinging to her lush hour-glass figure. She lifted her hand, her cold fingers threading through his. "I knew you'd come."

Their breath mingled in the icy air. He inhaled the intoxicating scent of her. "You have the most beautiful voice."

Nuala smiled. "I wrote a song for you today."

He lifted her hand, brushing his frozen lips over her icy skin. "Would you sing it for me?"

"It's about true love." She took his hand, leading him out into the waves. "And finding it in the most unlikely places."

CHAPTER TWENTY-TWO

*H*unching his shoulders against the rain, Sam knocked on Glenna's door. He inhaled the stench of something burning and stiffened. When she didn't answer right away, he kicked the mud off his work boots, scraping them over the rocks lining her garden and knocked again. When she still didn't answer, he stepped into the squishy garden bed, peered through the rain-streaked glass. There were no candles lit. No lanterns burning. No fire in the fireplace.

But there was no doubt about it. The air smelled of smoke. Testing the knob, he found it turned and glancing over his shoulder he pushed into the dark cottage. He swore when he spotted her lying on the floor. "Glenna!" He rushed to her side, dropping to his knees. Turning her over carefully, he saw the soot smudges on her face, the black ash in her hair, the red welts on her forearms. She was breathing, but she was limp in his arms. "What happened to you?"

"Sam?" Glenna's eyes fluttered open and she tried to push herself up onto her elbows, but her face was pale as a ghost.

"Come on." Sam scooped her up, carrying her over to the

couch. Glenna sank into the cushions and looked up at him, dazed. Anger coiled up inside him as he spotted the black scorch marks on the wall above the splintered drawing table, the fallen painting and melted oil paint dripping onto the carpet. "Who did this to you?"

"There must have been a fire," Glenna whispered, pushing unsteadily at her heavy hair. Ash fell onto the front of her blouse.

"*Who* did this to you?"

"I-I don't know."

"Glenna, stay right here. I'm going to get Tara."

"Wait."

Sam turned. Glenna's hand snaked out, wrapping around Sam's wrist. Something shifted deep in her eyes, like a flame burning through the fog. "Where is he?"

"Who?"

Glenna's fingers bit into his wrist. "Liam."

Sam dropped back to the sofa. "That's what I came here to talk to you about." He took her hand, covering it in his own. "I think you might be in shock, Glenna. Tell me what happened here first."

"No. I..." Her gaze swept over the room, assessing the damage. "I must have had an accident with a candle. It's nothing."

"Bullshit," Sam seethed. "I know I'm the last person you want to see when your defenses are down, but don't treat me like a fool."

Edging her hand out of his, she brushed soot from her sleeve. "Really, it's nothing."

"It's not nothing!" Sam shot to his feet. "I saw the painting, Glenna. The one you conveniently took over to Nuala's cottage today. I find it *curious*," he said, drawing out the word, "that you would paint a white coral palace for that guest cottage *this* weekend."

"I painted it weeks ago," she argued. "It just finished drying today."

"That's a lie," Sam snapped, starting to pace. "You painted that palace for Nuala as a warning. To let her know you were onto her. Because it's her palace, isn't it?"

"I don't know what you're talking about."

"Really?" Sam's strides ate up the small room. "I find it *curious* that all this happened the day after you borrowed one of Brennan's books. The day after Liam came searching for that exact book."

"Sam, you don't know what you're talking about."

Sam stopped pacing, turning to face her. "I've heard the story, Glenna. I know what we're dealing with. I didn't need a damn book to figure it out. I went straight to the source."

Glenna swallowed. "What...source?"

"Brennan Lockley. The keeper of the fairy tales. He told us the tale of the white selkie."

Glenna lifted her eyes to his. "The white..."

"You think you can handle everything, Glenna. But you can't. None of us can." Sam ran a hand over his wool cap. His forehead felt hot and scratchy all of a sudden. "But there is one thing I can't figure out. Something I'd like *you* to answer. I know you painted that palace for Nuala. To show her you knew what she was. But how do you even know what it looks like?"

Glenna had gone very still, all the color drained from her face. "I see things, remember?"

Sam shook his head. "You said your visions last only seconds. You couldn't have painted that from a few seconds."

"I'm a very talented artist."

He stared at her. Her words were measured—the very study of calm. But there was fear in her eyes. And he didn't like the way her knuckles had gone white as she gripped the sofa cushion. He didn't like it at all. "You have two choices," he said carefully. "You tell me what you know and I'll help you figure out how to stop her. Or you pretend you don't know anything and let me figure it out myself. Either way," he challenged, "I *will* figure it out."

"You need to stay out of this, Sam." But her voice had gone cold and grave. "I'll handle it."

He watched her run her sleeves back down her arms to cover the burn marks, watched her try to compose herself. And damned if he didn't respect her for thinking she could handle everything on her own. But not this time. This time, he wasn't going anywhere. "Why won't you let me help you?"

"Because I don't trust you." Glenna stood and a new resolve smoldered deep in her tawny eyes. "I don't want you hurting any more of the people I love."

Sam stared at her. "I'm not going to hurt anyone."

"Maybe not on purpose," Glenna admitted. "But you told me about your knack for finding things that don't want to be found." She brushed past him, rounding the edge of the couch and heading toward the bedroom. "Do us all a favor and go back to the farm."

The wind tore over the fields, rattling the windows. Sam stalked after her. "Might I remind you of the part I played in solving the legend this summer?"

"That was a lucky break." She paused by the drawing table, her foot shifting almost imperceptibly over the rug. He glanced down at the last minute, catching the small round objects rolling under the table into a pile of pale ash.

"It wasn't *lucky*." Sam bent down and scooped up a pearl, watching it glitter in his palm. "If Nuala's a white selkie, why can't we find her pelt? Like we did with Tara's ancestor? Maybe it's hidden somewhere on this island?"

Glenna snatched the pearl from his palm, slipping it into her pocket. "Stay out of this, Sam."

"Why? Why can't we just find out where it is and dig it up?"

Her eyes flashed as she looked up at him. "Because you cannot *steal* a white selkie's pelt!"

"Why not?" he demanded. "Tell me or I'm going to track down a shovel and start digging—starting in *your* garden!"

"You can't steal a white selkie's pelt because no one is allowed to see her, or even *know she exists* when she's on land! The only one who can see her pelt is the man she's come here for! And even he has only a matter of seconds before she gives him his own pelt and takes him under!"

"Then we'll destroy it!"

"You can't destroy a white selkie's pelt, Sam! It's *protected*! And any human who lays eyes on it will either die instantly or go mad trying to follow her into the sea!"

"Owen!" Kelsey hissed, pelting rocks at his bedroom window. When he pressed his face to the glass and held up his finger to his lips, she shrank back behind a scraggly rosemary bush, peering through the other window. It was too dark to see anything, but the glow of firelight flickering over the pale walls. Rainwater rushed down the slope, filling her sneakers and her feet squished around inside them as she shifted, moving so the trowel tucked in her pocket wouldn't jab into her side.

She heard the scrape of the window being lifted. Chips of white paint broke off, falling into the garden as Owen pushed it up far enough so he could slip out. "Come on," Kelsey urged. The boats in the harbor knocked into each other. The smell of fish and a faint stench of gasoline drifted up as the ocean slammed into the rocks.

Owen stuck his leg out, scooting his small body through the narrow opening, and hopped down to the soggy earth. Together they forced the window shut and ducked as they crept past the living room windows. Kelsey put a hand on his arm, stopping him before they crossed the flooded street. "Is she in there?" Kelsey whispered.

He nodded. "With your uncle. Where do your parents think you are?"

"At Ashling's. We don't have much time."

She looked both ways, making sure no one saw them before dashing out into the street and waving for him to follow her. They snuck past the statue of the Virgin Mary, standing watchful over the curve in the road leading up to the village. A flower had slipped out of the stone vase in her hands and Kelsey grabbed it before it swirled away, sticking it on the flat stone by the statue's feet, protected from the wind.

She dug a flashlight out of her jacket pocket and switched it on. A small beam of light illuminated a thin soggy trail leading north through the village to the bogs. She led the way through the fields, shining the light over the stiles and helping him clamber over them. Cows lifted their heads, watching them as they passed. Sheep scattered at the sound of their voices, jumping over fallen fences and squeezing through breaks in the stone walls.

When they came to the crumbling cottage, the lone rose shimmered and glowed through the darkness and Kelsey switched off her flashlight. More petals had fallen, but even though the water moved, the petals stayed perfectly still around it, like a circle of white stones protecting it.

Owen knelt. "You're sure it's under here?"

She shoved the trowel into the mud under the rose, scooping out a shovel full of soil and tossing it aside. "It has to be."

"Trapped in a selkie's spell?" Dominic stared at his wife. "Liam?"

Tara nodded, wringing her hands. "We searched everywhere, all through his room, all through his things. We went through every book, every piece of paper. But I know what I saw. The document...it just disappeared before our eyes."

"And you're sure of the title? *The White Selkie?*"

Tara nodded. "Caitlin's gone over there. To warn him. But I don't know if he'll listen to her. She said he was starting to remember things. That he was starting to remember *her*. But they were in her cottage earlier and he heard a voice, like someone singing. She said she couldn't hear it but he followed it out into the rain. It was like he couldn't stop himself. She said his eyes... they changed color and his skin grew cold. His clothes, even his shoes, were covered in ice. She came straight here looking for this document—this fairy tale—he told her he lost."

Dominic thought back to the times he'd walked in on his brother this weekend in his room, bent over his laptop, searching through his things. He'd said he had writer's block. But maybe he'd been lying, trying to cover up the memory loss. How had he missed all the signs? Dominic searched his wife's eyes. But Nuala? A selkie? His brother, caught in a spell? There was only supposed to be one curse on this island, and they had broken it this summer. "Caitlin said that he told her...that he lost this document?"

Tara nodded. "It was all he'd talked about before coming here this weekend. He was going to tell her about it on their date. Apparently, he discovered a new fairy tale in the Trinity Library in Dublin. I went to ask Sam earlier if he'd heard anything about it—"

"Sam?" Dominic stared at her. "You talked to Sam about this?"

"I thought I was being ridiculous. I wanted to run it by someone first."

"And you didn't think to run it by me?"

"I was afraid you might not be able to listen objectively. With Liam being your brother and Caitlin your best friend. I didn't know enough. I just had some suspicions. I didn't want to worry you…"

"You didn't want to worry me?" A muscle in his jaw started to tick. "Tara, I'm your husband. If there's anyone you should be willing to worry, it's me!"

She put a hand on his arm. "Dom…"

Dominic ground his teeth. "Is that why Sam was here earlier?"

Tara nodded. "He wanted to talk to Owen."

"Owen? What's Owen got to do with it?"

"That's what I'm trying to figure out. If Nuala's only here for Liam, then who is Owen? Is he even really her son?"

"Now hold on a minute. You were in here earlier asking me if I was descended from selkies. What's that got to do with anything?"

The front door swung open and Dominic bit back his next question as Ashling and her parents walked in.

"I hope you don't mind us dropping by." Mary Roark shook the rain off her sleeves and started to peel off her jacket. "With everyone up at the Dooley's we thought you all might want some company during the storm."

Dominic watched the door swing shut behind Ashling. "Where's Kelsey?"

"What do you mean?"

"She was supposed to be with you."

Mary glanced up at him, puzzled. "She stopped by for a little while earlier. Just to say hi. But she left soon after."

"I thought you were making candles tonight?"

"Candles? No." Mary shook her head. "I haven't a clue how to make candles. Where'd you get that idea?"

CHAPTER TWENTY-THREE

*C*aitlin spotted the glow of candlelight through the gauzy curtains, the shadow of two figures moving around inside Nuala's cottage. She took a deep breath and knocked, listening for the murmur of voices through the door. She stepped back when Liam's broad-shouldered frame filled the doorway, her eyes widening at the sight of him. Gone was the shimmer of blue on his skin, the ice in his hair, the frost on his clothes. Even his eyes were back to their normal color.

But there was no recognition in them, no apology for walking out on their kiss. No explanation for where he'd gone or how he'd ended up back at Nuala's. He gazed down at her curiously. "What are you doing out in this storm?"

"I need to talk to you."

He stepped back. "Come inside, then."

"No," she said. "I need to talk to you alone."

"About what?"

Her gaze darted over his shoulder into the cottage. "About Nuala."

"What about her?"

"Would you walk with me to the pub? I need to...discuss something with you."

"Discuss something?" Liam lifted an eyebrow. "I think you better tell me what's on your mind now."

Out of the corner of her eye, Caitlin spotted a flash of white. Nuala turned from the kitchen, cradling two drinks in her hand. "Liam," Caitlin said quickly. "I think Nuala's put a spell on you."

He blinked. Then smiled. Then started to laugh. "*That's* what you came here to tell me?"

"I'm serious," she hissed as Nuala started toward them.

"All right, then," he chuckled, crossing his arms over his chest. "What sort of spell is it?"

"I don't know yet, but it has to do with the fairy tale you found in Dublin. I found a file on your computer—"

Liam's smile faded. "What were you doing on my computer?"

"Looking for the story." Caitlin let the words come out in a rush. "I found one about a white selkie." She searched his eyes for something, anything that would give her a clue. "Does that ring any bells?"

Liam's dark brows snapped together. His puzzled gaze combed down her rain-soaked sweater, flickering back up to where her wet hair was plastered to her head. "How long have you been wandering around in the rain looking for me?"

Nuala sidled up to him and handed him a glass of whiskey. "Hello, Caitlin." Her lips curved. "What brings you here tonight?"

Liam took a sip of whiskey, looking at Caitlin over his glass. "I'm afraid Caitlin's been a bit shaken up by this storm. She's not feeling well."

Caitlin's mouth fell open. "I feel fine!"

"Come on," he scoffed, lowering the glass. "Even you have to admit that what you're suggesting is pretty ridiculous." He swirled the liquor around the glass. "*Especially* coming from you."

"You've forgotten," Caitlin breathed. "You've forgotten everything all over again."

"Forgotten what?" Liam frowned and the worst possible expression crossed his face—one of sympathy. He looked over at Nuala. "I think we better get her to Tara's. I think the storm's taken her ill."

"Tara was there when I found the document!" Caitlin snapped. "She believes me!"

"Nuala," he said, draping his arm around the blonde's shoulders. "I'm afraid there's been some talk."

She leaned into him. "What kind of talk?"

"Apparently, some of the villagers think you've cast a spell on me."

"Have they? Well, then." She looked up at him, lowering her lashes. "I think *you're* the one who's cast a spell on *me*."

"Liam!" Caitlin cried. "Can't you see what's happening? She's trying to steal you away from me!"

Nuala clucked her tongue against her cheek. "Jealousy doesn't become you, Caitlin."

"I'm not jealous! She's erased your memories, Liam. She's trapped you in some kind of awful spell! You have to believe me!"

He looked down at her, his eyes still filled with sympathy. His words, when he spoke, were as condescending as if he was talking to a child. "Did you happen to bring it with you? This story you found on my computer?"

"No." Caitlin kicked at the water. "It disappeared the second we brought it up."

"Isn't that convenient," Nuala suggested.

"I'm telling the truth!"

"I'm afraid Nuala's right, Caitlin. You do sound jealous. And I am sorry things didn't work out between us the other night. But

I'm sure it was all a misunderstanding." He stepped back, guiding Nuala into the shelter of the candlelit cottage. "Why don't you come back when you have actual proof of this story? And until then, stop spreading rumors about Nuala."

He closed the door. Caitlin stared at the rain dripping from the gold claddagh knocker, inches from her face. "Since when have you ever needed proof?"

Caitlin turned when she heard footsteps splashing through the puddles behind her. Voices called out to her, shouting her name. She spotted Dominic and Tara running up to the house. "What's wrong?" She sloshed through the flooded streets to meet them. "What happened?"

"Is Kelsey in there?" Tara asked, breathless.

"Kelsey? I don't think so. Why?"

Tara's eyes were wild with worry. "She's missing."

Dominic strode past her, pounding on the door.

"What do you mean, *missing*? Since when?"

"She was supposed to be at Ashling's all night." Tara's gaze darted over Caitlin's shoulder to the door. "But her parents just came into the pub and she hasn't been there for at least an hour. We checked Sarah's. And Fiona's. But she wasn't there. No one's seen her."

Caitlin spun around as the door opened and Dominic came face to face with his brother casually nursing a glass of whiskey without a care in the world. Dominic growled, shoving him aside and striding into the cottage. "Where's Owen?" he barked at Nuala.

"He's in his room." Nuala set her drink down on the table, her eyes flashing. "Do you make a practice of barging into others' homes without an invitation?"

"This isn't your home," Dominic retorted. "And I think I'll have a look myself if you don't mind." He headed for the back rooms when Liam stepped in his path.

"What if she does mind?"

"Your niece is *missing*." Dominic grabbed his brother by his shirt, shoving him hard against the wall. "If you're not going to do anything about it, get the hell out of my way!" He didn't wait for a response, didn't bother glancing back when Liam's glass fell from his hand, shattering over the floor. When a strange look crossed his face when he spotted the gold liquid seeping into the ivory carpet. Dominic slipped into the back rooms, coming back out only moments later, his face grim as his eyes met Tara's. "He's not back there."

"What do you mean he's not back there?" Nuala snapped. She brushed past him, her heels crunching over the broken glass. "He was in there a moment ago."

Caitlin edged into the cottage, snagging a candle from one of the tables. She ran into the room after Nuala. The candle cast a small circle of light and her eyes swept over the sparse furnishings, searching for clues.

"We were in the cottage the whole time," Nuala protested, throwing back her son's sheets. "We would have seen if he'd gone out..." But her voice trailed off, her hands stilling on the covers when she spotted the three rocks stacked up on the sheets.

Caitlin shone the light over the rocks and spotted the white paint chippings scattered over the foot of the bed. She crawled across the bed to the window, running her fingers over the sill. "It's still wet."

"Here," Kelsey shouted over the rain, pointing to a spot under the rose. "Shine the light here."

Owen aimed the beam of the flashlight at the base of the rose. A web of roots—ice white and glittering like diamonds—snaked deep into the soil. Kelsey jabbed the tip of the trowel into the roots. It bounced off the surface. The hollow sound of metal clanging against rock rang in the night.

Kelsey sat back, blowing out a breath. "I don't remember it being this hard."

Owen leaned closer, peering down into the hole. "How much deeper could they go?"

"I don't know." Kelsey pushed her dripping hair out of her eyes, smearing mud across her forehead. Her arms ached from digging. She had soil caked in her fingernails. The cold was starting to seep into her bones, making her teeth chatter. This had seemed like such a good idea before. But now that they'd started digging, she was starting to get a bad feeling about this. A really bad feeling. "Maybe we should stop."

Owen shook his head, reaching into the hole and digging out more wet soil with his free hand. Kelsey looked over at the bogs. They felt restless tonight—dark and restless and menacing. She heard something splash in one of the pools and jumped. She wasn't afraid of the dark. She'd never been afraid of the dark. The ocean thundered against the northern shore and she huddled under the hood of her jacket. Okay. Maybe just this once, she might be a little afraid. "Owen, I think we should stop."

"We can't stop!" he shouted, dropping the flashlight and digging with both hands. "I think I feel something."

Kelsey crawled over him, fumbling for the flashlight and shining it into the hole. Owen scooped out more soil, and they both stared when the rain washed the dirt off a web of roots twisting out in every direction.

"It looks like they're wrapped around something," Owen said, tracing the rectangular outline of where each root disappeared, curving back down into the earth.

"But how are we going to get it out of there?"

Owen felt around the spongy earth for the trowel. "I'm not giving up."

"I'm not saying we should give up." She ran her hands up her arms, trying to warm them. "But maybe we should get help. Or at least a bigger shovel."

"I don't want a bigger shovel." Owen wrapped both hands around the wooden handle. He forced it down as hard as he could, ramming it into one of the roots. The trowel slipped out of his wet hands, the curved metal clattering over the roots. He bit his lip, picking it back up and jamming it down into the hole.

They scrambled back as a flash of white light shot into the night, blinding them. Kelsey slipped, skidding over a patch of mud, groping for Owen's hand as she fell. At the first sound of ice cracking, she covered her eyes. The scent of the rose and the bogs swirled up around them. She gasped when she heard the stabbing. She peeked through her fingers, and saw Owen bent back over the gap in the earth, crushing the roots with the trowel.

"Owen!" Kelsey yelled as the sound of glass shattering, of icicles breaking, skated into the night. "Stop!"

"It has to be down here!" The frozen rose toppled, falling to the earth. Three more petals snapped off, swirling into the puddle. Kelsey's heart raced as she reached for it, but he grabbed her hand. "Don't touch it!"

Owen reached down into the hole, struggling to wrench the object free. With one last tug, he fell back, breathing hard, clutching a dirt-covered chest in his hands.

Kelsey stared at the pale, knotted wood. "It's...small."

Owen's eyes flickered up as he swiped at the mud, searching for the opening. "Too small?"

"I don't know." She shook her head. "The last time the box was a lot bigger."

Voices echoed over the bogs. The beam of a flashlight swept

through the darkness. She heard footsteps, saw the outline of a handful of people running toward them. Kelsey shot to her feet. "Mum?"

"Kelsey!" Tara's panicked voice cut through the rain.

Kelsey squeezed her eyes shut as the beam of the flashlight blazed into her eyes.

"Owen!" Caitlin cried, sprinting toward them. Rain kicked out from under her sneakers and she waved her arms frantically. "Stop! Don't open that!"

Owen fumbled for the opening, lifting the top off the chest.

CHAPTER TWENTY-FOUR

*N*o!" Caitlin sank to her knees. A cold winter blast shuddered over the bogs. The rain turned to sleet, spitting down pellets of ice. She grabbed the chest from Owen, all the color draining from her face when she looked inside.

"It's not in there," Owen cried, looking frantically up at Kelsey and then scrambling back over to the rose. "Maybe there's another box buried under it!" He dipped both of his arms—black now from the mud and soil—back down, scraping the watery bottom.

"There's nothing else down there," Kelsey shouted over the howling wind, reaching for her father as he pushed through the crowd.

Dominic scooped her up and hugged her hard to his chest. "Don't ever do that again," he whispered brokenly.

"I won't." She clung to him, shivering as sleet bounced off her hood. She was right. This was a bad idea. A very bad idea. "I promise."

"Owen!" A cold female voice lashed out into the night.

Owen's head snapped up. He spotted his mother and scrambled back against the wall of the cottage.

"What on *earth* were you thinking?" Nuala's white cloak swept out around her as she stalked toward him, grabbing his hand and yanking him to his feet. "Look at you! You're filthy!"

"We can talk to them later," Dominic's voice bit out. "Together. This isn't the time or the place."

Kelsey reached for her mother's hand. "I'm sorry, mum."

"It's okay," Tara murmured, smoothing Kelsey's wet hair back from her muddy forehead. But her troubled gaze stayed on Nuala and Owen. "It's okay. You're safe now. That's all that matters."

Nuala brushed past them, pulling Owen with her.

Dominic turned. "Why don't you come by the pub in an hour? We'll get this sorted."

"If it's all the same to you, Mr. O'Sullivan," she seethed. "I'll sort out this particular matter on my own."

Kelsey felt her father tense. "I think it might be best to discuss it together," Dominic suggested.

Nuala's arm curved around her son. "My son won't be coming anywhere near your daughter, ever again." She turned, yanking Owen's hood up to cover his face. "Not after this ridiculous charade."

Dominic's arms tightened around Kelsey. "So this is all *my* daughter's fault?"

"Dom," Tara said, never taking her eyes off the woman and child. "Let it go. Let's talk about this later."

"I'm sorry," Kelsey whispered. She felt so terrible for getting Owen in trouble. "It is my fault. I'm the one who planned this." She saw Owen glance back over his shoulder and she mouthed, "*I'm sorry.*" But he didn't see her. He was looking back at Caitlin, still kneeling in the mud, clutching the box to her chest.

Kelsey flinched when Owen tripped over a rock, his leg

splashing into a pool of water. His mother caught his hand, pulling him through a narrow path in the stone walls. Kelsey buried her head in her dad's shoulder, watching the seam of Nuala's cloak split, floating out behind her like a shimmering white fan.

ROOTED TO THE EARTH, Liam stared at Caitlin. The wind tore his hood back, but he didn't bother to reach for it. Sleet pricked Caitlin's pale face like falling thorns, but she didn't even blink. Rainwater dripped from her curls, a tangled mess framing her stricken face.

She wasn't wearing a raincoat. Mud streaked up the legs of her jeans. Her thick wool sweater was soaking wet and clinging to her, the hem fully submerged in the water. Numb, Liam stripped off his jacket, his boots squishing into the soggy patches of moss as he walked over to her, settling it around her shoulders.

She didn't look up, didn't even notice when he knelt down beside her. She was gripping the box so tightly her knuckles were white. He peered inside it, but all he caught was a flash of silver before the wind blew the lid shut with a sharp crack.

Caitlin clutched the box to her chest, staring at the rose. He heard a faint clicking, saw her shallow breath coming out in foggy puffs. He wrapped his arms around her, trying to warm her, stiffening when he realized her whole body was shaking.

"We need to get you home." He started to help her to her feet, but she twisted out of his arms. She sheltered the box inside the jacket, her wide eyes staring at the pile of dirt and the fallen rose.

He followed her gaze, his heart rate kicking up a notch when he saw the broken glass. Or...wait. What was that? He stood, walking over to the hole. Were those...roots? He stared at the web of white roots snaking into the earth, the glittering pieces floating in the rising water.

Tara's voice drifted toward him. She was standing not too far away, talking to Dominic. "Why don't you take Kelsey back to the pub? There's still enough of a fire left to warm a pot of water. Let her soak in a hot bath for a while. I want to check on Caitlin first, make sure she's okay after what happened earlier."

After what happened earlier? What *did* happen earlier? The hair on the back of Liam's neck stood up when he saw the circle of petals surrounding the fallen rose.

"It's okay, Kelsey," Tara cooed, soothing her daughter who still hadn't lifted her head from her father's shoulder. "No one's blaming you for anything. Let your father fix you some tea and I'll be right behind you."

"Are you sure you'll be all right?" Dominic asked.

Liam glanced up as Tara's troubled gaze drifted over to Caitlin. "Yes. Just give me a minute."

The last thing Liam remembered was walking into Caitlin's cottage and kissing her. And now here they were in the middle of a storm, running after two kids trying to dig up a box under a rose?

What the hell was in that box? He glanced back at Caitlin. Whatever was in it, she didn't want him to know. She didn't want anyone to know. But what could be inside that was so important? And why had she hid it all the way out here?

Liam looked back at his brother and saw that Dominic was watching him. There were questions in his eyes—questions, confusion and worry. He didn't want to leave, but one of them needed to get Kelsey home where she could warm up before she caught a cold. Dominic reached out for Tara's hand, squeezing it and then turned, carrying Kelsey back toward the village. His long, lumbering strides splashed through the puddles, the outline of them fading into the darkness.

Tara walked slowly over to Caitlin, crouching down beside her. "Caitlin," she said softly. "Are you all right?"

Liam bent down, picking up the fallen rose, marveling at the sharp, jagged end of the silver stem. He turned it over in his hand, careful not to touch the thorns. There were only two petals left, clinging to the frozen bud, but they showed not the slightest bruise from the battering this flower had taken out in this weather. They were perfectly formed and hard as glass.

He glanced down as a fallen petal swirled toward him, as bone-white as the ones that still clung to the rose. He picked it up and it shimmered in his palm, like a pearl plucked from an oyster, like beauty trapped in a hollow hidden shell. A memory from the ferry ride floated back to him and his fingers closed over the petal.

"May I ask..." Nuala's pale eyes lifted to his. "Why did you choose yellow?"

"It's her favorite color."

"But it's also the color of friendship."

"It is?"

"You didn't know that?"

"Do all women know that?"

"I don't know. But maybe it's good that a white one found its way in here."

"Why? What does white mean?"

"White can mean anything you want it to."

"That's a powerful rose."

"It is. What do you want this one to mean?"

"I don't know. I guess I'd have to think about that."

"Is it new, then? This relationship with the woman you're having dinner with tonight?"

"You could say that."

"Then maybe it means new beginnings."

"New beginnings. That sounds right."

"New beginnings can be wonderful."

Liam turned, walking over to Caitlin. He dropped to his knees and took her hand. He pried open her stiff fingers, turned her palm up and opened his, dropping the petal into her hand. It was a warm butter yellow now, glowing like a ray of sunlight in winter.

A flash of light in the distance had his gaze snapping up. A beam of white light bounced over the fields, heading toward them. He squinted through the rain, and could just make out the shadowy forms of two figures running—a man and a woman. When he saw it was Glenna and Sam, he curled Caitlin's fingers over the petal. He started to rise when his hand met something hard and flat like a stone and he pulled it up, out of the mud.

He wiped the dirt off the top of the stone, revealing three letters engraved in careful script. They looked so familiar—these letters—like he'd seen them somewhere before. And the handwriting—the loopy *M*, the long dash in the *G* that almost met the inner curve, the elongated *O*—he'd know it anywhere. He looked down at Caitlin, still gripping the petal in her hand, still hugging the mysterious chest in her other arm. "What is this?"

The beam of light flashed over them, illuminating her face. Water dripped from her hair, into her eyes. Raindrops glistened on her lips, so cold now they were turning white around the edges.

"Caitlin," Tara urged, laying a hand on her arm as Glenna and Sam ran up, breathless. "What's going on?"

Liam traced his fingers over the initials. "What do these letters stand for?"

"Michael Grady O'Sullivan," Caitlin whispered.

Liam took a step back. "But that..."

"I know." She nodded. "I named him after your grandfather."

Liam felt the earth give, like it was sinking away under his feet. "Named *who*?"

Caitlin lifted her eyes to Liam's. "Our son."

CHAPTER TWENTY-FIVE

S on? Liam stared at her, frozen. No. It couldn't be.
She'd said it was a mistake. "I don't understand." He
shook his head, refusing to believe. "You said it was a false
alarm."

"I lied."

The wind ripped a patch of thatch from the roof. It landed in
a wet splat in one of the puddles near his feet. "But...why?"
Liam's legs felt numb as he stepped over the rotted thatch. "Why
would you lie?"

"I was sixteen. I made a choice—a decision based on what I
thought was best for our child."

A decision based on what *she* thought was best for their
child? Which was...what? Not telling him? How could he not
have known they had a child?

"I wasn't going to keep it from you forever." Caitlin lifted her
eyes to his. "Just for a little while. Until we both got on our feet."

Liam stared at her. "But I would have supported you. I would
never have left you alone with this."

"I know. But I didn't want you to stay because I was pregnant. I didn't want to marry someone out of honor and tradition. I wanted to marry for love."

Liam closed the distance between them. "But I did love you."

"It was one night, Liam. We were teenagers."

"But what if I wanted the child?" Liam asked. "What if I wanted a life with you, here on the island? What if that's all I've ever wanted?"

Caitlin shook her head. "We were too young. As much as I wanted that life with you, I knew how it could turn out. I grew up in a house with parents who married young because of children, with a father who resented his wife for holding him back. I wanted a different life for my child, and for me."

"Your father resented your mother because he was an angry, bitter man," Liam argued. "He was always trying to make everyone miserable. He might have taken care of you, managed to put a meal on the table each night, but he was drunk half the time. He might not have been mean with his fists, but he had a mean tongue. I thought you knew never to listen to him."

"I did," Caitlin conceded. "But this was different. I had someone to take care of now, someone to protect."

"You could have come with me to Galway," Liam said. "We could have gotten a place. I could have found a second job and still made it through school. We would have figured it out along the way, made it work."

"But I would never have known if you were with me because you wanted to be, or because you felt it was your duty."

"My duty?" Liam took a step back. "How could you ever have thought...?" Sleet rained down around him as more pieces of the puzzle fell into place. "When you left the island..." he breathed. "You didn't go to an all girls' school..."

"No," Caitlin admitted. "I went to live with an aunt in Donegal—one of my father's sisters. I thought I could handle everything on my own." She scrubbed the heel of her palm down her mud-streaked denim. "I wasn't planning to hide it forever. I was going to tell you. As soon as I found work, as soon as I knew there wasn't a chance of you dropping out of school."

"But you didn't..." Liam shook his head. "You never told me anything."

"I know." Caitlin looked up at him. "Because everything fell apart."

The wind cut through Liam's sleeves and he felt a bitter cold take root inside him. "What happened?"

"Our son...Michael..." Caitlin clutched the box to her chest. "He was stillborn."

Stillborn? Liam sank to the ground in front of her. How much had she gone through without him? How much grief had she hidden from him, how much pain and heartache? "How could you have kept this from me? Why didn't you come to me afterwards? I would have been there for you. Even if you had kept it from me in the beginning. I would never have let you go through this alone."

"I wanted to tell you." She swallowed. "I went to Galway once, a few months after...I went to your school to tell you the truth. But then I saw you standing on the steps of this beautiful stone building surrounded by a group of students. You were talking and joking. Making plans for the night. You looked so carefree and happy. And I...couldn't do it. You had the whole world at your fingertips. I didn't fit in there. I didn't belong there. I thought you would grow, change into someone different. I thought you would change into someone I hardly knew."

"Did I?" Liam asked brokenly. "Did I change into someone you hardly knew?"

Caitlin shook her head. "No. You didn't. But that only made it harder. I moved back here because this was the only place I'd ever felt at home. I thought you'd stay in Galway, but you kept coming back. And you kept...bringing girls with you, a different one every weekend. And when you didn't, you'd try to talk to me, and flirt with me like I was one of them. But I wanted so much more than that."

Liam pulled her into his arms. He could feel her pulse racing through her soaking wet clothes. "All I ever wanted was to be with you, Caitlin. Since the first time you snuck in my bedroom window and gave me that fairy tale. Since the first time you kissed me on a dare when we were thirteen. Since the first night you let me lie with you when you were sixteen..." He looked up, realizing where they were for the first time. "...in *this* cottage."

At the scuff of boots behind them, Liam glanced over his shoulder. Glenna held out her hand. "Give me the box, Caitlin. We're running out of time."

"No." Caitlin shook her head, pulling out of Liam's arms. "I can't. It's... Someone's tampered with it."

"Tampered with it?" Tara asked, sliding out of the cottage behind Glenna and Sam. "What do you mean?"

Caitlin pushed at her wet hair. "Someone's played a terrible joke."

Glenna took a step toward her. "Give me the box, Caitlin."

Caitlin shook her head. "I want to get rid of it. Forget this ever happened. Whoever did this..."

"Did what?" Tara asked gently, walking over to kneel down beside her. "Caitlin, what was supposed to be in that box?"

Caitlin cradled it to her chest, her eyes meeting Liam's. "Michael's ashes."

"Caitlin," Tara put her arm around her friend's shoulders, her voice soothing. "Please show us what's inside."

Liam took the box from her hands. He loosened the top and lifted the object out for all of them to see. The rain tinkered down on the gleaming silver baby's rattle, in the shape of a seal.

CHAPTER TWENTY-SIX

*D*ad?" Kelsey asked as he set her down inside the pub and helped her out of her soggy rain jacket. "How much trouble am I in?"

"Don't worry about that, Kelsey." He shook out the jacket and hung it over the hook. "We'll talk about it later."

Striding over to the fire, he unlatched the heavy cauldron from the iron hook, carrying it back to the sink to fill with water. His footsteps echoed through the empty barroom and he paused when he saw Kelsey lingering in the stairwell, chewing on her lip. "Go on up and change into something dry while I get the water boiling. It won't be long but you shouldn't be in those wet clothes any longer than you have to. There should be a few things left in your old bedroom."

She scampered up the steps and he shook his head, carrying the cauldron back to the fireplace. When he had it settled in the hanger, he added a fresh brick of peat and used the poker to stoke what was left of the flames until they caught fire and licked up the sides.

Kelsey came back downstairs and he turned, his heart

clenching at the sight of his daughter in a lavender unicorn sweat-shirt and a pair of pink stretch pants an inch too short.

"It's all I could find." She crossed the room to join him by the fire, glancing down at the puffy white unicorn with a braided mane on the front of her shirt. "Who gave this to me, anyway?"

"I think it was Sarah Dooley." Dominic handed her a towel. "A few years ago for your birthday."

"Someone should talk to her." Kelsey sat on the floor next to her father, twisting the towel around her wet hair and holding her hands out to the fire. "She gives terrible gifts."

Dominic let out a long breath, one he hadn't even known he'd been holding, and caught her in another bear hug, squeezing her to his side.

"Dad!" she protested, wriggling out of his grip.

Dominic shook his head, refusing to let go until she sighed and gave up. He pressed his chin to the top of her head. She looked so precious in that silly outfit from a few years ago. It reminded him of how fast she was growing. And he wanted to hold onto her for a minute, before everything started to change. There was still mud on her face, dirt still caked under her finger-nails, but that was Kelsey. She was always getting into things, always the first to stir up trouble if she could find it. Damned if she wasn't going to cause him one heart attack after another as she grew up.

"Dad?" Kelsey inched back. "How did you know where to look for us tonight?"

"Tara had a hunch."

"Because of the rose?"

He nodded.

"So, she'd seen it before?"

"She had, yes."

"Didn't she think it was strange? That it was growing in the middle of winter?"

"I imagine she did." And they still needed to talk about why she had kept it from him. But that was another conversation, for another time. It seemed his family would have *a lot* to talk about over the coming weeks. But that was the nature of family, wasn't it? Just like everything in life, you figured it out as you stumbled along. All that mattered now was that they were all safe. At the sudden guarded shift in his daughter's expression, he angled his head. "What exactly did you think you were going to find under there, Kelsey?"

Kelsey looked away. "Owen thinks his mum's some kind of a sea creature."

"I see..." Dominic said slowly, remembering his conversation in the kitchen with Tara earlier. About the document she and Caitlin had found on Liam's computer. About the missing fairy tale. She'd been convinced he was trapped in some kind of a spell.

Kelsey nodded. "When we heard Brennan's story this afternoon, we thought she must be a selkie. I thought if we could find her pelt, we could prove that Owen was right."

"Brennan's story?"

"The one about the white selkie."

Wasn't that the same thing Tara had seen on Liam's computer? "So you thought that because Tara's ancestor's pelt was hidden under the roses, this one might be, too?"

Kelsey nodded.

"But it wasn't?"

"No." Kelsey picked dirt out from under her nails. "I was wrong. I'm sorry. I just wish..."

"What?"

"Never mind."

"What, Kelsey? What is it?"

"I just wish I knew how to help him. I don't know what to do."

"About Owen?"

She nodded.

"Do you think he'll be in a lot of trouble tonight?"

Kelsey looked into the fire. "I do."

He studied his daughter's worried face, firelight flickering over her fairy-like features. "Is there anything I can do?"

Kelsey shook her head. "I don't think so."

He reached for her hand. "Next time you think someone's mum is a sea creature, would you tell me?"

Kelsey bit her lip and looked away.

"What is it?"

"I still think she might be a sea creature."

Dominic's pulled his hand back. "*What?*"

"I can't help it." She grabbed the poker, started jabbing it into the fire. "I think Owen's right. He's sure he's been living under-water. He can't remember anything else from his past except for starfish and seashells and selkies. And yet, he's terrified of it. You'd think if he was from there, if he belonged there, he'd want to go back. But he doesn't. He's afraid of it. And he's afraid of his mother. He doesn't even want to be around her."

Dominic stared at her. "Go on..."

Her anxious eyes flickered up to his. "He can't read. I don't think he's ever been to school. I don't think he's ever even played with children his own age. I think he..." She lowered her voice to a whisper even though they were the only ones in the room. "I think he was *taken*."

"Taken?"

Kelsey nodded, dropping the poker. It fell against the floor-boards with a clatter. "Like a changeling. Liam has a book upstairs. I can show it to you." She started to jump to her feet and he pulled her back down.

"I know what a changeling is," Dominic said tightly.

"I think he might be one," Kelsey whispered. "I don't think

Nuala is his real mum. I think she stole him and took him underwater."

Dominic stared at his daughter. It wasn't possible, was it? A strange sensation, like ice crawling over his skin, had him brushing a hand over his arm, like he was imagining it. But impossible things *had* happened on this island. And that *would* explain why nothing about Nuala's past added up. Why she couldn't seem to remember anything about Limerick. Why her son was always wet and looking at her with that strange distant expression, almost like he was afraid of her. And it would explain why Liam had fallen head over heels for her when he was supposed to be falling for Caitlin. "But why?" Dominic stammered, still trying to wrap his mind around it. "Why would she do that?"

"I don't know. She must have had a reason."

"But how would we prove it?" Dominic stood, starting to pace. "Even if what you suppose is true, it would be her word against ours. And how would we ever find his real parents? It would have been ten years since he was...taken."

Kelsey crept closer to the fire. She huddled beside it, hugging her knees to her chest. "Haven't you noticed how much Owen looks like Uncle Liam?"

Dominic froze. He stared at his daughter.

"I'd know, right?" Kelsey asked, looking up at him worriedly. "If I had a cousin?"

"Of course," Dominic said slowly.

"I mean," Kelsey picked at the dirt under her nails again. "If Owen's ten...then Uncle Liam would have been eighteen when he had him. That's not too young, is it?"

Eighteen. That would have been the year Liam left for university. There was only one girl on this island Liam was after at that age. The same girl who had left to finish her last two years of high school on a *scholarship* a few weeks after he had left for his first term. *Holy shit.*

"Kelsey, I want you tell me everything Brennan told you this afternoon."

"About the white selkie?"

"Yes." He dropped to his knees in front of her, putting both hands on her shoulders. "Everything."

"Where are we going?" Owen asked when they passed the cottage at the edge of the cluster of white-washed homes and the road curved down toward the docks. A yellow fog slithered through a gap in the stone walls. The rain had thinned to barely more than a mist and an eerie silence swept over the harbor.

"It's time to go home."

"Home?" Owen dug his heels into the pavement. "But I don't want to go home!"

"Maybe you should have thought of that before you snuck out tonight." Nuala pulled him along, dragging him down the dark path. In the village, an owl hooted. Owen looked frantically over his shoulder at the silvery cottages. The shutters of many of them were crooked and barely hanging on. Garden gates were splintered. Stones had spilled into the streets, causing the runoff to bubble and split, streaming out around them.

He could yell. But what if no one heard him? The lines in the harbor sang as whispers of wind shivered over the quiet waters. His muddy shoes slipped on the wet pier as she led him onto the planks. The boats rocked, rubbing against each other.

When he saw what waited for him at the end of the long stilted pier he started to tremble. A woman stood in a narrow wooden boat, her face shadowed by a red hooded cloak. A single oar lay across the hull, and a small dark bundle was folded on the seat.

"This is only temporary," Nuala said as she pushed Owen

toward the woman. "I will reclaim him before the end of the night."

The woman smiled and extended her hand to Owen. Her fingers winked with glittering amber jewels. A strange black bracelet twisted around her arm and when her cloak shifted, it hissed like a snake. He shrank back from her when those green-gold eyes lifted, locking on his. "It's nice to see you again, Owen."

Owen scrambled back, his shoes slipping on the wet surface. "I-I don't know you."

"Oh, but *I* know *you*." The woman swept the hood back from her face. Her red-gold hair tumbled down over her shoulders, streaming down to her waist.

Owen's fingers scraped over the wind-weathered wood, struggling to back away from this woman as his mother pushed him toward her. "Who are you? How do you know me?"

"My dear," she said. "I helped bring you into this world."

Owen's heart pounded. A high-pitched ringing sounded in his ears. He looked up at his mother. "What does that mean?" He gripped the ends of her white cloak, clinging to her. "What does she mean?"

"You mean, she hasn't told you?" The woman asked, the joy in her voice crackling over the water. Nuala pried Owen's fingers off her cloak, and lifted him off the pier, settling him into the boat. He felt a tingling, a strange warmth spreading into his skin. The boat shifted, rocking in the water as the woman smiled and patted the seat beside the dark bundle. "Why don't you slip this on." Her eyes gleamed as she dipped the long oar into the water and pushed them away from the dock. "Go on," she urged when Owen's fingers brushed the oily seal-skin. "I'm sure it'll fit."

CHAPTER TWENTY-SEVEN

Glenna plucked the silver rattle from Caitlin's hand. She heard the soft ringing like bells through the wind. The rain had thinned to barely more than a mist, but the silence felt somehow more sinister than the relentless drumming rain. Especially now that she'd seen the token tucked into this hidden box—a token that was never meant for Caitlin.

It was meant for her.

But how? Her gaze swept over the fields, shrouded now in a thick blanket of gray. How could Moira have known ten years ago that Glenna would come to this island? How could she have known that she and Caitlin would become such close friends?

"The chest," Glenna asked, her voice strained. "Who gave it to you?"

"My aunt," Caitlin answered as Liam helped her to her feet. "Or...maybe it was the midwife? I...I don't remember. I wasn't thinking clearly at the time. I just remember they...took care of things. It was already done by the time I woke up."

"Have you ever looked inside it?"

"No." Caitlin shook her head, rubbing her muddy palms over

the front of her soaking jeans. "But it was supposed to be filled with his ashes."

Glenna's gaze flickered up again, sweeping over the maze of stone walls, the knotted patchwork of pastures stretching south to the village. Sam's hand caught her elbow. He leaned down, his voice a whisper in her ear. "Who are you looking for?"

She pushed him away, stepping out of the cottage. The air was thick and full of moisture. Secret warnings shuddered over the bogs. "This midwife," she said quickly, walking over to Caitlin. "What did she look like?"

Liam narrowed his eyes. "What does it matter?"

"It matters!" Glenna snapped.

Liam's arm curved around Caitlin protectively, and Glenna took a deep breath. She could feel Sam's eyes on her. Could sense him watching her. She needed to keep calm, not draw any of them into this. They only needed to know what was absolutely necessary. She would deal with the rest.

"It's okay," Caitlin murmured to Liam. She glanced back up at Glenna. "She was young. She couldn't have been more than thirty-five. She had long strawberry blond hair, but she usually wore it tied back in a bun. She had green eyes, I think." She nodded, remembering. "Yes. They were an odd color green, with flecks of gold in them. They used to change colors in certain lights."

Glenna looked north toward the bogs, searching for signs of smoke in the night. She breathed in the wet air, trying to catch a whiff of it, but all she could smell was the salt from the ocean and the faint perfume of the fallen rose drifting up between them. "And your aunt?" She bent down, picking up the cold, stiff flower. "Where is she now?"

"She passed away. Some kind of accident. I should have kept in touch..." Caitlin shook her head. "But I didn't."

Glenna rolled the icy stem around in her fingertips. "So the only two people who ever saw this child"—Glenna lifted her eyes to Caitlin's—"are your aunt and this midwife?"

Caitlin nodded slowly and Glenna watched the subtle shift deep in her friend's eyes.

Liam's arms tightened around Caitlin. "What are you trying to say?"

"Liam." Tara laid a hand on her brother-in-law's arm. "Sam has a theory that I think you should hear."

Liam's jaw clenched as Sam stepped out of the doorway. He didn't like Sam any more than Dominic did. "What?"

Sam's gaze shifted to Glenna, then down to Caitlin, then back up to Liam. "Have you ever heard of a changeling?"

"Of course, I've..." Liam stiffened. "Why?"

The box fell from Caitlin's hands. It splashed into the puddle of rainwater at her feet. She pulled out of Liam's arms, shaking her head, her eyes wide. "No."

"What if your child didn't die?" Tara breathed. "What if he was taken?"

Caitlin's panicked gaze fell to the silver baby's rattle—a rattle in the shape of a seal. "Owen."

"Owen?" Liam grabbed her, spinning her around to face him. "What about Owen?"

"It's him, isn't it?" Caitlin cried. She screamed his name into the night. "Owen!"

His name echoed over the bogs, shivered over the stone walls. Liam grabbed her hand. "Are you sure?"

She nodded. "We have to find him!"

"Then we will," Liam breathed. "Come on!" They broke into a run, heading for the village. Their feet pounded over the fields, splashing through the puddles.

Sam started after them, but he stopped short when he realized Glenna and Tara weren't following him. He turned, shielding his eyes from the mist. "What are you waiting for? If we split up, we can find him faster!"

Glenna shook her head. She reached behind her, fumbling for the wall of the cottage. The rose tumbled back to the saturated earth and another petal snapped off. A river of rainwater swallowed it, sucking it under.

"Glenna!" Sam raced to her side. "What's wrong? What's happening?"

Glenna shook her head again. She had failed them. She had missed all the signs. She knew now that Owen was only a pawn. That all Nuala had ever wanted was Liam. And all Moira had ever wanted was her. She stared at the silver rattle in her lap. The one *she* had played with as a child.

Sam grabbed her shoulders in both of his hands, shaking her. "What do you know? What are you still hiding?"

A curl of smoke rose from the water, drifting into the cold, gray haze. It smelled of sulfur, of fires sparking to life deep underground. A yellow fog rolled in over the bogs. "It's too late," she whispered. "Owen's already gone."

DOMINIC KNOCKED on Nuala's door. Drops of water leaked from the saturated thatch into the dark streets. Kelsey pressed her face to the window but there was a layer of moisture creeping up the glass and she could barely make out a blurry outline of furniture.

"It doesn't look like anyone's in there," she whispered.

Dominic knocked again and Kelsey flinched when the curtain stirred, a ripple of white lace through the frosted glass. She jumped back from the window when she heard the faint click of heels on pavement. Her gaze darted up to her father and Dominic squeezed her hand, placing a finger on his lips for silence as he pulled her behind him. The clicks got louder, the steps echoing through the empty streets and coming from the direction of the harbor. Nuala rounded the corner of the cottage and stopped short.

"Out for an evening walk?" Dominic asked casually.

Nuala's face was tight as she measured them up, like she was deciding what to do with them. Kelsey huddled behind her father, staring at the mist clinging to Nuala's white cloak. "I thought I left something down at the docks earlier," Nuala answered. "I was wrong."

"Where's Owen?"

"He's inside sleeping."

"After all the activity tonight?" Dominic lifted an eyebrow as she brushed past them and slid her key into the latch. "I'm surprised he could fall asleep so easily and not hear the door."

She turned, not bothering to open it. "Is there anything else I can help you with this evening?"

"I thought we could talk," Dominic suggested. "About what happened."

"I told you." She looked pointedly down at Kelsey. "I don't want Owen near your daughter."

"But they must have had a reason for sneaking out tonight," Dominic argued. "Don't you even know what it is?"

"No. I don't."

"You don't even want to know what they were trying to dig up?" Dominic pressed. "We could at least have a discussion about it so we know how to prevent it from happening in the future."

"It's not going to happen again, Mr. O'Sullivan. Because Owen and I will be leaving this island on the first ferry out tomorrow morning." She turned, grasping the knob and pushing the door open. Stalking into the dark cottage, she turned back to face them, blocking the small opening so Kelsey couldn't see into the room. "You can discuss this matter with your own daughter as much as you want."

Kelsey flinched as she slammed the door in their face. Dominic's eyes narrowed and he lifted his fist to pound on it again, but tugged him away from the door. "Come on," she whispered, waving for him to follow her around the back of the cottage. She let go of his hand as they rounded the back corner, clambering over the hedge of rosemary bushes and pushed up on her toes, cupping her hands around her eyes to see inside Owen's bedroom window. "He's not in there."

"Are you sure?" Dominic whispered, crouching down beside her.

"I'm sure," she said, climbing back over the thick winter stalks.

"Where do you think he'd be?"

"I don't know." Kelsey glanced over her father's shoulder at the shadow of boats in the harbor below. "He might have snuck out again. He could have gone anywhere."

"Then we'll start looking." Dominic said, pushing to his feet. "Nuala's footsteps came from the docks." He grabbed her hand and they ran down the muddy path to the harbor. The boats rocked restlessly against the pilings as they came to the edge of the pier. They spotted the two sets of footprints leading out onto the planks. "Look." Kelsey pointed to the faint marks in the wood. "She must have brought him here."

They followed the prints to the end of the pier, where one set disappeared and the other turned around—the larger set—leading back to the island. "We're too late," Kelsey breathed.

"No," Dominic's gaze combed the deserted harbor, but only a shiver of breeze danced over the surface. "That's not possible." He twisted, counting the boats tied to the pilings, trying to see if one was missing. "What if he took one of the rowboats? What if...?"

A dark head eased out of the quiet waters. "Dad! Look!" Rings teased over the surface as a handful of sleek black heads edged out of the sea. "Look how many of them there are!" More seals swam up to the surface, bobbing their heads in the dark waters, watching them.

Dominic stared at the circle of seals, at their pleading eyes. "We need to find Tara."

Kelsey lowered to her knees. Holding onto one of the pilings, she stretched her arm out over the water trying to touch one of them. But just as her fingertips brushed a velvety nose, a low cry, like a howl, tore over the harbor and she shrank back from the edge. The seals dove, splashing back under the water, their fins propelling them toward the beach.

"What's happening?" Kelsey whispered.

The wind kicked up and more seals slipped into the water from the rocks by the cliffs. Metal rings clanged against the splintered mast of a sailboat moored in the harbor. More seals edged out of the caves along that sheltered stretch of white sand. They lifted their heads to the rain, barking frantically as the first notes of the siren's song drifted into the night.

CHAPTER TWENTY-EIGHT

*L*iam threw open the door to Nuala's cottage. "Owen!" A cold draft swirled into the living room. The white curtains danced through the empty darkness like ghosts in the wind.

"Owen!" Caitlin wailed, running to his bedroom and grasping the handle of the door. She twisted it, but it jammed. She cursed, pounding on the door. "It's locked!"

Liam took her by the arms and pulled her out of the way. He shoved his shoulder into the door. The wood splintered and he threaded his hand through the jagged opening, unlocking it. They pushed into the room, but it was dark, the bed empty. They searched the closet, tore back the bedspread. Liam pried the window open and shouted out into the growing mist. "Owen!"

"Where did she take him?"

"We'll find him," Liam said, grabbing her hand and leading her back out into the hallway. Caitlin stumbled over a piece of wood, catching sight of a single candle burning on the floor of Nuala's bedroom as she righted herself.

"Look!" She pointed at where the carpet was flung back,

exposing the floorboards. "One of the boards is missing!" She ran into the room, dropping to her knees and dipping her hands into the gap. Her heart raced when she fished out a half-empty bottle of oil. She felt around inside again, in case she'd missed anything else, but all she found was a soiled rag. "Liam," she breathed, her pulse ringing in her ears. "Her pelt wasn't hidden under the rose. It was here the whole time."

"Come on," Liam pulled Caitlin back to her feet, already running for the door. "They must have gone down to the water. We might be able to stop them!"

They fled back out into the night, racing for the rocky path leading down to the sea. Stones slipped out from under their feet, spilling over the edge. Dark shapes edged up out of the water, covering the sand. The siren's song drifted into the night and Liam fisted his hands to his ears. A glow, like a white light shone from one of the caves, illuminating the harbor an eerie metallic silver.

"What is that?" Caitlin breathed as they stumbled onto the sand. A single wooden rowboat drifted up to the beach through the mists. The woman inside rose slowly to her feet, a long red hooded cloak draped around her. Silver mist swirled up around her like smoke. She let the boat float to a stop in the sand before stepping out.

A scream cut through the night as the white glow vanished from the cave, shrouding them in a veil of darkness. Nuala ran from the rocks, her white cloak streaming out behind her. The woman tilted the boat and a small seal tumbled out into the waves, flopping around in the surf.

"No!" Nuala cried. "What are you doing? You were supposed to take him away from here!"

"I changed my mind." The woman swept back her hood, revealing her face.

Caitlin froze when she saw the strawberry blond hair, the

luminous green-gold eyes. It was her—the midwife—the same woman who helped her bring Owen into this world. Her gaze fell to the seal. She backed up, shaking her head. "That can't be..."

"My dear," Moria said, lifting her eyes to Caitlin's. "Don't you recognize your own son?"

Moira vanished in a curl of smoke. Seals slid from the rocks, swimming to the beach, calling out to each other. Liam caught the strap of Nuala's leather satchel, spinning her around to face him. "Is that him? Is that Owen?"

"Let go of me!" Nuala cried.

"Is that *Owen?*" Liam shouted.

"Yes!" Nuala clawed at his wet clothes. "Let me go!"

Caitlin ran, stumbling over the soft white sand to the small seal struggling in the surf. Voices echoed over the harbor. Kelsey shouted, waving frantically from the end of the pier. Dominic hauled her back from the edge, pulling her with him as he ran. Their footsteps pounded over the planks as they made for the path leading down to the beach.

Caitlin splashed into the surf, lifting the floundering seal from the icy waves and pulling him back with her onto the sand. She fell to her knees, cradling him in her lap. His big black eyes stared up at her. He opened his whiskered mouth and let out an anguished cry.

"Owen?" she whispered, when he curled up into her, trembling. She ran her hands over his sleek seal-skin, rubbing off the white sand stuck to him like salt. She laid her hands on either side of his frightened face. "Owen?" she whispered. He nudged her back and a rage so strong, so powerful welled up inside her, she shot to her feet. "I don't care how much *power* you have!" Caitlin cried, lashing out at Nuala. "You can't take my son from me!"

Nuala's eyes darted over her shoulder as more voices, more shouting drifted down from the village. Her fingers fumbled to unhook the straps of the leather satchel. "There is only one way your son can take on his human form again."

More seals edged up out of the water, gathering around Caitlin and Owen. Dozens of seals formed a circle, a protective shield around the mother and child. Seawater rolled off their pelts as they rose, puffing out angry breaths. "Whatever it is," Caitlin cried. "We'll do it!" The seals pressed in on her, closing the wall, blocking her view. "Tell us what it is!"

Nuala untied the straps, lifting the leather flap. A blinding white light pulsed from the satchel as she pulled out the pelt. "Liam in exchange for Owen."

THE SEAL-SKIN SHIMMERED, sparkling like diamonds through the silver mists. In the distance, Liam heard voices calling out to him. Friends, people he knew, shouting for him to...do something. But he could not tear his eyes away from that beautiful white seal-coat. It called to him—whispering his name, a restless lure over the waves. He lifted a shaky arm, reaching for it, as the memories unraveled like pearls spilling from a broken chain.

The white selkie. She had come. His fingers brushed over the pelt—the white fur as soft as velvet, as delicate as silk. She had come to claim her land-man. To take him with her, into the sea. Liam fought the pressure building inside his chest, the ringing in his ears. He was never supposed to find the fairy tale. It was supposed to remain hidden.

But he had unearthed it, threatened to expose the deepest secret of the sea in the name of research. Foolishly assuming they had all passed into legend. She must have known. She must have known he was planning to unveil his findings and had come to stop him.

Because she could not let this tale spread. Modern humanity would never accept a human sacrifice. They would not accept that a man—a human man—would give his life to keep the peace between the land and the sea. They would see her as a threat—some pagan witchery—and they would seek to destroy her.

He stumbled back, his heels sinking into the sand. "There has to be another way."

"There is no other way!" Nuala fished out a second pelt—a soft silvery-gray, larger than the first—and pushed it toward him.

He shook his head, backing away from it. The sea lapped up over his feet, teasing him, tempting him. He remembered, now, finding his mother's name listed in the Trinity Library's registry. She had checked out the same book only weeks before she had run off and left him and Dominic alone with their father in Dublin. His mother had hidden the tale so he would never find it. Somehow, she had known that he would be looking for it one day. "This is madness."

Nuala's eyes flashed. "I thought you of all people would respect tradition, would find *honor* in sacrifice." She pushed the gray pelt into his chest. "You're a man of history, Liam. A man of the past. You know why you were chosen for this. This is who you were *meant* to be."

A selkie king. A ruler of the seas. Liam struggled to hear the voices of his friends. But the sound of rushing water, of waves rolling over a rocky beach drowned them out. Wet mists crept up, curling around his wrists, tugging him closer to the water's edge. His arms felt numb as they lifted, as his fingers grasped the sealskin. A light glimmered deep in Nuala's eyes.

He would live out the rest of his days underwater, separated from his home, from his family. He would be forced to marry Nuala. He would never see Caitlin or Owen again. But his family would be safe. They would not struggle. They might grieve, but they would find a way to move on. And his friends, his home, this island—they would be spared.

He heard the sudden sound of choking, of someone trying desperately to suck air into her lungs. He whirled, but the wall of seals shielded Caitlin from his view. A young seal's cry, desperate and high-pitched, rang out in the night.

"Listen to me, Liam. Listen very carefully," Nuala said. "If you want to save them, you must come with me."

He heard footsteps pounding down the cliff path, the voices getting closer. They could not see the white pelt. No one could see it or they'd be driven mad by it. He heard Caitlin suffocating behind the wall of seals, the young seal's cries growing louder, more frantic. "Can you promise me that my son will be safe? That my family, my friends will be protected?"

Nuala took his hand. He felt the whisper of cool air, the crackling of ice in his veins. He heard the song in the distance, the voice floating in from the sea. "For as long as we both shall live."

Forgive me, Caitlin. He dove into the icy waters, expecting the shock, the sudden loss of air from the cold. But instead, the seal-skin slid over him like a glove. The rush of the water surrounded him, sucking him under. He caught the flash of white and followed it. Into the darkness. Into the pulsing beat of the heart of the sea.

CHAPTER TWENTY-NINE

Seals slipped from the sand, into the water. Their desperate cries echoed over the harbor as they fled. Owen thrashed in Caitlin's arms. He let out a distressed howl and Caitlin dropped back to her knees. She laid him down on the sand. He twisted, writhing as the sound of something tearing, like leather splitting open, peeled through the night.

Kelsey ran up, sinking down beside Caitlin, her hands shaking as she reached for the wrinkles in the dark seal-skin, edging the slippery coat down Owen's back. "He's *shedding*."

Caitlin caught a fleeting glimpse of Dominic running out into the waves, screaming his brother's name. She heard her friends shouting, the sound of their footsteps pounding over the sand as they ran toward her. She felt the kick of sand, the sting of it as it met her eyes. But she couldn't move. She couldn't breathe as Owen's sleek black head of hair emerged from the seal-coat.

She reached for him, cradling his head as it crested the mouth of the pelt, the oily skin stretching and curling back over his shoulders. She gasped as his arms slid out, extending toward her, covered in a clear odorless mucus. The slap of the seal-skin suctioning back to his skin had Kelsey grabbing the hind fin, tugging it down. Tara stripped off her jacket, covering his naked body as the rest of the pelt peeled away.

Owen let out a strangled sob as he crawled into Caitlin's arms, kicking at the pelt until it was no more than a dark lifeless shell at his feet. He shuddered, trembling in her lap. His dark eyes were haunted as he searched the faces huddled over him. Fear swam into his eyes as they transformed from liquid black to a frightened blue-gray.

His sticky hands inched up Caitlin's sweater, curling into the threadbare wool at her neck. "Mum?"

RED HOT FURY whipped through Glenna, shooting down her arms, exploding from her fingertips like lightning. A scream tore from her throat as she released it—the fury, the rage, the helplessness. The wooden rowboat at the edge of the beach burst into flames. The wet wood splintered, crackling like bones breaking.

Moira stepped out of the flames, dropping her red cloak, letting it spill to the sand. "Losing your temper again, darling?"

"You cannot do this to them!" Glenna screamed when Sam grabbed her, pulling her back against him. "You cannot *play* with their lives!"

Smoke curled into the night, a black chimney of grief. Moira laughed, low and wicked. "You surprise me, Glenna." She walked slowly over the sand, flames snapping from the end of her hair in fiery sparks. "It's not a bad trade, when you think about it. Liam in exchange for Owen? A husband in exchange for a son?" She looked at Caitlin, narrowing her eyes. "At least Owen will love her. A husband's love can fade. But a child's love never strays."

"You *knew*." Glenna struggled against Sam, scratching her

nails down his arms. "You knew all along. You knew I would come here. You fixed it so this awful thing would happen."

"Of course, I fixed it." Moira lifted her chin. "I fix everything."

Glenna tore free of Sam's arms, hurling a ball of fire over the beach. But Moira merely held up her hand. A wall of ice sealed around it. It fell like a ball of hail, shattering when it hit the sand and crumbling into dust.

"How?" Glenna stumbled back, tripping over the sand. "How is that possible? You don't have those powers!"

"Do you think I make these trades for sport?" Moira's dress crackled around her as she stalked over the sand, furious with her daughter. "Nuala's foolishness was my gain. She took someone who was never supposed to be taken. She made a mistake—a grave one. And now, with every step closer they get to the kingdom, her powers fade. And feed into mine."

"I don't understand." Glenna backed up, shaking her head. She saw it now, the lightening of her mother's strawberry blond hair, the slight sparkle on her high cheek-bones. A powerful, unbeatable force—ice united with fire. "What do you mean, he was never supposed to be taken?"

"Liam was not a *true* land-man," Moira explained. "The same blood runs in his veins that runs in ours—selkie blood. That's why Nuala was able to change Owen when he was a child." Her gaze shifted to Caitlin. "She took Owen because she thought he would be enough to replace the selkie child she had lost—and the man she'd been stupid enough to run off with, turning her back on her fate at eighteen."

She took a step toward Owen, smiling. "But you weren't enough for her, were you dear? No," she hissed as Owen shrank back from her. "She wanted more. She wanted a husband. A man who would help her get back into the kingdom she'd been banished from for stealing you. When she discovered your father was a scholar of myths and legends, when she realized he was looking for *her* legend, she took the bait. As I knew she would."

Moira laughed, a hollow empty sound. "Nuala thought if she took your father, it would appease the king and queen. But she did not take the time to do her research. She did not know that Liam was already from that line. That *you* were already a part of their family. They did not know when they banished her that *you* were the child she had taken. They were too blind to see the truth then. And she will never be forgiven for stealing the great-grandson of a king."

"But *you* knew," Glenna realized. "*You* knew about Owen. *You* set this whole thing up!"

"Of course, I knew," Moira snapped. "The queen kept an eye on their lineage—on Liam and Dominic. But they did not keep a careful enough eye on the teenage girl who stole Liam's heart." Moira's eyes gleamed as she looked back at Caitlin. "They wrote you off when you rejected him. They thought that was the end of it. But *I* didn't. No." Moira shook her head, walking across the sand to where Caitlin cradled her child in her arms. "I watched you carefully, my dear. I knew you were hiding something when you went to Donegal. I suspected what it was. And I followed you there. Knowing all I had to do was offer my services as a midwife and things would be set into motion—things that could not be undone."

"You *cannot* do this to them!" Glenna raged. "You cannot throw away lives like this!"

"I have not thrown away Liam's life, darling." Moira brushed her hair back. It glowed like sunlit straw in the mist. "I have done nothing to him except reunite him with his family."

"His family is here!" Glenna shouted. "On the island!"

"I'm afraid you're wrong, Glenna. Liam's grandmother is the daughter of the last white selkie. She holds the throne now, guarding it until the next white selkie comes. But now that

Nuala's powers have been stripped, his grandmother will continue to rule the sea. With Liam by her side."

"No!" Glenna's voice echoed over the harbor. "You have to stop this! These people are my friends!"

"Friends?" Moira turned, her long dress cracking around her ankles like a whip. "Glenna, do not make the same mistake Liam's mother made. Do not let these people get under your skin."

Glenna cried out as her skin began to smolder, as smoke seared from the burns on her arms, glowing red. Sam caught her when her knees gave out, when all the power drained out of her, seeping into the sand like liquid fire.

"Who is this woman?" Sam hissed into her ear. "Tell me who she is so I can help you!"

The woman's eyes twinkled, warming as she looked back at him. "You mean, you haven't told them about me?" Moira lifted a perfectly winged eyebrow, feigning a look of hurt. "I thought you would have at least told your *friends* about your own mother."

Caitlin let out a strangled cry.

"Don't worry." Moira smiled wickedly at Caitlin. "You may never see your precious Liam again, but he will grow to like his new life. He may even grow to love another one day."

Glenna sank to the sand, struggling to breathe over the icy seawater clogging her lungs. Her fingers curled into Sam's jacket when Caitlin rose, when her friend pushed to her feet, facing the woman who had been the cause of so much grief, of so much destruction in her life.

Glenna watched the blind rage flood into Caitlin's eyes. She saw her stance, one of strength, one of a mother preparing to fight for her family. A small ray of hope burned in her heart and she squeezed her eyes shut, sending what little was left of her own power, her own strength into the earth, channeling it to Caitlin.

Caitlin stared at Moira across the long stretch of beach. The waves curled over the sand like angry slaps. "Bring him back."

"I'm afraid I can't do that, my dear."

"You said she failed," Caitlin challenged, stepping between her son and the woman who had stolen him from her. "That Nuala is losing power as we speak." Her hands clenched at her sides, her heels digging into the sand, drawing more power from the earth. "You have what you want," Caitlin shouted. "*Bring him back!*"

"What's done is done, my dear. There is no magic powerful enough to reverse a white selkie's spell." Moira smiled down at Owen. "Perhaps one day you will find that Owen is enough for you. Perhaps you will find happiness where Nuala could not."

"I will find him," Caitlin breathed, her words like frozen feathers falling in the night. "I will find Liam and I will bring him back. You will not get away with this."

"Oh, my dear." Smoke curled around Moira, pulling her out of sight. "I already have."

CHAPTER THIRTY

$\mathcal{T}$hey spent days combing the beaches, searching the harbor, scouring the cliffs and calling his name. Grief settled like a gray cloak around Caitlin's shoulders. Like a bird nesting in the hollow of tree, broken and beaten. At dusk each night, she and Owen went back to the beach—the one where they'd lost him. They built a small driftwood fire and listened to the crackle of the flames as the sky grew dark. They watched the surf curl over the sand, waiting for a sign, for a clue that he was there.

The islanders came with candles, with jars of black sand and bowls of seashells. They brought dried herbs and stones from their gardens, sprinkling them over the sand. They huddled under wool blankets, forcing Caitlin and Owen to sip thermoses of hot tea, steeped in Tara's rose petals. Sometimes they brought books, children's stories they found in Caitlin's cottage. Sometimes they stayed and read them out loud. Even when they knew she wasn't listening. They read them to the wind.

Dominic came each night to sit with them, to hold a silent vigil. He said nothing as the pile of trinkets grew around them, adding to it when he could. When Kelsey crawled into his lap, closing her eyes and laying her head on his shoulder to fall asleep as she did every night now, Caitlin picked up a jar of black sand. The tea light flickered inside it. These trinkets—these *things* from their past—they were meaningless without the man who completed them. She would gladly trade all of it for the chance to see him one last time.

And she would see him again. They would find him. They would find a way to bring him back. Even if it meant *she* had to go into the water. She would do anything to save him. Glenna was regaining her strength every day and they would go after him. They would face down her mother and they would win. She tilted the candle, letting the white wax spill over the edge into the black sand. Liam *had* remembered. These things—these objects that represented the love that had never stopped growing between them—they *had* brought his memory back. Even if it was only for a moment. He *had* remembered.

If these trinkets could bring back his memory, then surely her love could bring *him* back. She had not thought her love was strong enough to bring a healthy child into this world at sixteen. But she'd been wrong. She had been strong enough. Just not strong enough to see through the black magic of a sea witch. She might not have been ready for it then, might not have understood even if she'd seen the signs.

But she was ready now. She was strong enough. And no one was going to take her family away from her. Her fingers curled around the jar. She might not have magic. But she had something stronger, and ten times more potent. She had the power of love— real, lasting, true love for both Liam and Owen. And she was ready to wield it. She glanced up when she heard a soft thud in the sand where the waves curled over the beach. The ocean receded, leaving eleven long-stemmed yellow roses in its wake.

SHE'D SENT him on an errand. Again. Sam scoured the scraggly plants growing along the edges of the rocky footpaths, using his pocketknife to slice off a handful of what he hoped was the right weed. He'd been pacing outside Glenna's cottage for days. Tara was inside, healing her with all her powers, both human and selkie. She kept sending him for herbs, for different balms and tinctures she kept in her office. And now she'd sent him for some winter weed that grew around the edge of the bogs.

He was starting to wonder if she was even using the things he brought back, or just making things up and trying to give him something to do, so he wouldn't stand outside and worry and pace. But how could he not worry? When someone as strong as Glenna fell to pieces in your arms, it was hard not to think that the world was falling apart.

A gull cawed, swooping low over the stone walls. He followed its path west along the row of pastures, picking his way over the trail leading back to Glenna's cottage. He let himself in, pausing in her doorway when he spotted Tara helping Glenna to her feet.

"No." He shook his head, closing the door and walking into the room. "You're not ready yet." He dropped the handful of weeds onto the table, taking her elbow when she wobbled unsteadily. "You can barely stand on your own."

Glenna looked up at him. "It's time."

Sam kept shaking his head. He caught the determination in her eyes, the subtle lift of her chin. But it was going to take so much more than that. It was going to take all of her strength when she called her mother back, when she tried to break this terrible spell. "What's going to happen to you? If this is how drained you were from the last time?"

Glenna's gaze dropped to the marks on her arms, the burns

that were no more than scars now. "You accused me of never asking for help earlier. I need you to help me now, Sam. I cannot do this alone."

"There has to be another way—"

Glenna laid a hand on Sam's arm. "Bring me my cloak, Sam. It's time."

Every muscle in Sam's body clenched at the thought of what might happen to this woman when she called her mother back. But he fetched her cloak, draping the soft material over her shoulders. He let his fingers linger there when he felt her bones protruding. Rage coiled like a snake inside him when he realized how much weight she'd lost this week. "I want you to tell me what's going to happen." He turned her around, catching her chin in his hand and holding her gaze. "Exactly what's going to happen when your mother steps out of that fire."

"I don't know," Glenna admitted. "If I knew the answer to that question, I promise I would tell you. But all we can do tonight is try to open a passageway for Liam. Once a land-man is turned into a selkie, he has to choose to come out of the water on his own. Liam will have already lost all his memories of his friends and his family. Of his home, this island. His love for Caitlin. The only way we can bring him back is to find a way to get that memory to him. If we can find a way to reach him, we might be able to bring him back."

"And if we succeed? If we open this passageway, will Liam be able to walk through it on his own?"

Glenna shook her head. "All we can do is help open a passageway. Caitlin will have to pull him through."

"What happens if it doesn't work?"

Glenna looked away. "He'll be lost forever."

Sam waited until her eyes swung back to his. "What happens to *you*, Glenna?"

Glenna reached up, brushing his hand away. Sam gritted his

teeth when Glenna hooked her arm through Tara's, letting her friend lead her toward the door. He grabbed the flashlight off the table and switched it on. He stalked to the door, opening it for these two stubborn, reckless women and followed them out into the darkness.

If they made it through the night, he would personally make sure Glenna put every ounce of the weight she'd lost back on. He would drag her to the pub every day for a month if he had to, and make sure she ate every bite of every meal. Even if she refused to talk to him, and shot daggers out of her eyes at him the whole time, he wouldn't stop until she was as strong and healthy as she was the first time he laid eyes on her.

They walked in silence through the deserted village—the homes dark and empty. When they got to the top of the bluff and the rocky path leading down to the beach near the harbor, Glenna paused. Candles flickered over the sand where groups of islanders huddled together, praying for Liam's return. She spotted the keepsakes, the piles of mementos the islanders had built in his honor. "How long have they been here?"

"All week."

"They don't have to stay for this."

"They won't leave her," Tara said gently. "They won't let Caitlin—or *you*—face this alone."

"They know that if they join us, if they cross a white selkie— even one whose powers have been stripped—they could be destroyed. Their homes, their livelihoods, this *island* could be destroyed."

"They know," Tara said quietly. "We all know."

Glenna's honey-colored cloak floating out around her ankles as she started down the cliff path. "So be it."

~

CAITLIN CLUTCHED Owen's hand tightly in hers when she heard the footsteps in the sand behind her. She turned, watching Glenna walk across the beach with Tara and Sam. Her friend's face had grown thinner, her cheekbones more prominent. She'd lost some of her color, too. But she was still Glenna. She held her shoulders straight and the amber eyes that met Caitlin's were focused and determined. "Is everything ready?" Glenna asked.

Caitlin nodded. The roses lay in a circle now around the driftwood fire, petals to stems. All of the most precious memories of her and Liam's love were inside the circle, inches from the flames. She held Owen close to her side, the most precious gift of all. No matter what happened tonight, she would love and cherish Owen more than a mother had ever loved and cherished a son.

Glenna stepped toward the flames, watching them curl and hiss. Steam rose up from the fire as a thick yellow fog spread over the beach. The stench of sulfur drifted into the night and Glenna reached for Caitlin's hand. "Whatever happens, I want you to know that Liam did love you. I knew it the moment I first saw you together. And every moment since."

Caitlin nodded as the islanders rose, stuffing trinkets and mementos into their pockets and shuffling over to join them. Tara took Glenna's other hand, linking her with Kelsey and Dominic. Sam hooked his hand through Owen's, reaching for Sarah Dooley and the string of islanders she'd begun to form. One by one, they came together, forming a circle, a ring of linked hands around the fire.

Glenna bowed her head, closing her eyes, and began to chant. The flames danced, kicking up into the night. They stretched higher, the heat building until they grew as high as the cliffs. An orange ribbon of fire illuminated the islanders' faces through the yellow fog. Caitlin held Owen to her side as Glenna's voice rose over the waves like an ancient song. The fire crackled and popped. The sea shuddered under her words, the surface stretching and snapping together as fingers of smoke dripped from the cliff edge into the sea.

When a familiar laugh floated out of the flames, Caitlin stepped inside the circle. Glenna reached for Owen's hand, closing the ring as Moira's image formed. Caitlin stood her ground, facing the woman who'd tried to take everything from her. She was so close to the fire, the heat of the flames nearly scorched her skin. "You cannot come through."

Moira laughed louder as the flames swirled up, snapping and crackling. "Says who?"

"Says me."

"With what power?"

"With this power," Caitlin breathed, stepping into the fire.

Moira's eyes flashed as the flames parted. Seals edged out of the water, calling out to each other in the fog. Moira lifted her arms, sending a bolt of lightning twisting up into the sky. It shot through the night, illuminating the ocean. She gasped when she spotted the seals—a mass of them coming up out of the sea—heading straight toward her.

All over the beach, the islanders called out to each other through the fog, squeezing each other's hands, refusing to let go of the circle. They formed a wall around the fire, both man and seal. Moira hurled a ball of fire at Caitlin, but she just stood there as it split, passing around her.

"How is this possible?" Moira cried. "You don't have magic! You don't have powers!"

"I'm protected," Caitlin answered. "By something you could never understand."

Glenna's chants grew louder. Moira writhed, twisting in the flames. She hurled daggers of ice at Caitlin, but they melted in the flames. The sea surged into the cliffs. The waves built, crashing over the sand. The water rose, spilling over the beach as more seals came, howling into the night.

Caitlin stood in the flames, inside the circle of islanders, protected by the love of her friends, protected by her love for Owen and Liam. Through the fading image of Moira, she could see the pulsing ocean. The surface opened, revealing the glittering gates of a kingdom far below. She reached for it, the passageway leading into the sea. But her hands shrank back when she spotted the lone seal swimming back and forth outside the gates.

The seal turned, and Caitlin staggered back. She recognized the pale, colorless eyes—Nuala's eyes. But her pelt was no longer white. It was dark now, as dark as the rest of the seals. Nuala stared back at her through the ocean, her eyes wide and pleading. She was trying to tell her something. But what? What was she trying to tell her?

Nuala turned, rubbing against the gates, trying to get into the kingdom. She was locked out. But where was Liam? Nuala looked back at Caitlin, her eyes begging her to do something. What? What was she supposed to do? Caitlin took another step into the fire, toward the ocean. She heard Owen shout, breaking free of the circle. He ran to her. She caught him, pulling him away from the flames as the passage closed and the image vanished.

"Wait!" Caitlin cried as the flames shrank around her. A wave crashed over the beach, the tide swallowing what was left of the fire.

THE FOG SLITHERED AWAY. The sea sucked back, leaving a pile of wet wood and smoke. Caitlin watched the line of the horizon, her heart pounding. Please. Please come back, Liam. She squeezed Owen's hand. She could hear Glenna's labored breathing, Tara's whispered prayers. The circle of islanders had turned. All of them were watching the sea, waiting to see if he would come.

The surface quieted, the storm clouds passing. They stood for what felt like hours, until Glenna collapsed.

"Glenna!" Caitlin ran to her friend, trying to lift her friend up. But she was so weak, she could only hang limp in her arms. Her eyes fluttered open. "I'm sorry."

Tara knelt beside her, feeling for her pulse. She looked up at Sam. "We need to get her back to the cottage."

Sam lifted Glenna into his arms, carrying over the sand. Glenna glanced back at Caitlin, tears in her eyes. "I'm so sorry."

Sorry? Sorry meant it didn't work. Sorry meant there was no other way. She shook her head. No. Her gaze searched the horizon, scouring the line of the surf. But there was nothing. Not a single shift in the wind, not a single wave in the harbor. One by one, the seals bowed their heads, laying them down on the sand.

No! Caitlin pulled Owen into her arms, hugging him to her. "He's not gone. He can't be."

Tara walked up to her, tears streaming down her face. "Caitlin," she whispered brokenly. "He's gone."

CHAPTER THIRTY-ONE

*C*aitlin stayed on the beach until dawn, in denial. Unwilling to believe. She stayed until everyone else had gone. When a red sun rose, shimmering over the surface of the sea, Owen stood and held out his hand. It was over. He was gone.

They walked in silence back to the village. When they got to her cottage, she knelt in front of the door, putting her hands on Owen's shoulders. No matter how painful this was, she had to be strong for Owen. He was the only thing holding her together right now. And she had to make sure he knew every day how happy she was to have found him. How much he meant to her. How much she loved him and would cherish the rest of their days together. Despite everything that had happened.

"I want you to know that I don't blame you," Caitlin said gently. "This isn't your fault."

Owen nodded, but he looked down at his feet. She knew he didn't believe her. "Do you think, before we go in, we could go to the cottage one more time?"

"The one by the bogs?"

He nodded.

"Why?" She brushed a lock of dark hair from his eyes. "We've looked everywhere. He's not going to be there."

"I know." He scrubbed his toe in the mud gathered outside her door. "I wanted to see if the last petal had fallen."

"And if it has?"

"Then I'll know." He lifted his eyes to hers. "I thought it was marking my time here. But I was wrong. It was his. I just want to see it. One last time."

Caitlin nodded. What would it hurt to go one more time? If it meant something to Owen? If it would make him feel better? The raw ache settling into her chest was only the beginning. It would be years before either of them—before anyone on this island—got over this storm. She was not going to sleep anytime soon.

"Of course," she said, taking his hand and leading him back out into the wet fields. They walked slowly, their shoes seeping into the squishy earth. Birds flew over the sunlit pastures. The sparkling ocean stretched out calm and subdued in the distance. The sunrise glowed over the walls of the cottage when it came into view, painting the stones a warm peachy-pink.

Owen slipped his hand free from hers, jogging over to the pile of dirt and the fallen rose. "Look!" He snatched it up off the ground, holding it out to her. "There's still one petal left!"

She saw the hope swim into his eyes and she swallowed the lump in her throat. A cool breeze quivered over the bogs, blowing the last petal off and Owen grabbed it before it fell. Dropping the white stem into a puddle, he walked over to Caitlin, lifting her hand and placing the petal in her palm. "Close your eyes and make a wish."

"Owen."

"It's a magic rose. It has to be. It couldn't have grown in winter if it wasn't."

She felt the pulsing in her palm, saw the warm glow as the

petal started to change colors, as the textures softened from ice white to velvety gold.

"See!" he said, cupping his own hands around hers to protect it from the wind. "I knew it! There is some power left in it. Maybe if we both hold onto it together and wish for him to come back at the same time, we can bring him back."

Caitlin felt the petal throbbing in her hand, but she shook her head. "We tried using magic, Owen. It didn't work."

"But we didn't try using *this* magic."

"I'm not a magical person. What happened last night was all Glenna. She drew power from my love for Liam. From my love for you. But it wasn't our magic. We couldn't have done it without her."

"I think you're wrong. I think last night opened up a doorway for Liam. And we have to help pull him through. I think that's what my...what Nuala was trying to tell us. You said you saw her. You said she was trying to tell you something."

Caitlin bit her lip, nodded.

"Maybe she was trying to tell you to come here, to find this last petal. Maybe if we wish hard enough for both of them, we can pull Liam through *and* she can get back into the kingdom."

Caitlin swallowed. "Is that what you want, Owen? Do you want us to help Nuala get back in?"

He looked up at her. "I don't think it was all her fault. She doesn't deserve to be punished forever."

Could she do this? Could she forgive this woman for stealing her child? For taking the love of her life away from her? Even if Nuala was a pawn in the sea witch's master plan, it was still Nuala's doing. But when she looked down at Owen and she saw the kindness, the compassion, the sheer love in his eyes, she knew. She had to find a way to forgive Nuala. She had to let go of this terrible hurt and move on. Maybe that was what Nuala had been trying to tell her. Maybe all she had been asking for was Caitlin's forgiveness.

"I think we need to help her," Owen whispered. "And I think we can. We can help Nuala and we can bring Liam back. But you have to believe first."

"Okay." Caitlin nodded. She didn't know if she had the heart to hope again. But she could forgive. And she could find the strength to believe. One last time. For Owen. "I'll try."

Owen put his hands over hers. "You promise you'll really try? That you're not just saying it?"

"I promise." If she did anything to keep the spirit of Liam's memory alive, it would be to dream and wish and believe. To teach Owen to have an imagination. Even after everything that happened, she would not take that away from him. She closed her eyes and Owen's small hands squeezed hers.

"SELKIE ROYALTY?" Dominic stared at the single candle burning on the table in the pub. "How?" His face was pale, grief-stricken. His clothes were still damp, covered in sand. "How is this even possible?"

Tara sank into the chair beside him and Kelsey crawled up into her lap. There were strings of seaweed tangled in her hair. Mud from the caves streaked up the arms of her sweatshirt. Her eyes were red and puffy from crying. "Uncle Liam can't be gone." Her voice faltered. "I mean, he can't *really* be gone...can he?"

"I don't know." Tara fought back tears, running a soothing hand over her daughter's blond curls still damp from sea spray, from the hours spent searching the shoreline. "I don't know, Kelsey."

Dominic and Kelsey had stayed on the beach with Caitlin and Owen, searching the caves for hours in case they'd missed anything. Sam had carried Glenna home and Tara had done all she could. Glenna was stable and Sam was still with her. He wouldn't leave her side until she was healed. "Glenna says they'll let Liam into the kingdom. But Nuala will be banished forever and without her powers to protect her, she won't last long."

Kelsey buried her face in her mother's shoulder. "What does that mean?"

"It means Glenna's mother—the sea witch—got Nuala's powers in exchange for her time here on land. But since Liam was never supposed to be taken, since he is not a true land-man, they will let him stay."

Dominic's eyes lifted, haunted and bloodshot. "I knew there was something off about Nuala. The first time I saw her. The first time I spoke to her. But I didn't heed the warnings. I didn't look any closer. I could have saved him."

Tara squeezed his arm. "You cannot blame yourself for this, Dominic. This was bigger than any of us could have foreseen."

"Except for Glenna." Dominic looked away, his face tight.

Tara pulled her hand away, wrapping her arms around Kelsey. "I think there's a lot more to Glenna's story than she's ever told anyone."

Dominic shook his head, his fingers curling around the glass candle-holder. "Her mother is a sea witch who's been playing with our lives since we were children. What else is there to know?"

"Her *mother* did this to Caitlin and Liam," Tara argued softly. "Not Glenna."

"But she knew things," Dominic growled, tilting the candle so hot wax spilled over the edge, dripping onto the table. "She held things back that she should have told Caitlin. That she should have told us."

Tara took the candle from his hand, peeling his fingers off it and setting it back on the table. "We still don't know how much

Glenna knew. She told me what she could, but there were still gaps. There were still missing pieces from her story."

"That she left out *on purpose.*"

"Maybe not," Tara disputed. We still don't know how close she is to her mother. How much she really sees in her visions. I think there's a reason for Glenna's secrecy. That maybe she wasn't trying to hurt us. That maybe she was trying to protect us."

"From what?"

"From something bigger."

Kelsey stirred and Tara cooed into her ear, gently laying her head back onto her shoulder.

Dominic lowered his voice to barely more than a whisper. "Not everyone deserves our forgiveness. I suppose you think Sam was trying to protect you by staying on the island after trying to kill you."

"Sam was wrong to lead my deranged husband here. But Philip was the one who tried to kill me. Not Sam. And as soon as Sam realized what he'd done he switched sides and fought alongside us."

"Whose side is Glenna on?"

"I don't know," Tara said after a long time. "But I won't push her away. Not yet. Not until I know the truth. Dom..." Tara took a deep breath. "Caitlin told me about how Liam found a connection to your mother in the library, to this fairy tale. That she was the last one who checked it only weeks before she left you."

Dominic looked away, shaking his head.

"You and Liam were right to be angry with her for leaving you when you were children. For leaving you with a worthless drunk of a man. But now we know there's more to her story." Tara laid her hand on Dominic's arm. "Your mother was the grand-daughter of a selkie queen—of a *white* selkie. Don't you think it's possible she might have had a bigger reason for leaving, and a reason for burying that fairy tale?"

Dominic lifted his eyes to Tara's—disbelief and anger swimming in them. "I don't care *why* any of them did what they did. I just want my little brother back!"

Kelsey lifted her tear-streaked face from Tara's shoulder. "Do you think..." Kelsey whispered when Dominic put his head in his hands, his shoulders shaking in anguish. "That there's a way we could bring him back?" She looked up at Tara. "Maybe we could make a wish? All at the same time?"

"Of course, Kelsey." Tara squeezed her hand, swallowing the lump in her throat. "Whatever you want."

"Maybe if we all think the same thing together at the same time..." Kelsey's eyes swept over the barroom. "Maybe if we all hold onto something that's really special to all of us." Her face lit up and she crawled out of Tara's lap. "I'll be right back." She jogged up the stairwell, running into her old bedroom, her footsteps echoing over the floorboards. She padded back down the steps in her socks, cradling a bowl filled with dried rose petals.

"These were yours," she said to Tara, setting the bowl on the table and the scent of roses drifted up between them. "Caitlin saved some of the petals. We dried them last summer. She gave me these and said I should keep them to remember."

Kelsey sprinkled the red petals into each of their hands. "Maybe there still some magic left in them. Maybe if we put some in our hands and wish together, we can bring him back."

"Kelsey." Dominic shook his head, but his voice broke over the words. And his fingers closed tightly around hers when she laid her hand in his. Tara slipped her hand inside his other hand and they formed a circle of three. They bowed their heads around the candlelit table, and closed their eyes as a red sun rose over the ocean, streaming in the windows of the pub.

SAM SAT on the edge of Glenna's bed, holding her hand, watching the gentle rise and fall of her breath. Her rich brown locks were splayed out over her pillows. He'd lit every candle in the room, thinking the familiar smells might help her heal. But no matter how long it took, he wouldn't leave her. Not until she opened her eyes. Not until he knew she would be okay.

And when she did, he would find a way to convince her he had changed. That he could be trusted. That he was worthy of her love. He picked a single dried rose petal from the dish tucked into the corner of the shelf behind her bed. He knew Caitlin had given her these. That they were the magic roses from Tara's cottage last summer. Caitlin had dried them and given them each a handful, to remember. He knew because she had given him some, too.

He'd pretended, at the time, that it wasn't necessary. That she didn't have to include him. But it *had* meant something to him. It had meant the world to him. After everything he'd done, she should have hated him. She should have never spoken to him again. But, instead, she'd thanked him. She'd included him. She'd given him a handful of dried rose petals, which he kept in the same spot, right next to his bed.

Swallowing a lump forming in his throat, he laid the petal in Glenna's limp hand, pressing his palm to hers so the petal was between them. He closed his eyes and did something he hadn't done since he was a child. He prayed. For Glenna. For Caitlin. For Liam. For Tara. For Brennan. For every person on this island who had shown him what it meant to believe in hope again.

And as the first rays of a brilliant sunrise glowed through the curtains of the room, he opened his eyes and saw that Glenna was watching him. A faint smile played at her lips and she curled her fingers around his palm, squeezing his hand.

Caitlin held her breath, waiting. There was only silence, a cool breeze rustling through the taller grasses edging the bogs. She listened for the sound of footsteps. For the sound of his voice. But nothing changed. She waited for what felt like an eternity. But when she opened her eyes again, it was still only the two of them. "Owen," she said brokenly. "Please. It's time to go home."

"Wait," he said squinting into the distance. "I think I see something."

Caitlin followed his gaze and it did look like something, far off in the distance, like a faint wisp of smoke. She rubbed her eyes and when she looked back it was darker, almost like a shadow, or an outline of a person. When it started to move, she froze.

"Come on!" Owen said, tugging her with him onto the stone-and-boulder path that led to the northern shore.

Caitlin's heart skipped a beat when she saw the dark shape form into a man, when she recognized Liam's long, lanky strides heading toward them.

"It worked!" Owen yelled, letting go of her hand racing through the bogs, splashing through the puddles to meet him.

When she saw him standing there, the shells woven into his dark hair, a thin silver crown encircling his head, her breath caught in her throat.

"We did it!" Owen jumped up and down. "We brought you back."

Caitlin paused, a yard away from him. What if he was just a figment of her imagination? What if none of this was even real? "Is it really you?"

He nodded, holding out his hand to her.

She saw the sea still shimmering on his skin, the starfish clinging to the hem of his dark pants. "Are you...here to say goodbye?"

"No." He caught her hand, pulling her into his arms. He felt real. Warm. Muscular. Strong. Like Liam. She leaned into him, breathing in the scent of the ocean. When she started to shiver, he edged back, lowering his mouth to hers and pressing a soft kiss to her lips. "I don't understand..." Caitlin breathed, looking up at him. "We tried to bring you back. Last night, Glenna tried everything. But it didn't work."

He took her face in his hands. "It did work."

"How?"

Liam smiled. "*You* brought me back."

Caitlin shook her head. "But I don't have any magic. I'm not..."

He cradled her face in his hands, brushing his lips over hers like the first rays of sunlight shining through a long winter's snow. "There is no magic stronger than true love."

CHAPTER THIRTY-TWO

*C*aitlin was waiting outside for him when he walked up the hill from the village. She'd seen the ferry come in, making its slow crossing over the sea and into the sheltered harbor. She smiled when she saw the roses, shaking her head when he held them out to her. He grinned. "I thought I'd give it another shot."

"And look," she joked, "all twelve of them are yellow this time." She closed her eyes, taking a good, long sniff. When she opened them again, they were shining. With love. For him. He would never tire of seeing that look in her eyes. Ever. She held out her free hand. "I missed you."

He rubbed his thumb over her cheek, leaning down for a kiss. "And I missed you."

She laughed when he pulled his hand back and showed her his fingers, covered now in pink paint. "Yes, well." She gestured to her paint-splattered apron. "I thought it might be fun for the kids to help me paint the set of chairs I picked up at that flea market a few weeks ago. I haven't decided on a place for them yet, but they'll find a home in one of my cottages, someday."

"Cait, you've talked about turning the cottage by the bogs into a home—into *your* home—for a long time. Since we were children. Do you still want to do that?"

"I'm not sure," she admitted. "I used to think that's what I wanted. But I rather like living in the middle of the village, being a part of the hustle and bustle." She rolled her eyes at herself. "As much of a hustle and bustle as there ever is on the island. But we can talk about it, if you..."

"No." He shook his head, relieved. "I'd much rather be here, too. I had some time to think on the ride over and I wonder if you might want to turn that cottage into your workshop. Then you wouldn't have to worry about where to store things."

She laughed. "I think when you see inside the house, you'll want that particular project to get moving sooner rather than later."

Children's laughter and conversation bubbled out into the street through Caitlin's open door. Liam spied Tara inside, her hair covered in paint, pointing at the furniture and trying to talk the kids—Owen, Ronan, Ashling and Kelsey—into painting the chairs instead of each other. "Looks like she's got her hands full."

"I'm afraid we lost control hours ago." She angled her head. "Are you sure you're ready for it? You've lived a pretty quiet life up until now."

He grinned, reaching for the door. "I've never been more ready for anything." When she caught his hand, he paused.

"What's that?" She pointed to the envelope sticking out of his pocket.

He pulled it out, sending her a lopsided smile. "I almost forgot."

Caitlin saw the official stamp and her eyes widened. "It came."

He nodded. "Today. Sarah stopped me on my walk up. Asked me to bring it to you. She knew you'd want to see it right away."

She didn't bother wiping her hands. She tore into it, reading the letter and letting out a long breath. "He's ours. The test results came back positive."

"Not that we needed that letter to know."

"Still." She tucked it in her apron pocket, looking up at him. "I'm glad we have it. And it'll make things easier from a legal standpoint. For doctor's visits. For when he applies to university."

He smiled, tucking her hair behind her ear. "That's a bit of a ways off, I hope."

She smiled. "He's a fast learner. He'll catch up in no time."

Liam nodded, glancing through the doorway again and watching Owen try to dab Ashling's cheek with a brush of paint. She ducked, squealing and batting his hand away. "He seems to be adjusting well."

"He is." Caitlin nodded. "But he'll be glad you're back. He's been after me to stay up with him and read late into the night. You've been spoiling him."

"And I plan to continue spoiling him. For a very long time." He grinned and pushed open the door. The children squealed and rushed over, all wanting to show him what they'd done at the same time. Liam scooped Owen up in a bear hug, not caring at all when he rubbed his paint-covered hands all over his sweater. "I see you've been helping your mother."

"She let me mix the colors. I came up with a new one. It's called chocolate mint."

"It looks more like slime," Kelsey argued.

Liam looked down at Owen's greenish-brown hands, a mixture of every paint color in Caitlin's stash. "I can see that." He laughed, setting him back down.

Tara walked over, picking paint out of her hair. "Kelsey, Ashling, Ronan, time to go."

"You don't have to leave," Liam said.

"Oh, believe me," Tara said. "It's way past time to go." She shook her head as the three kids dashed out into the street. "Ash-ling and Ronan's parents are going to kill us when they get a look at their clothes." She picked another glob of paint out of her hair. "I take it the presentation at the conference went well?"

"Very well," Liam answered. "Though, I might have left out a few bits and pieces of the ending."

Tara winked. "Best not to let the general public in on *all* of our family secrets. By the way," she lowered her voice. "I've talked to Sam about tracking down your mother. He's agreed to look into it."

"And Dominic's okay with it?"

"Not quite yet," Tara admitted. "But he will be." She smiled, waving goodbye to Caitlin as she followed the children into the street. "I'll see you both at the pub later for dinner tonight."

Caitlin nudged Owen into the hallway. "Go on into the washroom and scrub the paint off your hands. And use the faucet in the tub," she called out, shaking her head when she heard the one in the sink turn on.

Liam wandered over to where Caitlin was cutting the end of the stems off, fussing and fluffing the flowers, moving them around until they were perfect and then carrying them over to set in the center of the kitchen table. "I've been meaning to ask...why are yellow roses your favorite?"

Caitlin glanced up. "Because they're the color of friendship."

"You knew that?"

"Of course, I knew that. Did *you* know that?"

"I found out...recently. But, then, would you have preferred I brought you a dozen red ones this time? If only for the meaning?"

"Not at all." She moved one of the flowers around again. "I've always thought love—true love—should be based on friendship. Love can't last unless it has a strong foundation to grow from. And I believe the strongest foundation is real friendship." She edged one more flower a quarter of an inch, and then stepped back, satisfied. "I want to know that when we're wrinkled and gray and hobbling around with sticks, we'll still have things to talk about. We'll still enjoy each other's company. We'll still be able to make each other laugh."

"Love based on friendship..." Liam echoed. "Like a childhood friendship?"

"Yes." Caitlin's lips curved. "Exactly." Her eyes sparkled as they met his across the room. "In my opinion, that's the best kind."

The sound of the water running stopped and Owen dashed into his bedroom—the spare room they had fixed up for him—and came back out holding a book. "I read a full sentence while you were gone," he told Liam. "Do you want to hear it?"

"Of course," Liam answered, feeling a rush of pride well up inside him as he listened to Owen reading him a line from one of his old children's books. It was hard to believe this was his life now. That Owen was his son. That Caitlin had finally admitted her true feelings for him. That after all this time, all he'd ever wanted was finally going to be his.

Half-painted furniture cluttered the living room. A tarp, covered in paint cans, was pushed up into a corner. There were dirty paintbrushes piled up in the kitchen sink. It was exactly the kind of chaotic but simple life he'd always wanted to live here on the island with Caitlin. "Owen, I have a sentence I'd like you to read out loud for me. It's a question I have for your mother."

He unfolded a piece of paper from his pocket. "I wrote it down on the way over. Would you read it to her, from me?"

Owen took the paper, his mouth forming a thin line like it did whenever he was trying to concentrate. "Will you...mah...mah..." He glanced up at Liam, who looked down at the paper.

Liam touched his hand to the paper, sounding out each syllable. "Mar-ry."

Owen's eyes lit up. "Will you marry me?!"

Liam withdrew a ring from his pocket. He dropped to one knee and Caitlin sucked in a breath when he held out a sparkling circle of gold, glittering with an exotic cluster of pearls, sapphires and diamonds. "It was my grandmother's," he whispered, his heart in his throat. "She wanted you to have it."

"Your grandmother...?" Caitlin's eyes went wide when he slipped the ring onto her finger.

Liam rose, his eyes twinkling. "From my mother's side. She wants to meet you one day—the human woman whose love was so strong it could break a white selkie's spell."

"Mum," Owen tugged on her hand. "Are you going to say yes?"

Liam grinned down at her. "How would you like to be a princess?"

Caitlin stared down at the ring. She let out a long shaky breath. "You can't lord it over me, you know—that you're selkie royalty." She looked up at him, a warning in her eyes. "Even if I say yes, you're still the same ordinary land-man as far as I'm concerned."

Liam took her face in his hands. "I don't care who I am." He pressed his lips to hers. "As long as you'll be my wife."

Caitlin wrapped her arms around him and he lifted her up off the floor. "God help me, Liam O'Sullivan. I thought you'd never ask."

On a lonely stretch of beach, a driftwood fire burned. Glenna stood in the sand, gazing out at the sea, her long hair whipping around her face.

Her mother stood beside her, watching the fishing boats bob around the string of islands to the north. "You're getting soft."

"I only gave them a nudge."

A gull cawed, swooping low over the horizon. "First Tara and Dominic. Now Caitlin and Liam." Moira lifted an eyebrow. "If I didn't know any better, Glenna, I'd think you were starting to believe in true love."

"I'm not."

The pale wood shifted, crumbling under the heat. "You know they're going to look for her now—the mother."

"I do."

"You know what that means."

Glenna nodded, staring out at the sprinkles of sunlight dotting the sea.

"They've talked to the man—the detective. They've asked him to find her." The flames danced in the fire pit, black smoke curling into the sky. "You know what will happen if they do."

"I know."

Moira turned, facing her daughter. "You can't let that happen."

"I won't."

"What are you going to do, Glenna?"

Glenna lifted her eyes to her mother's. "Stop him."

THE END

A NOTE FROM THE AUTHOR

Dear Reader,

I hope you enjoyed *The Selkie Enchantress*. The Seal Island Trilogy continues with Sam and Glenna's story, *The Selkie Sorceress*, which is available now. Read on for a special preview. For updates on future books, please sign up for my newsletter at sophiemossauthor.com.

Also, I have a small request. If you enjoyed the story, it would mean so much to me if you would consider leaving a brief review. Reviews are so important. They help a book stand out in the crowd, and they help other readers find authors like me.

Thank you so much for reading *The Selkie Enchantress*!

Sincerely,

Sophie Moss

ACKNOWLEDGMENTS

Thank you to my mom and dad for sharing your love of stories, for reading me my first fairy tale, and teaching me about magic. Thank you to my big brother for believing in me and supporting my dreams. Thank you to Juliette Sobanet for your friendship, pep talks, and positive spirit. And thank you to Margot Miller and Martha Paley Francescato for your incredible attention to detail in editing this book.

ABOUT THE AUTHOR

Sophie Moss is a *USA Today* bestselling and multi-award winning author. She is known for her captivating Irish fantasy romances and heartwarming contemporary romances with realistic characters and unique island settings. As a former journalist, Sophie has been writing professionally for over ten years. She lives in Maryland, where she's working on her next novel. When she's not writing, she's testing out a new dessert recipe, exploring the Chesapeake Bay, or fiddling in her garden. Sophie loves to hear from readers. Email her at sophiemossauthor@gmail.com or visit her website sophiemossauthor.com to sign up for her newsletter.

BOOKS BY SOPHIE MOSS

Wind Chime Novels
Wind Chime Café

Wind Chime Wedding

Wind Chime Summer

Seal Island Trilogy
The Selkie Spell

The Selkie Enchantress

The Selkie Sorceress

Read on for a special preview of *The Selkie Sorceress*!

THE SELKIE SORCERESS

CHAPTER ONE

Sam Holt stripped off his jacket and laid it over the railing of the ferry. He stood at the helm, watching the rocky cliffs of Seal Island come into view. A beat-up pair of aviator glasses shaded his eyes from the reflection of the midmorning sun. He hadn't expected to be gone this long.

Or to return with so little.

The ancient motor hummed, cutting a slow path over the surface of the ocean. Inside the leather satchel at his feet was the only clue he'd found so far in his search for Dominic and Liam O'Sullivan's mother, a woman who'd left them over twenty years ago.

Brigid O'Sullivan had done a damn good job of covering her tracks.

Not that that had ever stopped him before. But there was something about this case that nagged at him, that reminded him too much of *Tara* O'Sullivan. It was Tara's case that had first led him to this island. He'd come in search of a runaway wife, only to find an innocent woman seeking shelter from her deranged husband. He'd realized too late that his client—her husband—had no desire to reunite with Tara; he had wanted to kill her.

Tara had managed to defeat her husband, and Sam had switched sides at the last minute to help her, but he'd come far too close to getting her killed. Sam rolled his neck, working out the kinks. He'd fallen asleep at his desk the night before, as he did most nights now. He glanced at the captain, eyeing the sheen of sweat on the elderly man's forehead. "It's rather warm for January."

"Aye." Finn spoke out of one side of his mouth, a pipe dangling from his cracked lips. "But it's been good for the cleanup." He rested his leathery hand on the wheel. "The village is almost back to the way it was before the storm."

Sam nodded. When he'd left the island in November, it had been to the sound of hammers patching broken shutters and splintered fences, the bark of sheepdogs herding animals from flooded pastures to the highest fields.

Now, he took in the cluster of white-washed cottages dotting the sunlit hillside. Stone walls crisscrossed the blankets of moss leading up to the soaring limestone cliffs. The deep blue waters around the island were calm and surprisingly deserted.

"It's a nice enough day for fishing," Sam remarked. "How come we're the only boat out on the water?"

Finn puffed on his wooden pipe, and the sweet scent of tobacco floated into the salty air. "Haven't seen a fish in these waters for weeks."

"Weeks?" Sam picked up the paper cup he'd set down when he'd taken off his jacket, eyeing the instant coffee grounds lying on the bottom. He was starting to get used to the coffee in Ireland. It was the only thing keeping him awake at this point. "I thought the waters around these islands were some of the best fishing on the west coast?"

"They are." Finn steered them toward the quiet harbor, where the crumbling ruins of an ancient stronghold dipped into the sea. "At least, they used to be."

Sam knocked back the rest of the coffee. "Until what?"

Finn sent him a sideways glance. "You don't know?"

Sam shook his head slowly.

Seagulls alighted from a thin sliver of white beach, their cries echoing over the water. Finn glanced up, following the path of the birds. "It's fallout from the white selkie curse."

Sam lowered the cup. Last fall, when Liam had uncovered an ancient Irish fairy tale, it had trapped him in a dangerous enchantment. The white selkie, who was every bit as real as the pages in that tale, had chosen Liam as her mate. She had come on land for three days to tempt him into following her back into the sea. It had been a very close call, but in the end they *had* managed to save him. "I thought we broke that curse?"

"We thought so, too," Finn admitted. "Turns out, it's not that simple." The motor propelled them through the water, the wake fanning out behind them the only ripple in the glassy surface. "When Nuala failed to bring a suitable land-man into the sea, the selkies lost their ruler."

"What about Liam's grandmother?" Sam turned to face Finn. "I thought she held the throne until the next white selkie came?"

"She passed."

"When?"

"About six weeks ago." Finn shifted gears, slowing the ferry. The ocean churned beneath them. "The white selkie and her land-man have kept the peace between these islands and the sea for thousands of years. Without them, everything falls out of balance."

"What about the king?"

Finn shook his head. "The selkies need a queen."

Sam's gaze shifted back to the island. Long strands of kelp curled on the sand, cooking in the sun. The stench of dried seaweed floated over the sea and he noticed for the first time how low the tide was.

A lone seal bobbed in the water at the edge of the shallow harbor. She dove, disappearing from sight, but when she resurfaced several meters behind the boat, she bobbed in the water until their eyes met.

Sam took a step back. He would recognize those pale eyes anywhere. But what the hell was Nuala doing here, so close to the island?

The sound of laughter drifted down from the village and Nuala slid underwater, her sleek black shadow darting away toward the deeper waters.

Sam turned to see if Finn had seen her, but the captain's filmy eyes were gazing up at the village, at the woman walking out of *O'Sullivan's* pub.

"Glenna's doing well," Finn said over the hum of the motor. "Almost fully recovered."

Glenna. The coffee grounds in Sam's throat turned to dust. The mere mention of that woman's name could spark every nerve-ending inside him until all he could hear was the pop and sizzle of his own flesh burning with need.

"I thought she might have mentioned something to you," Finn said, glancing back at Sam, "about the curse."

Sam pushed back from the railing, crumpling the paper cup in his hand. "I haven't spoken with Glenna since I left."

Glenna McClure stood outside *O'Sullivan's* pub in the village, watching the ferry motor up to the pier. She knew Sam would be on it. She'd prepared herself for this moment. But she hadn't expected the wave of emotions that would sweep through her at the first sight of him in two months—like a thousand moonflowers unfurling at dusk.

Her fingers closed around the fire agate pendant hanging from a long silver chain around her neck. She breathed in the calming energy of the stone and let its protective powers ground her. The last thing she needed right now was a distraction. She couldn't afford to lose focus.

Behind her, the door to the pub was propped open. Dominic was writing up the day's specials on a chalkboard. A handful of children chased a soccer ball through the streets, their cheerful shouts echoing over the water.

From the outside eye, it would appear things had gone back to normal on Seal Island. The villagers had spent weeks cleaning up the island and riding out the aftershocks of the storm in November. But that storm was only the beginning of what the people on this island were going to have to face.

Glenna watched Sam step off the ferry, his long purposeful strides carrying him toward the one road leading up to the village. She heard Kelsey O'Sullivan's excited squeal when she spotted him and Sam's deep gravelly laugh as the children ran down to meet him.

She gripped the pendant tighter, her knuckles turning white around the fiery red stone. The man was trouble. He'd brought nothing but trouble since the moment he'd set foot on this island last summer. The sooner he left, the better it would be for all of them.

The children's chatter grew louder as they climbed the hill, surrounding Sam. And then there he was, not twenty feet away from her, batting the ball back and forth with the kids, without a care in the world.

Ronan O'Shea let out a triumphant cheer as he knocked the ball free from under Sam's foot. It rolled down the rutted street toward Glenna. She released the stone, lowering her hand to her side and lifting the toe of her heeled boot to stop the ball.

Sam's eyes followed the path of the ball, then cruised up the front of her, wandering up every inch of her body. He lowered his glasses from his face and those tawny eyes—the same eyes that had haunted her dreams for weeks now—met hers. She felt a punch of heat swim all the way through her. "Sam."

"Glenna." She expected him to say something witty, something clever to break the ice. But she saw only raw concern and something else—something she couldn't place—in his eyes. "You look well."

Glenna nodded. She hadn't forgotten how he'd stayed with her every night until she recovered, how he hadn't left her side until she was strong enough to walk back and forth to the pub on her own.

Sam kept his eyes on hers as he walked slowly toward her, easing the ball free. With a twitch of his boot, it sailed lightly up into the air and he caught it, tucking it under his arm.

Glenna lifted a brow. "I didn't know you could play football."

Sam leaned in so she could catch his scent—earthy with a touch of wood smoke. "I bet there are a lot of things you don't know about me."

Desire pooled inside her, but she could see the fatigue in his eyes now that he was so close. He hadn't shaved in days and his thick blond hair, tousled from the ferry ride, had grown even longer.

The case was wearing at him. She could sense the tension in his muscles, the frustration building inside him. Good. She wanted him tense. Frustrated. On edge.

He was more likely to make mistakes that way.

They both glanced up as Dominic O'Sullivan walked out of

the pub. He slipped his hands in the pockets of his worn jeans, leaning against the doorway. He didn't offer Sam even a hint of a smile. "We thought we'd hear from you. A call. Something."

Sam hooked his sunglasses in the neck of his shirt. "That's not the way I work."

No, Glenna thought. It wasn't. Sam didn't waste time with phone calls to update his clients when he could be working. He wouldn't stop until he got his answers, until he found out the truth. She knew how hard he'd been working.

Because she'd been working just as hard to stop him.

"Do you have any news?" Dominic asked.

Sam nodded, peeling back the flap of his tattered satchel. He walked over to Dominic, pulling out a bulky object. "I thought you should have this."

Dominic breathed out a curse when Sam unfolded the battered seal-skin.

They waited until everyone was gathered at the pub. Sam helped Dominic and Glenna pull up enough seats for Tara O'Sullivan, Dominic's wife; Liam O'Sullivan, Dominic's younger brother; and Caitlin Conner, Liam's fiancée. Fiona O'Sullivan, Dominic and Liam's grandmother, coaxed the children back out into the street to play. As soon as Fiona closed the door behind them, Sam laid the pelt on the table.

Tara gasped at the burn marks singed into the leather. There were cracks along the creases where it had been folded for so long, and teeth marks where rats had nibbled at the edges.

"Where did you find it?" Dominic asked.

"Inside your old house," Sam replied. "The one where you grew up."

"Was anyone living there?"

Sam shook his head. "The neighbors said a building down the block caught fire several years ago and it spread to the rest of the houses. Yours was right on the edge of the worst of the damage, but the city condemned them all. They haven't gotten around to rebuilding."

"I'm not surprised," Dominic murmured. "It wasn't the best section of town."

No, Sam thought. It wasn't. It was about as bad as it gets.

Tara reached out, brushing the tips of her fingers over the pelt. It crackled when she touched it. She jerked her hand back as a moldy dust puffed up from the table.

Caitlin looked at Sam. "If it was boarded up, how did you get in?"

Dominic pushed away from the table and walked to the open window. "I'm sure Sam has his ways."

A balmy breeze blew into the room, ruffling a stack of cocktail napkins on the bar. A few fluttered to the floor. No one bothered to pick them up.

Liam pulled out the chair beside Caitlin. He reached for her hand, lacing their fingers together. "What else did you find?"

"Not much," Sam admitted. "I searched the place twice, but something kept nagging at me to go back. I found a tear in the ceiling of one of the bedrooms last night. I thought it was water damage, but when I touched it, it fell away. The pelt was hidden inside, behind about three layers of insulation."

Dominic gazed out at the fields. "If our mother never went back for her pelt, that means she's still on land."

"But why wouldn't she go back for her pelt?" Liam asked. "Doesn't every selkie need to return to the sea?" His gaze met Tara's across the table. "Isn't that what they are desperate for?"

"Unless she couldn't go back for it," Tara said slowly, "because she was in some kind of trouble."

Sam looked at Glenna. She'd been uncharacteristically quiet, her gaze never leaving the pelt. Her hands were clasped calmly in her lap, but Sam could tell something was wrong. "Glenna, what do you think?"

"I think," she said, lifting her amber eyes to his, "that you have a knack for finding people who don't want to be found."

Made in the USA
Middletown, DE
19 November 2017